W9-ABM-039

WITHDRAWN
FROM THE RODMAN PUBLIC LIBRARY

GOOD AND DEAD

Other Books by Jane Langton

Emily Dickinson Is Dead
Natural Enemy
The Memorial Hall Murder
Dark Nantucket Moon
The Transcendental Murder

GOOD
AND
DEAD

Jane Langton

A
Joan
Kahn
BOOK

St. Martin's Press
New York

RODMAN PUBLIC LIBRARY

"He Who Would Valiant Be" by Percy Deamer (1867–1936), after John Bunyan, reprinted by permission of Oxford University Press.
"Turn Back, O Man" by Clifford Bax, reprinted by permission of A. D. Peters & Co. Ltd.

GOOD AND DEAD. Copyright © 1986 by Jane Langton. All rights reserved. Printed in the United States of America. No part of this book may be used or reproduced in any manner whatsoever without written permission except in the case of brief quotations embodied in critical articles or reviews. For information, address St. Martin's Press, 175 Fifth Avenue, New York, N.Y. 10010.

Copyeditor: Mildred Maynard

Library of Congress Cataloging in Publication Data

Langton, Jane.
Good and dead.

"A Joan Kahn book."
I. Title.
PS3562.A515G6   1986   813'.54   86–13802
ISBN 0–312–33865–1

First Edition
10 9 8 7 6 5 4 3 2 1

For Elvira

Thou New England, the Lord looks for more from thee than from other people, more zeal for God, more love to his truth, more justice and equity in thy ways. Take heed lest for neglect God remove thy candlestick out of the midst of thee. . . .

Reverend Peter Bulkeley
Concord, Massachusetts, 1646

The Congregation of Old West Church,
Nashoba, Massachusetts

Reverend Joseph Bold, incoming minister
Claire Bold, wife of the minister
Homer Kelly, scholar, professor, ex-lieutenant detective
Mary Kelly, scholar and professor
*Edward Bell, retired lawyer, presiding officer of the Parish Committee
Lorraine Bell, homemaker and community volunteer
Eleanor Bell, high-school freshman
Jerry Gibby, proprietor of Gibby's General Grocery
Imogene Gibby, homemaker
Wally Pott, insurance adjuster
Arlene Pott, homemaker, gardener
Betsy Bucky, knitter, crocheter, good cook, committeewoman, murderer
Carl Bucky, retired machinist
Parker W. Upshaw, executive of the General Grocery Corporation of America
Libby Upshaw, business executive (fashion imports)
Howard Sawyer, furniture buyer (wholesale)
Joan Sawyer, homemaker, former controller of inventory at Acme Lumber
Fred Harris, distributor of personal computers
Ethel Harris, homemaker
Bo Harris, high-school junior
Augusta Gill, organist and choir director
*George Tarkington, retired civil engineer
Hilary Tarkington, retired kindergarten teacher
*Philip Shooky, retired veterinarian

Deborah Shooky, bookstore clerk (part-time)
*Rosemary Hill, active member of the prison-visiting committee
*Agatha Palmer, library volunteer
Bob Palmer, director of an industrial real-estate corporation
*Percy Donlevy, investment counselor, amateur actor, baritone in the church
    choir
Maureen Donlevy, editor of Emerson Hospital Quarterly
*Bill Molyneux, technical writer
Judy Molyneux, high-school English teacher
*Eloise Baxter, retired consultant (market research)
*Thad Boland, retired building inspector
Maud Starr, woman-about-town
Charlie Fenster, president of Nashoba Building & Loan
Barbara Fenster, guidance counselor, Middlesex Community College
Bob Ott, financial adviser, tenor in the church choir
Geneva Jones, proprietor of Concord Card Shoppe
Felicia Davenport, church secretary
Dr. Arthur Spinney, local physician
Jill Marx, Marigold Lynch, Julie Smith, Mollie Pine, Mabel Smock,
    Priscilla Worthy—good women of the church
Donald Meadow and Jonathan Sinclair, righteous defenders of the needs
    of the parish

---

*Members of Ed Bell's Sunday-afternoon society

Miscellaneous Agnostics, Freethinkers, and Baptists

Josie Coil, practical nurse
Paul Dobbs, parolee
Flo Terry, reference librarian
Peter Terry, chief of the Nashoba police department

1

. . . we are as a City set upon an hill.
Reverend Peter Bulkeley
Concord, 1646

*T*his is a story about too many funerals in a single church, and a congregation of good men and women.

Well, it would be going too far to pretend that everyone in the parish was a model of rectitude. Most were the usual confusing mixture of virtues and faults. It would be more truthful to say that the story concerns only three good men: the Reverend Joseph Bold, parishioner Homer Kelly, and that stalwart pillar of the church, Edward Bell.

No, once again the list is too long. Homer Kelly's name should be withdrawn right away, since Homer was certainly afflicted with many grievous flaws.

And to say baldly that Joseph Bold, the new minister in the Old West Church of Nashoba, Massachusetts, was a good man would be giving him too much credit. It's true that Joe had once been an example of peerless benevolence, but lately he seemed to have lost the knack.

So that leaves only the presiding officer of the Parish Committee, Ed Bell. Surely no one would question Ed's goodness. As you would describe a spiral staircase by twisting your hand in the air, so you would define human virtue by pointing at Ed. It came to him so naturally he didn't even have to think about it. What's more, it drew people to him rather than driving them away as some kinds of pious behavior are apt to do.

As for the funerals, they began slowly, then came in a rush, one after the other. They didn't seem strange at first—except for the murder, of course. A murder isn't exactly normal in a little suburban town like Nashoba. But neither was the frequency of the other deaths something you would expect in a place like that. As the funerals went on and on, people began to be upset and bewildered.

In the matter of the actual murder, Homer Kelly was useful, drawing on the experience of his old days in the office of the district attorney of Middlesex County. But he wasn't very helpful in explaining the rest. He simply couldn't understand why the angel of death was suddenly so interested in Old West Church. What about the other two parishes in the town of Nashoba? "Look at the Catholics of St. Barbara's," he complained to his wife. "All in rude good health, so far as I know. And the Lutherans are skipping right along to the Church of the Good Shepherd, right? Rollicking in marriages and baptisms? Are the Methodists sick? Or the Jews? The Baptists? The Quakers? The Christian Scientists? No, indeed, they're all in the pink. Even the atheists are thriving. It's only the Unitarians and Congregationalists of Old West Church who are keeling over. What does it mean?"

Unfortunately the new minister, Joseph Bold, seemed forlornly unable to reassure the people of his congregation. And certainly the chief of the Nashoba police, Peter Terry, was as much in the dark as anybody else.

So once again there was only the steadfast support of Ed Bell, with his comforting reminders that most of the deceased parishioners had been ill anyway, that coincidences do happen, even in dying, and that his fellow church members should set their faces forward, because life had to go on, after all.

Good old Ed. What a treasure he was to the whole parish, and of course to his friends and family. It's true that his prodigies of kindness sometimes irritated his wife, Lorraine, but how could you complain about a husband who was a community institution, whose disposition was sunny, whose judgment was sensible, whose actions were compassionate and without guile?

"It's just that he's so stubborn," said Lorraine, confiding in her friend Geneva Jones.

"Can't you argue with him?" said Geneva.

"Argue! What good would that do? He's got this inner compass, that's the trouble. It's as if he could see the needle pointing north. Of course sometimes he's wrong, dead wrong, but do you think he ever feels guilty afterward? Guilty? Never! The man was born without any sense of guilt. Isn't that amazing?"

"Incredible," agreed Geneva solemnly.

Sometimes Lorraine wondered how Ed had become the kind of man he was. It surely hadn't been his parents' doing. Oh, they had been all right, in their way, but they certainly didn't account for a phenomenon like Ed. "He was just born like that," Ed's mother had told Lorraine, tossing her hands helplessly. "I used to wish he would do something naughty, but he hardly ever did. His sister, now—good gracious, did I ever tell you about the time Doris was expelled from school?"

So it was one of those random mysterious things, perhaps even an interference by God in human affairs. Who could tell? Taking everything together, Lorraine knew she was lucky to be married to a man like Ed. Therefore she put up with his amiable charities as cheerfully as she could, although their consequences were often extremely awkward.

There was the madman who had arrived on the doorstep with all his possessions, to be invited in by Ed and installed in the guest room. He had stayed for a month, shouting without cease, departing at last for a mental hospital, leaving behind him a plague of cockroaches.

There was the dear old widow to whom Ed had lent money and given comfort, who had stood up one day in church to accuse him of robbery and rape.

And there was the good cause for which Ed had exhausted himself raising money, until the treasurer pilfered the funds and took off for parts unknown.

"Honestly, Ed," Lorraine had said, "you should have known

3

better. I could tell right away the man couldn't be trusted." But even Lorraine had to admit there were plenty of other times when Ed had knocked himself out for somebody and yet nothing actually bad had happened, as far as she could determine.

As for the selection of the new minister, it was too soon to tell. Lorraine didn't know whether Ed had been right or wrong in persuading the rest of the selection committee to choose Joseph Bold, even when everybody on the committee knew the man's wife was in awful trouble.

"We'll see them through it," Ed had told them. "Why not? What's a church for anyway?" And this question had knocked the rest of the committee members back on their heels. They had looked at each other, dazed, and voted to accept the candidacy of Joseph Bold.

On the dawn of the Sunday morning in March when the new minister was to appear for the first time to his congregation, Lorraine still hadn't made up her mind about him, although she and Ed had helped the Bolds move into the parsonage and had brought home three loads of their laundry because the parsonage washing machine wasn't hooked up yet. Oh, they were nice people, all right, but they seemed terribly young, and they were certainly headed for grief.

It was typical of Ed that he had more to do that morning than there was time for. He had been up most of the night writing a welcome to the new minister to be read by the members of the selection committee, and now he had to deliver his typed copies all over town.

"I'll be back soon," he said. "We've got to get there early. Is Eleanor up yet?"

"I haven't heard a peep," said Lorraine, pulling bobby pins out of her curlers, unwinding her hair.

"Well, no wonder. Poor kid, she must be worn out. Did you know she was reading half the night? When I went up to bed, it was four in the morning, and I saw a light under her door, so I poked my head in and told her to go to sleep, and you know what she said?" Ed laughed. " 'Oh, that awful Lydia,' she said. 'Poor Elizabeth, she has to go home because of Lydia, just when Mr.

4

Darcy is being so incredibly nice.' So I shut the door and let her alone."

"I wish I were fourteen again," said Lorraine, tumbling the curlers into a drawer. "Imagine reading Jane Austen for the first time."

But in Eleanor's bedroom down the hall, *Pride and Prejudice* lay neglected under a copy of *Seventeen*. Eleanor was sitting on the edge of her bed, studying the cover of the magazine with intense interest, noticing the luscious pinkness of the cover girl's lipstick, the dark mascara of her eyelashes, and the headlines under her chin: SUMMER ROMANCE, CAN THE MAGIC LAST? SHOULD YOU KISS AND TELL?

Eleanor's mother was knocking on the door. "Eleanor, dear, get up."

"I am up," said Eleanor loudly. Then, tossing the magazine aside, she went to the mirror and got to work on her face, devoting herself to the task with total absorption. Choosing a lipstick called Kissing Pink, she outlined her mouth, then worked over

The Bells' house, Acton Road

her cheeks with Naturally Glamorous Blush-on in Enchanted Orchid and did subtle things to her eyes with Soft Plum eyeliner and Flame Glo Brown Velvet mascara.

The makeup was for the benefit of Bo Harris. Would Bo be in church this morning? Bo didn't often come to church, but today was sort of different because of the new minister. If Bo didn't turn up, then all this work was a big waste of Eleanor's time.

Eleanor Bell was fourteen, the last of the five Bell children still at home, the apple of her father's eye. It wasn't that Ed had not been a good father to Stanton and Margie and Lewis and Barbara. It was just that he had more time to be with Eleanor. After forty-two years of practicing law for an international corporation manufacturing valves, boilers, and radiators, he was at last retired, although he still went to a lot of meetings because he was on the boards of a bunch of other companies.

"Now, Ed, don't get trapped on the way," said Lorraine. "The last time you went out on an errand, you helped somebody bury a dog and you were gone for hours."

"Oh, I promise," vowed Ed. "I'll just slap these copies around to my committee members and hurry right back."

2

When we New Englanders undertake to set the world aright, we assume a task that is far more formidable than we imagine.

Reverend Edward G. Porter
Lexington, 1898

*B*ut Ed was Ed. The man was incorrigible. On the way to the Buckys' house he stopped to help Maud Starr with her flat tire.

"Oh, hi, there," said Maud, a little disappointed to see a happily married man pulling over to lend a hand. When her car had lurched to a stop, she had recognized her predicament at once as an opportunity, a doorway to adventure. Maud had always believed in snatching at the brass ring, in taking the bull by the horns, in drinking the cup of life to the dregs. *Knock,* she told herself sanctimoniously, *and it shall be opened unto you. Seek, and ye shall find.*

This morning Maud's flapping garment was of buzzard black. Standing to one side, she babbled enthusiastically while Ed opened the trunk of her car. "Isn't it thrilling? Getting our first look at our new minister? Now, Ed, tell me, what's all this about his wife?"

"His wife?" Ed struggled with the spare tire. It was stuck. "What's all what about his wife?"

"Oh, come on, Ed. You've met her. I hear there's something queer about her." Maud's famished face peered at Ed as she crouched beside him to get the lowdown. Her predatory perfume billowed around him in a suffocating cloud.

7

The tire pulled free. Leaning it against the rear bumper, Ed looked around in the trunk. "No jack?" he said, remembering with chagrin that he had lent his own to another stranded motorist. "You don't have a jack in the car anywhere?"

"A jack? No, dear, I'm afraid not. Now come on, Ed, tell me about Mrs. Joseph Bold."

Ed folded his arms and looked at Maud gravely. "Claire Bold is a brilliant young woman, an authority on Celtic literature and the early Irish church. Look, if you don't have a jack we're going to have to borrow one. Stay here. I'll be right back."

"Oh, Ed." Maud fumed, then shook out her black cloak and climbed into her car to wait, adjusting feathers, claws, and wattles as Ed walked along the road, inspecting the neighborhood, looking for the likely possessor of a jack.

This stretch of Lowell Road was ornamented by a development of four new houses. Ed walked up to the first, a mini-château with a tiny tower and a mock drawbridge. The name of the owners, THE POTTS, was written in Gothic script over the front door. Beside the house a large rectangle had been plowed for a vegetable garden, even though the spring season was barely under way. Ed was acquainted with Arlene Pott, because she attended church services regularly at Old West, but his recollection of her husband was cloudy. Wally Pott seldom turned up on Sunday mornings.

Ed lifted his hand to ring the bell, then stopped with his finger in the air. Was that a dog in the shrubbery? No, it wasn't a dog, it was a woman in white slacks, escaping, getting away, wriggling through the rhododendrons. Ed pressed the doorbell. At the same instant, a racket broke out inside the house, feminine shrieks and angry masculine shouts.

It was obviously a family squabble. What should he do now? Ed backed away, intending to beat a tactful retreat, but he was too late. The door was jerked open by a surly man in a bathrobe, Wally Pott.

"What the hell do *you* want?"

"Oh, sorry to bother you." Beyond Wally, Ed could see Arlene trying to squeeze herself out of sight behind a fancy lacquered highboy. She was fully dressed in a suit and blouse. There was a flaring red mark on her jaw. Her eyes were brimming. Her husband had struck her, that was plain. "Might I trouble you people for the loan of a jack?" said Ed innocently. "We've got a flat tire out there on the road."

"Oh, for Christ's sake." Wally Pott glowered at Ed and slammed the door in his face.

Ed turned away, astonished as always by human frailty. What precisely was the relation between the vanishing woman in the rhododendrons and the screams of Mrs. Pott? One could only guess. It was better to let such things be.

At the ranch house next door, he was without luck once again. The curtains in the window beside the door twitched aside and a woman looked out. Then she opened the door a crack and looked at him suspiciously. It was the lady of the rhododendrons. Above the white slacks she wore a white tunic. Her shoes were white with thick rubber soles.

"I wonder if I could borrow a jack for my friend's car," said Ed. "She's got a flat tire."

The woman in white was cozily built, with a pearly complexion and a mop of platinum curls. "I'm sorry," she said sharply. "I can't let you in. I don't live here. I just take care of old Mrs. Hawk."

Strike two. The next house was also a failure, but at least its owner was polite. The man who came to the door of the Mount Vernon plantation was in his sock feet, holding a pair of shoes. "Oh, gee, I'm sorry," he said in response to Ed's request, smiling at him genially. "We just moved in. The tools are in a box in the cellar someplace. I can't even find the shoe polish." Then he transferred the shoes to his left hand and offered his right to Ed. "Jerry Gibby here. We just moved to town. Maybe you know my supermarket, Gibby's General Grocery? In Bedford?"

Ed introduced himself and passed the time of day courteously for a minute, then hurried across the brand-new lawn to the last house in the row, the big builder's Colonial with the lamppost and the split-rail fence. Here the foundation planting had been clipped into perfect geometric shapes. The points of the cones looked sharp enough to prick Ed's finger. Even in March the grass was a faultless emerald green. Ed lifted his hand to grasp the knocker, on which the name Harris had been engraved, but he was forestalled by a hail from the garage, where a tall boy in a grubby T-shirt stood looking at him, wiping his hands on a rag.

"Hi, there," said the boy. "You want something? My mom and dad just went to church. There's this new minister, so they went real early to get a seat."

"I'm supposed to get there too," said Ed, "but right now we've got a flat tire out here. I wonder if I could borrow a jack?"

"Oh, right," said the boy. "Come on in. We've got one in here someplace."

Ed followed young Harris into the garage, pleased by the contrast between the boy and his environment. The kid was scruffy and dirty, with grease all over his face and arms, while the garage was like the house, excruciatingly neat. On the wall the garden tools hung beside their labels: GARDEN FORK, LEAF RAKE, PRUNING SHEARS. The storm windows glittered in a polished row. One of the cars was a gleaming Mercedes sedan. The other car matched the boy. It was the worst-looking automobile Ed had ever seen, a Chevy Chevelle with a buckled door.

"Mine," said the boy, looking at it proudly. "How you like her? I just brought her home. You know, with a hitch on my dad's car."

"Well, she must have been really handsome once upon a time," said Ed graciously, looking around for the jack.

But the boy was eager to talk about his new treasure. "What the guy said was, basically, he said, you got a body and four tires. Not too much rust. Everything else is shot, he said, your engine, your exhaust system, your clutch, your differential, your universal joints, your brakes. Pile of junk, the guy says."

"Well, then, I hope you didn't pay too much for it," said Ed. "Might there be a jack in the trunk, by any chance?"

"Ten bucks, that's all it cost me. A steal. Of course I've got to replace everything. There's this guy in Medford's got a rebuilt engine. Only thing, I've got to find a used transmission and differential assembly." The boy opened the trunk of the Mercedes, took out a jack, and followed Ed to the road.

Maud had been nodding in the front seat of her car, but now she got out and watched eagerly as the good-looking Harris boy changed her tire.

Squatting beside the car, the boy talked ceaselessly about his new automobile. "Trouble is, my mom says no way. I can't work on it in the garage, she says. They need the space for their two cars. And I can't do it in the driveway." The boy looked up sorrowfully at Ed as he tightened the lug nuts. "The neighbors wouldn't like it, she says."

Finished, he stood up and accepted Maud's effusive gratitude in melancholy grandeur and stood beside the road with Ed as she drove away.

"Listen here," said Ed, his generous nature coming rashly to the fore. "Tell you what. You could work on your car in our back yard. Of course you'd have to get an okay from my wife."

The boy's somber dignity gave way to excitement. "No kidding? Hey, that would be great."

"My name's Bell," said Ed. "Do you know where we live, on Acton Road? Perhaps you know my daughter Eleanor. She's a freshman in the high school."

The Harris boy's formal gravity returned. "Actually," he said, "I'm a junior myself," and he waved the jack solemnly as Ed drove away in the direction of the Buckys' house.

Betsy and Carl Bucky had bought their house on Lowell Road forty years ago with a G.I. mortgage. It was a small Cape Cod with a shrine to the Virgin Mary in the front yard. The shrine was an embarrassment to Carl Bucky. He thought it looked Catholic. Whenever visitors came to the house, he made jokes about mackerel-snappers, to make it plain that the Buckys were not in thrall to the Pope in Rome. Betsy liked the shrine because it was cute, in a sublime sort of way. Everything in Betsy's house was cute in one way or another. Cuteness to Betsy was the same as the good in the dialogues of Plato.

The shrine had been bought at a roadside stand, but most of the adornments in the Buckys' house had been made by Betsy herself, embroidered, patchworked, knitted, crocheted, quilted, smocked, or tatted. Betsy was also a superb cook. Her highest competence, however, was for something else. Betsy was murdering her husband. She was killing him cleverly, skillfully, continuously. This morning she got to work on it right away by shrieking up the stairwell, "Carl Bucky, get up. It's almost time for church. Your breakfast's ready."

Silence upstairs, then a groan. The bed creaked as Carl rolled over.

"You heard me, Carl Bucky. Get up this minute."

When Carl came down at last, he looked ill. "Listen, Betsy, I don't feel so good." Carl spread his big hand across his chest. "I've got a pain right here."

"Nonsense," said Betsy, bustling him into his chair at the table. "You're just hungry."

Carl looked doubtfully at the big pile of sausage fritters on his plate and the cup of pitch-black coffee. "Honest, Betsy, I think I ought to call the doctor."

"Carl Bucky," scolded Betsy, "if you don't eat those fritters after I made them special, I'll never speak to you again. You just need your coffee, that's all. You know how grouchy you are without your coffee."

As Ed Bell turned in to the Buckys' driveway and drove up the steep hill to the house, he wondered if he should have called Betsy to tell her he was coming. But the truth was, Ed rather liked dropping in on people, finding them in their natural state, not all cleaned up and formal with the domestic mess cleared away. Besides, he knew there would be no mess at Betsy's house. She could be dropped in on at any time, and her house would be spic-and-span. Betsy Bucky could be taken to her Maker any hour of the day, and the undertaker would find her in clean boiled panties.

At the door, Ed gazed sideways at the shrine to the Virgin Mary, wondering mildly when the mother of Jesus had become a Protestant. "Oh, Betsy," he said as she opened the door, "I've brought you the piece you're supposed to read this morning to welcome Joe Bold."

Betsy took the paper and her face assumed an expression of gleeful rapacity. Her button eyes sparkled. "Will Mrs. Bold be in church this morning? What will people *think*? What will they *say*?"

Once again Ed made tactful noises. "They'll think she's a charming woman. They'll want to help out. You'll see."

The Shookys' house, at the Concord end of Carlisle Road, was nearly surrounded by cyclone fences. The fences had once been cages for dogs, because Phil Shooky was a retired veterinarian. Now there were only two dogs left, Phil's pets, a couple of big German shepherds.

This morning there was no sign of the dogs, no barking welcome. And Deborah Shooky, answering the doorbell, was in great distress. "Oh, Ed, I'm glad you're here. I can't find Phil. He went out in his bathrobe to feed the dogs and he hasn't come back. He isn't anywhere."

"He's probably just picking up firewood or something," said Ed comfortingly, but he set off with Deborah into the woods behind the house to look for her husband. Soon distant barking put them on the right trail. They found Phil standing in a clearing with his dogs. His face was ashen.

"Phil, dear," said Deborah, taking his arm. "Come on home. What are you doing out here in the woods?"

Shivering with cold, Phil huddled into his bathrobe. "I don't know. I was just starting to pour chow into the dogs' dishes, I remember that. I don't know how I got here. I just don't remember."

"Now, now, old man," said Ed, "let's go back." Together they made a parade, three people and two dogs, walking to the house. "Listen," said Ed, thinking about the massive heart attack Phil had suffered last year, "don't you think you ought to stay home from church? You don't have to read this stuff I brought you. We've got plenty of other people on the committee who can do it."

"No, no," said Phil. "I'll be there. I'll just sit down for a minute. I'll be okay."

But as Ed said goodbye to the anxious Deborah, he could see Phil behind her, dropping exhausted into a chair. His face was gray with dread.

Rosemary Hill was having a bad morning too, but she didn't tell Ed when he appeared on her doorstep. Rosemary lived on Carlisle Road in the house she and Rob had moved into with their first baby after Rob finished law school. Now Rob was dead and the children were grown and Rosemary was rattling around in the big Victorian all by herself. Sometimes she wondered if she ought to move into a condominium like her widowed friends Jill Marx and Marigold Lynch.

This morning Rosemary had felt a heavy dull pain in her abdomen as she lay flat on her bedroom rug doing her exercises. She had felt it before, at Christmastime, but she had been too busy at Christmas to go to the doctor, and after that the pain had gone away and she had forgotten about it. Here it was again. What did it mean?

When the doorbell rang, Rosemary got up carefully, wincing, and went downstairs.

"Oh, Ed, it's you." Rosemary took Ed's typed sheet and looked at it blankly. The pain was goading her again.

"I'll see you in church," said Ed, turning away, wondering why Rosemary was so brusque this morning. It wasn't like her at all.

The next to last member of Ed's committee was Joan Sawyer. Joan's house on Hartwell Road was newer and grander than the

Buckys' or the Shookys' or Rosemary Hill's. It was a handsome structure with redwood decks and big sliding glass doors.

As Ed pulled into the driveway, Joan Sawyer was dressing for church. Joan was glad to be going out, grateful to be escaping from Howie for an hour or two, relishing the thought of a break in the interminable togetherness of the weekend.

Pulling on her left shoe, she tensed, hearing Howie's heavy step on the stair. *Ten more seconds to myself, five more seconds . . .*

Howie was surprised to see Joan in her good clothes. "What's up, sweetie-pie?" he said loudly.

"Going to church," said Joan calmly, pushing the strap into her shoe buckle.

"No kidding?" boomed Howie. "Is this Sunday?"

Joan glanced at him. He looked genuinely puzzled. "Of course it's Sunday. Yesterday was Saturday."

"Well, say, why don't I come to church too?"

"Fine," said Joan, standing up quickly, whirling around, whipping open a drawer.

When Ed Bell knocked on the big glass door and handed Joan her typed sheet of paper, he couldn't fail to see how tense she was. But then Joan had always been like a wire in the twisting grip of a turnbuckle. She looked at him now without speaking, then said, "Won't you come in?" Her voice was soft and quick. She was thinking a thousand things, decided Ed, rushing them through her mind but saying none of them aloud.

"No, no, thank you. No, no, I guess not." Ed could feel himself dithering. It was the effect on him of Joan's tingling pauses. He smiled foolishly and turned away.

Joan closed the door silently as Howie came downstairs in his brown suit.

"Ready, hon?" he said.

"Yes, of course," said Joan, swinging the door open again, walking stiffly out to the car ahead of Howie.

Ed still had one last rumpled sheet of paper to deliver. Swiftly he raced his car up the road in the direction of the Upshaws' house. But he didn't need to hurry. Parker W. Upshaw was coming to meet him, pounding down the road in his sweatpants, the drawstrings tied in neat bows at waist and ankle. *Pound, pound, pound,* ran Parker W. Upshaw, clocking off the miles of country road, recording them meticulously in his mental record book. When Ed Bell got out of his car and waved a piece of paper at him, Parker didn't stop running. He merely galloped past Ed, put out his hand, and grabbed the paper from Ed's fist like an express train roaring up the track and snatching a mailbag without slowing down.

Ed's surprised hand stayed aloft for a few seconds as he gazed after Upshaw, but Parker didn't look back. His morning run was a sacred thing, a serious matter. Some people just didn't understand the importance of a steady pace and absolute regularity. And anyway he didn't have time to stop and pass the time of day. If he didn't get home in a hurry and change

The Terrys' house on
Hartwell Road

clothes, he'd be late for church. He wanted to be there when Claire Bold came in. He wanted to see people's faces. He wanted to behold their reaction, to feel their shock.

From across the street, Flo Terry watched Parker Upshaw disappear around the bend as Ed Bell climbed back into his car. Parker and Ed were parishioners at Old West Church, and Flo was reminded of the fact that the new minister was about to meet his congregation for the first time.

"It's a big morning for Old West," Flo told her husband, Pete. "I wonder how the new man will turn out."

Flo was not a member of the Old West congregation, nor was she a parishioner in the Lutheran Church of the Good Shepherd, nor did she take communion in the Catholic church of St. Barbara's. But Flo was a keen observer and a sharp critic of all these religious societies just the same, keeping track of their ups and downs, priding herself on her nimble perception and on a judgment that was so quick and accurate it was almost extrasensory. Actually, Flo's conclusions about life in the town of Nashoba were due to the careful way she did her homework and to her long practice as a highly trained reference librarian.

It was strange that her husband didn't share his wife's cleverness in judging his fellow citizens. You would think a chief of police would have a sharper understanding of what was going on in his own bailiwick, but poor Peter Terry seldom had a clue.

"I have a funny feeling about that new man Joseph Bold," said Flo, narrowing her eyes, preparing one of her famous predictions. "Have you heard the rumor about his wife?"

"Oh, go on, Flo," said Pete, chopping up his breakfast egg, "you and your funny feelings."

"He's headed for disaster," said Flo. "That's what I think. I wonder if the church will live through it."

But in Old West itself there was no such premonition of evil days to come. In the basement common room, George Tarkington was already at work, preparing for a possible overflow of the congregation from the floor above. He was setting up chairs and testing the public-address system. The choir was practicing upstairs, but their singing wasn't coming through the loudspeaker. "Rats," said George, fiddling with it some more.

Up in the balcony, Bob Ott, the choir's prize tenor, gave another pull on the bell rope. The rope scraped against the sides of the narrow hole in the ceiling, and in the steeple the small bell rang with a tinny clang, summoning the congregation, calling the new minister to his task.

3

*The bell that has sounded from this steeple over field
and hill has reminded men of higher realities than crops
and herds, and has called them to the pursuit of
imperishable riches. . . .*

Reverend Edward E. Bradley
First Parish, Lincoln, 1898

*T*he clang of Nashoba's Old
West Church was inaudible to Homer and Mary Kelly, because
their house was not in Nashoba at all. The Kellys lived in neighboring Concord, right on the shore of Fairhaven Bay where the
river turned the corner on its way to the Old North Bridge.

Homer Kelly was one of the three good men listed in the first
chapter of this book—that is, until he was eliminated on sober
second thought because of the blemishes and defects in his character. In spite of these inadequacies, Homer was a man of consid-
erable accomplishment, first as a lieutenant detective in East
Cambridge and then as an associate professor of American literature at Harvard University. Mary Kelly, too, was a professor
there. In fact, Homer and Mary together taught a famous course
in Memorial Hall.

Right now Homer was spending his days in the storage base-
ments of old churches and the reference rooms of local libraries
among the locked cabinets where precious materials were stored.
He was pursuing his latest colossal project. It was a book he
called *Hen and Chicks,* a study of the spread of daughter churches
from the First Parish in Concord, and of the further separation
of granddaughter parishes farther away. If he ever finished the

undertaking, it would be a model of the growth of New England, but Homer doubted it would ever be done. He would die, he told himself pathetically, in the freezing vault of some library, and his last glimpse of the world would be the pothooks and flourishes of some eighteenth-century parson's crabbed hand.

On the morning of Joseph Bold's first service in Nashoba's Old West Church, Mary had to keep going into the bedroom to badger her husband into waking up. But Homer only turned over in bed and made anguished stricken noises and insisted it wasn't time yet, and why didn't she go away because he was still sound asleep.

But even in his sleep Homer was fretfully aware that he had to get up, he had to get up, he had to get up and go to church. So heavily did this necessity loom over his dreams that the church itself burgeoned before him, swelling whitely, its edges knife-sharp, its clapboards smartly level, its tower ascending to the weathercock aloft. Something very odd was happening. Backing across the street, Homer stood on the misty grass of the Nashoba Common to stare upward at the tower. Two gigantic hands were removing it from the church, lifting it up and setting it down on the lawn. And now two huge thumbs were prying off the roof. The thumbs belonged to none other than God himself. He was

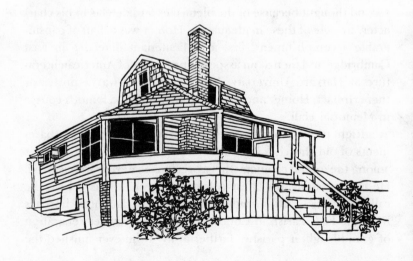

grunting with effort, succeeding at last, setting the roof down beside the steeple. Now he was leaning over to peer at the congregation within, one long strand of gray whisker trailing over the pulpit wall. Homer was further astonished to observe something he had never noticed before, a large faucet attached to the pulpit. He watched in awe as God reached down to turn it on, releasing the gushing stopcocks of all their individual souls.

But the sharp squeak was really the sound of the faucet in the Kellys' own bathroom, on the other side of the wall. Homer opened one eye as his wife came into the bedroom, fully dressed. "Okay, Homer, come on, get up," she said firmly. Taking him by the shoulders, she bounced him up and down. "I mean it this time."

The mattress jounced and twanged, and Homer protested loudly, but Mary took him by the ankles and dragged him off the edge. (Their connubial relation was more pugilistic than erotic.)

Soon they were zooming up their terrifying driveway and turning out on Route 2. Whizzing through the center of Concord, they made their way along Lowell Road in the direction of the town of Nashoba. Nashoba's Old West Church was actually one of the offspring churches Homer was writing about. It had set itself off in 1760 because the Sunday journey to meeting had seemed so long and difficult to the farmers in the northern quarter of Concord. Nashoba was a town of swamps and glacial eskers, of low hills and arable fields, of brooks running into the Assabet River, the Concord, the Merrimack. As a village it had a quarrelsome history, perhaps because its citizen farmers had been so maddened by the clouds of mosquitoes breeding in the swamps. Remoteness and poverty had kept it unspoiled for a long time, but now the Subarus and Saabs and Toyotas of software engineers tore down the narrow ways where apple-laden carts had once lumbered to market. Along Nashoba's winding roads there were still two-hundred-year-old farmhouses of supreme and simple beauty, but there were new houses as well, especially on Lowell Road and Heald Avenue and Blood Street. Homer and Mary passed one of the new developments on their way to church.

"Tsk-tsk, will you look at that," said Homer, shaking his head in disapproval. "They've finished that Southern plantation. There's the new owner in person, installing his birdbath."

The man with the birdbath was Jerry Gibby, the newly arrived citizen of Nashoba, the proprietor of Gibby's General Grocery. Homer and Mary didn't know it, but Jerry and his wife, Imogene, were about to become the newest members of Old West Church. Imogene and Jerry had fallen in love with the beautiful old building on the green, with its charming domed tower. It was part of their image of their new life in the suburbs. Jerry wanted to become acquainted with the church members, hoping to bring new customers into his store. Imogene, too, wanted to know everybody. She wanted to find out if there was a women's group in the church. She wanted to be part of the community right away.

This morning, as the Kellys' Ford pickup sped past the Gibbys' house, Jerry Gibby dumped his new birdbath beside one of the expensive boulders that were part of the flossy landscaping around his new house. Then, puffing with the effort, he went indoors to ask Imogene to come out and take a look. But Imogene was in the Jacuzzi. So, instead, Jerry wandered around the new kitchen, dazed with possessive pride, admiring the microwave oven, the trash compacter, the bar with its own little sink, the bay window with the maple table and the captain's chairs.

It was all a dream. Jerry couldn't believe it. If only he had known about this house when he was a kid, growing up in Somerville with a mother who was always sleeping off a binge and a dad who was missing half the time, it would have made things easier. What if he had known that someday he would possess a house in a fancy suburb and a gleaming white Coupe de Ville and a supermarket franchise! Well, of course the bank owned the house and the car, and General Grocery owned most of the supermarket. After all, Jerry still owed General Grocery seven hundred thousand dollars. Oh, God. For a second Jerry panicked. Once again he told himself he had been a fool to build the house and buy the car at the same time he was going so far out on a limb to acquire the store.

Distracted by the grim statistics of his debts, Jerry stared at the trash compacter and tried to persuade himself things were going to be okay. He had a formula for comforting himself whenever he got in a tizzy, *Everybody's got to eat.* Jerry had recited the formula to his brothers-in-law and his father-in-law—"Groceries! it's a cinch. Everybody's got to eat." And they had all nodded their heads and agreed with him and loaned him the hundred thousand for the down payment on the supermarket. The car and the house had been spun out of air, somehow or other. Jerry himself wasn't sure just how.

Worrying made him hungry. Looking in the refrigerator, Jerry found a piece of sausage left over from breakfast, and he ate it greedily, dripping grease on his lapel. Imogene saw the spot when she came flouncing into the kitchen in her pretty ruffled dress. Swiftly she scrubbed it off and kissed him. Then she got to work on the boys, straightening their ties, wetting down their cowlicks. The three fat little boys looked just like Jerry. They all wore identical suits. In the back of the Coupe de Ville they bounced on the seat, demanding to hear the stereo. They wanted to see the windows go up and down when Jerry pushed the buttons. They wanted to try the tape deck.

"Pipe down, guys," said Jerry, backing cautiously out of the driveway. "Just shut up, okay?"

Imogene patted the white leather of the front seat with her plump hand. "I'm scared about church," she said. "I won't know when to kneel and when to stand up."

"Kneel?" Jerry snickered. "You don't kneel in a Protestant church. You just sit there. God lets the Protestants sit there on the seat of their pants. Everybody's equal, you know? How do you do, God! Shake hands, okay, God?"

"Well, at least the minister will be new too," said Imogene. "We won't be the only ones walking into the church for the first time."

4

Suppose two men, both in fear of drowning by water;
one stands on a firme rock, the other on a quick-sand. . . .
Reverend Peter Bulkeley
Concord, 1646

*E*d Bell was long overdue at home. On the way past the parsonage, he slowed down, wondering if he should stop in for a minute to encourage Joseph Bold. But then he pulled away and accelerated again, because he really didn't have time. And anyway the man would be all right. He would handle his first service perfectly well. Confidently Ed drove home and apologized to his frantic wife and called upstairs to his daughter Eleanor, and soon the three of them were on their way to church.

As their car swept past the Bolds' house, Ed didn't even give it a second glance.

The parsonage of the Old West Church was a homely Victorian structure almost lost behind two enormous Norway spruce trees that threw the front porch into impenetrable shadow. Within the house, Ed Bell's angelic confidence was not the mood of the morning. But Joe Bold was doing his best to seem poised and self-assured in front of the Shookys, who had stopped by for Claire. Then, gathering up his sermon from his desk and throwing his black robe over his arm, he said goodbye and stepped out on the back porch to walk up to the church.

Instantly his attention was assailed by the washing on the line in the yard. He had hung it out himself the day before, and he should have brought it in after supper, because there had been rain in the night. Now the sheets and towels were drenched, but they billowed in the morning breeze and subsided, and filled again with air and fell back. One of his shirts hung between him and the low streaking sunlight, lifting its arms, flinging them wildly, dancing, hurling itself outward. It was ridiculously like himself, but transfigured. There in the backyard hung this phenomenon, half natural, half polyester, seizing his attention.

But Joe was used to that. Everything everywhere beckoned him, crooked its finger at him; that was the trouble. Rocks and clouds plucked his arm, crumpled paper bags on the sidewalk called to him, every petal on a flowering bush had its own voice. It dizzied him, wore him out, to keep turning and looking and gasping politely, "Yes, yes, I see, I see."

As he turned out on the road, for example, he couldn't help noticing the way the drops falling from the high trees were plummeting straight down, glittering as they fell. He couldn't help hearing the bird in the branches overhead make a tentative light remark before it flew away.

As usual, Joe was strongly affected. Ever since he could remember, his senses had been more intensely vulnerable than other people's. His first memories were of sharp visions, the blue sky above his playpen, ants on blades of grass, shadows tumbling on a blanket. Later on, walking to school, he had been transfixed by the sleek furry coats of dogs, by weedy thickets in a brushy field, by sandwich wrappers blowing across the playground. His teacher had complained to his mother: "Joseph always seems to be somewhere else. I can't get the boy's attention." Then, in adulthood, Joe had discovered the transcendentalists, and learned that these airy manifestations were metaphors, mystical pedagogical remarks by God, who never stopped talking in a language composed of the droplets in a cloud or the sap running up a tree, or the willful behavior of the elements of a dividing cell.

It was a garrulous communication that never ceased, a gabble of molecules, a continuous proclamation by cobblestones and the bark of trees, by constellations of stars and by cracks in the sidewalk, an endless monologue of visual splendors.

Now Joe was thirty-eight—too old, it seemed to him, for what he had accomplished. Six years of his life had been wasted as a student of zoology, attempting to transform the ignorant rapture of his childhood into a useful profession. For two long years in graduate school, he had been mired down in the examination of the skeletal differences among blowfish. When at last he had come to his senses, he had simply walked across the dingy parking lot from the Harvard Museum of Comparative Zoology to the Divinity School. There he had spent another four years, preparing for ordination as a clergyman.

His new career had seemed satisfactory, the right one for Joseph Bold. Until recently, the ministry had seemed his true calling. Throughout his years in the big Congregational church in Pittsburgh, he had spoken from a reservoir that seemed unfailing. His ecstatic apprehension of his surroundings had been like Henry Thoreau's intoxication with the song of the wood thrush. Like Thoreau, he had been *Drunk, drunk, drunk, dead drunk*. For Joe, Thoreau's wonder at a nutshell in his hand had become a talisman—*I looked at a walnut shell this morning, and saw that it was made for joy.*

For joy? Bitterly, Joe walked under the dripping trees in the cool, moist air. In his own hand Thoreau's shell had broken open to reveal a worm, and now the worm was rearing up like some dread creature of the jungle, swaying and coiling itself around Claire. All Thoreau's transcendent joy had been merely self-delusion. How could anyone be such a fool as to believe in it?

Above him now as he walked to church, the telephone wires looped from pole to pole, shining in the sunlight like strands of spiderweb. The tall grass beside the pavement was a mass of delicate parallels straining upward. Joe was compelled to see it, but he no longer had faith in it.

"You promise and promise and never deliver," he told the grass resentfully. Walking past the Civil War memorial on the Common, he crossed Farrar Road and entered the church.

5

*An humble spire, pointing heavenward from an obscure
church, speaks of man's nature, man's dignity, man's
destiny, more eloquently than all the columns and
arches of Greece, and Rome, the mausoleums of Asia,
and the pyramids of Egypt.*

William Ellery Channing

*O*f all the white wooden spires
pointing skyward from the green commons of suburban villages
in Massachusetts, from the public squares of cities, from rural
crossings surrounded by shopping malls, from abandoned
parishes where deer and foxes ran in the woods, the small-domed
tower of the Old West Church of Nashoba was among the most
demure. It housed a single bell and a family of barn owls. The
bell rang only on Sunday mornings, but the owl came and went
every night through a broken slat in the shutter, carrying live
mice and voles for her downy young to dismember.

It was called Old West because it lay a few hundred yards
west of the church from which its disgruntled orthodox founders
had detached themselves in 1836, shocked by the way the church
of their fathers was drifting into the Unitarian heresy. A century
later, the two churches had joined forces once again, and now the
united parish paid dues both to the Congregational United
Church of Christ and the Unitarian Universalist Association. The
reunion was not a matter of philosophical tolerance so much as
a recognition of their mutual poverty in the Great Depression.

Back in 1836, when the present edifice was built, tricky
points of theology had counted for much more. God was three,

not one. *Bang!* went the hammers. *Three, not one! Bang, bang, bang!* Christ the Son was coequal to God the Father, not subordinate. But, even so, the carpenters had not carried the cross of Christ up the ladder to the top of the steeple. A cross would have been suspect, smacking of popery. Instead they had crowned the building with a rooster weathervane.

This morning, after a century and a half of pointing to the four corners of God's vast creation, the same rooster was sweeping around on his creaking iron axle in the thrust of the brisk wind that tossed the bare tops of the maples and drove white clouds like puffy sofas across the cold blue sea of air.

When Homer Kelly's big pickup slowed down in front of the church, early comers were thronging across the road. "I'll drop you off here," he said to his wife.

"I'll save you a place as long as I can," promised Mary.

Driving up the hill beyond the church, Homer found a parking place in front of the parish house, the old building that had once housed the Unitarians. Opening the car door, stretching out his long leg to the pavement, he looked at his big oxford and imagined instead the high laced shoe of a Kibbe or a Farrar or a Blood descending from a buggy or a rockaway or a buckboard, or the worn boot of a Heald or a Russell or a Hutchinson stepping down from a cutter or a sleigh in the winter snow. This morning the snow was gone, the sun was shining, the grass at the edge of the green was gouged with tire tracks. Homer hurried along the dry asphalt of the road and joined the press of fellow parishioners moving up the wooden planks that had been set down on the lawn last fall.

The vestibule was crowded. People were shuffling toward the two doors, peering past each other, craning their necks. There were extra ushers this morning, dodging up and down the aisles, opening the little pew doors, handing people their orders of service, packing six bodies to a bench instead of five. Charlie Fenster crooked his finger at Homer and wedged him in beside Mary in a rear pew. Homer settled himself in the narrow space, Mary squeezed up against Joan Sawyer, Joan prodded her husband, Howie, to move over, Howie shoved massively against George Tarkington, and George crowded still closer to his wife, Hilary. There was a sense of expectation in the murmured greetings, the rustle of coats, the flutter of orders of service, the wooden noise of pew doors sticking, opening, shutting, the sound of whispering from the choir in the balcony, a blundered bass note from the organ.

The choir was a world unto itself. On the long varnished benches, the singers sat jammed together in their black robes, separated from the congregation, enjoying an undercurrent of hushed hilarity. "I can't find the damned hymn," muttered one of the baritones, Percy Donlevy, riffling through his hymnbook. "It's the punishment of an angry God," explained Bob Ott, and there was a burst of subdued laughter from the other tenors.

But then they didn't rehearse the hymn, after all. Glancing over her shoulder at the packed church, choir mistress Augusta

Gill shrewdly forbore. "It's too late," she said. "We should have started earlier." Then Augusta rearranged her music, took a deep breath, and launched into the prelude. Her fingers rippled on the two keyboards, swell and great, her feet ran up and down the pedals. The music pealed out over the congregation, and the sense of anticipation increased.

In the last pew on the south side, Homer was butted up against the shutter of the window. His back was stiff. The sun warmed his neck. From the three south windows, the light poured into the chamber, filling the hollow volume of the church, ricocheting from the white walls, the white pews, the white ceiling, multiplying itself in white upon white, losing itself in overlying white shadows in the crevices of the classical moldings behind the pulpit, in the carvings of the Corinthian capitals, in the slats of the shutters. It was a cheerful light, devoid of mystery. It said "Wake up," rather than "Adore." Homer thought of the forefathers and their pious teachings on original sin and total depravity and atonement and eternal punishment and predestination and the covenant of grace—mighty fallacies, sublime hallucinations, exalted errors. What was there in this sunlit space to equal them in majesty, in solemn grandeur? How did the church survive when it no longer believed in a God who heard the cry of every heart, who listened with fervent interest to the prayers rising like steam, who never failed in his earnest seeking of lost souls? Would the Reverend Joseph Bold measure up to the stature of the devoted and misguided men who had stood in the several pulpits of Old West in the past? Or would he be only a flea on the back of the last elephant in that long and ponderous parade, hopping up and down, emitting an insect whine? Well, they would soon find out.

Homer glanced across his wife and Joan Sawyer, and marveled at the way the morning sunshine had picked out Joan's husband for its full attention this morning. He had noticed it before, the sun's personal interest in the congregation, its habit of choosing one and then another to bathe in light. At this moment its warm slanting rays glowed lovingly upon Howie Sawyer's bald head, penetrating the freckled skin a fraction of an inch, illuminating the gray hairs that fluffed around the dome, turning the brown fibers of his polyester jacket into rainbows. Against the brilliance, Howie's face was nearly invisible. His glasses flashed at Homer. He was leaning heavily over his wife, describing an encounter with a traffic cop.

"I told the man, it's not my fault. And he said, whose fault is it? Ha-ha! So I said, the other guy's, right? So he said, listen, you want a citation? Me, he was going to give me a citation. So I said to him, listen, I said . . ."

Homer slumped on the bench and made an occasional low rumbling noise that spurred Howie to further meandering recollection, while the sun lit up his ears like the handles of an alabaster jar. Between them, crushed against Howie's wife, Mary Kelly could feel Joan Sawyer's mortification. Joan was a large-boned, sober young woman, far younger and cleverer than Howie. Why had she married the man at all? Now in the tight grip of Joan's hands in her lap, in the rigidity of her crossed knees, her chagrin was manifest.

Diagonally across the church, in the first box pew on the north side, Eleanor Bell sat alone. Now and then she glanced back at the two doors to the vestibule, hoping to see Bo Harris. But Mr. and Mrs. Harris had been helping out downstairs in the common room. When they came upstairs at last and hurried up the aisle, Bo was not trailing behind them, scowling gravely the way he always did in church.

Eleanor was crushed. Drooping forward, she stared at her homemade skirt, and poked her finger in an open place along the seam where the sewing machine had run off the edge. But then she stiffened her back and listened. Mr. and Mrs. Harris had settled into the pew directly behind her, and Mrs. Harris was talking to Mr. and Mrs. Palmer about Bo.

"He's got this new car," said Mrs. Harris. "It's the worst wreck you ever saw. He wants to work on it in the driveway. Can you imagine? An old heap like that? So of course I said no. So the poor boy is furious with me. So is Fred."

Eleanor could hear Mr. Harris make a demurring sound.

"Poor old Bo," Mrs. Harris went on. "He should have asked me before he bought the car. Nobody asked *me.*"

Halfway between the front of the church and the back, Arlene Pott sat in her customary pew, unaccompanied by her husband, Wally. Arlene touched her cheek, hoping the red mark didn't show. She had powdered it with peach face powder. Now she looked down at her new suit, and decided she had chosen badly. She should have worn her pink. The new minister wouldn't even notice her. Just another old lady, he would think, and then he would look past her at young Eleanor Bell or at Maud Starr with her big bust. It was lonesome coming to church without Wally. Arlene's perpetual sense of grievance enveloped her as she stared at her plump crossed ankles. "I am fifty-seven years old," she said to herself. It was a fact that haunted her every hour of the day. Then her heavy self-consciousness lightened as she remembered the peas she had planted yesterday in her vegetable garden. The peas would be up soon, their little pairs of leaves unfolding in the cold soil. The germination of the peas seemed mysterious and wonderful to Arlene. She was here in church this morning partly because she was curious to see the new minister, but also because of the peas. It was hard to understand exactly what they had to do with the minister and the Bible and religion, but there was some connection, Arlene was sure of it.

Betsy Bucky had no trouble knowing why she came to church. The Old West Church was the theater where Betsy displayed her talents, at after-church coffee hours, at church suppers and bake sales and noonings. Social events like these were the realms in which Betsy held sway, the stage where she won applause for her sausage fritters, her Sunshine cake, her Blackbottom pie. At the Christmas Fair everyone exclaimed at Betsy's aprons and afghans and potholders. But of course the cooking and sewing were only part of it. There were deeper reasons, really religious reasons, why Betsy came to church every single Sunday, why she never missed a service. As soon as Betsy sat down in her pew beside Carl, her thoughts soared up and out, romping in the blue sky among hosts of fluffy clouds, frolicking with angels and the Virgin Mary, and the Virgin always said to her, "Betsy Bucky, you're the cutest little woman! Oh, you're special, Betsy Bucky, really special!" Of course Betsy knew you weren't supposed to pray to the Virgin in Old West Church, but she thought that was silly. The Virgin was in the Bible, wasn't she? Jesus had a mother, didn't he?

Beside Betsy, her husband, Carl, sat sullenly, his feet wide apart on the floor, his belly tight against the button of his blazer, his face wadded and pale. The pain in his chest had come back. Carl thought of nudging Betsy to say he wanted to go home and lie down, but he knew she would only scold him in a fierce whisper and tell him to keep still. So he went on sitting quietly, one hand spread wide over his chest under his coat.

"Look, Carl," whispered Betsy, pinching his arm, "new people."

It was the Gibbys, Jerry and Imogene. While Betsy Bucky watched eagerly, they hurried up the aisle after Charlie Fenster to one of the pews at the front of the church. The three chubby boys walked in front, then Imogene came tripping gaily in her yellow dress, the frills catching every little breeze, and Jerry followed in the rear, his bald forehead gleaming, his sallow jowls glistening, his teeth showing in an anxious smile. Jerry felt like an interloper in this Anglo-Saxon Protestant church, but he was not troubled by any sense that he was betraying his Catholic boyhood. God was God, after all, and a tricky bastard, wherever you found him at home.

Taking his seat, Jerry was stunned to find himself in the pew next to Parker W. Upshaw's. Good God, Parker Upshaw, the big wheel in the upper echelons of General Grocery! Thank God, Upshaw was in some other department. He wasn't in charge of franchise holders like Jerry. The guy was a cold fish with a reputation for nosy interference. Uneasily, Jerry nodded at Parker W. Upshaw and yanked at his trousers, which were tight in the crotch. Then he focused his attention on the words printed on the front of the order of service. They were from the prophet Isaiah:

And the foreigners who join themselves to the Lord
. . . these I will bring to my holy mountain, and make
them joyful in my house of prayer.

Foreigners, thought Jerry, that's us. We're foreigners. Well, okay, go ahead, you Protestants, make us joyful. Bring on the new minister. What's his name? Bold? Joseph Bold.

Jerry and Imogene Gibby had heard no rumors about the minister's wife. Therefore they were the only ones who did not guess that the woman entering from the door beside the pulpit, limping into the chamber on the arm of Lorraine Bell, was Claire Bold. A tremor ran through the crowded rows of pews. In her customary place at the back of the church, Rosemary Hill winced with shocked compassion. The face of the minister's wife was a mask of skin and bone. Her arms and legs were bony sticks. Rosemary stopped staring and lowered her head. So that was the truth about Mrs. Joseph Bold. She was going to die! Then Rosemary felt a sympathetic pang beneath the belt of her skirt, and reminded herself to make an appointment with the doctor. She mustn't wait any longer. She had waited too long already.

From his front pew, Parker Upshaw looked inquisitively around the room to see how they were all taking it. He wanted to stand up and say, It's not my fault. I told the other members of the selection committee to pick another candidate. That guy from Pennsylvania, he had a wife with a doctor's degree in church-school administration, and the Chicago man's wife was a Harvard overseer, for God's sake. But Parker's intelligent suggestions had been overlooked. The rest of the committee had fallen for Joseph Bold in spite of Claire's desperate physical condition. Ed Bell had talked them into it. Parker raised his eyes and stared at Claire Bold as she faltered into her pew. *Look at the woman. She can barely stand up.*

Mary Kelly, too, was astounded by her first glimpse of the minister's wife, but for a different reason. "Homer," she murmured, "I know her. It's Claire Macaulay. She was my roommate freshman year. Oh, Homer, she used to be so—" Mary clutched Homer's arm, overcome with helpless pity, as the choir stood up

3 5

in the balcony to begin their anthem of welcome. The tenors exulted, the sopranos caroled jauntily, the altos droned on one note, the basses leaped with heavy agility from octave to octave. The music flooded the sunlit chamber as the door beside the pulpit opened a crack, then closed again, then opened wide to admit the new pastor into the presence of his congregation.

6

The Ministry is a Signal Blessing . . . one of those
Royal Gifts which our exalted Lord Jesus gave to
his Church, when he rode in Triumph into Heaven.

Reverend Joseph Estabrook
Concord, 1705

*J*oseph Bold had practiced going
up and down the steps of the pulpit, but this morning, approaching them in the company of Ed Bell, he paused on the first step
in flabbergasted surprise. It was as if a volcano had erupted in
front of him. Someone should have warned him about the way
the light rebounded from the windshields of the cars on the street
and rocketed through the windows of the church to land on the
pulpit wall in watery images of the old panes of glass. Pulling
himself together, he mounted the top step and sat down beside
Ed in one of the pulpit chairs.

Ed glanced at his protégé, and grinned encouragement. The
man seemed rattled. Joe smiled wanly in reply.

The two of them were nearly hidden behind the pulpit. Deprived, the congregation stared at the top of Joe's head, eager to
get another look. Their new pastor seemed plausible enough. He
was tall and gaunt. His receding hair fell limply forward over his
face, which was pensive, a little sad. The sadness was reasonable,
everyone decided, considering the illness of his wife. Homer
Kelly was reminded of Hawthorne's minister, the one who wore
a black veil to conceal his private woe.

Maud Starr was particularly pleased. She quivered with curiosity, quite taken with Joseph Bold. Her first glimpse of his ailing wife had whetted her vulturish appetite. It was obvious that Claire Bold was not long for this world. Carrion, thought Maud, not forming the word in her mind, only the image of what it meant. Shrugging off her black coat, she pulled her sweater tight.

Round balls, thought Joe Bold, looking out left and right at the visible portions of his new congregation. Round balls on stalks, the heads of his new parishioners. To Joe's nearsighted vision they were vague and out of focus. Soon they would become separate people with names of their own, eager for salvation of one kind or another. They were important people, Parker Upshaw had said, doctors and lawyers, professors and bank presidents, board chairmen and administrators. They certainly looked prosperous. In this church the problems of urban poverty were seventeen miles away in the city of Boston, although, according to Ed Bell, the outreach committees were stretching their arms north, south, east, and west, like the missionary societies of old who had spread their kindly interest far and wide, sewing for the remote populations of Africa, converting the heathen Chinee.

Joe tried to control his alarm. To his fuzzy vision the men and women sitting in the pews around him looked calm and undisturbed by trouble, as if they had solved all of life's problems. There were a great many gray heads among them. The congregation was more elderly than he had expected. What could he possibly say to them, when his own soul was clenched in despair? What did they want of him? Why were they all here, surrounded by the paraphernalia of Sunday morning, the fresh flowers, the red carpets, the old hand-planed pews, the pewter collection plates, the organ with its sacred measures, the high notes of the sopranos, the low notes of the baritones, the hymns and prayers? Didn't they know how shaky the whole apparatus was? Glancing up at the ceiling, Joe saw it full of holes, bare to the sky between ruined walls, smashed by sledgehammer blows. In the last century the corner posts had been buckled by Charles Darwin, and the shuddering vibrations were still cracking the plaster, rotting the joists and sills, unsettling the foundation. Why had the world been made two ways at once, so beautiful and so terrible, both at the same time? Joe glanced at the sermon in his hand, an outline on a single page. Then, dropping his gaze, he studied his polished shoes. His sermon was ready, his shoes were ready, he had cleaned his fingernails. For what? All at once Joe felt unequal to the task of giving meaning to the accoutrements of piety. He had an impulse to run down the pulpit steps and snatch up Claire and run away.

Ed Bell was rising to welcome him. The moment had passed. The service had begun.

Ed performed his task with easy grace. He was the benevolent spirit of the morning, the jocular intermediary between pastor and congregation. With comfortable affection and kindly jokes, he expressed the selection committee's pride in its choice. Then he called on the members of the committee to rise in the congregation and read their separate welcomes, the ones Ed had written for them in the middle of the night. When the readings were over, he clapped Joe Bold on the shoulder and shook his hand and sat down.

It was Joe's turn. Standing up, gripping the reading desk, he thanked Ed Bell, he thanked the committee. His melancholy face grew animated as he began to speak. To the congregation his voice was surprising. It wasn't strong and vibrant and oratorical. The Reverend Bold had apparently never learned to summon great drafts of air from his lungs. Only a trickle worked its way past his larynx. His speech came out cracked, a little absurd, with broken edges, as though he were merely talking, not declaiming from a pulpit. Impulsively he called for the first hymn as if the notion had just occurred to him.

Charmed, the parishioners rose to sing. At the organ in the balcony, Augusta Gill turned to her keyboard and congratulated herself on her new freedom to choose the hymns. Joe Bold had confessed to her his total ignorance, his helplessness in the face of printed music. "Oh, that's okay," Augusta had said, privately delighted. No longer would the congregation be forced to struggle with unsingable horrors chosen for their aptness of thought, no longer would the service be cluttered with ghastly musical frights that looped up and down the scale with frisky eighth-note runs and idiotic dotted rhythms. From now on she would have a free hand to choose the best and nothing but. Terrific. Augusta pulled out the stops for a majestic run-through of Old Hundredth, a hymn recommended for the beginning of worship. It had sixteenth-century words and music. You couldn't get older or better than that.

> *All people that on earth do dwell,*
> *Sing to the Lord with cheerful voice;*
> *Him serve with fear, his praise forth tell,*
> *Come ye before him and rejoice.*

Then the covenant was spoken. The minister recited it with the rest of them, reading it respectfully from the order of service as though he knew the words were still theirs, as though he hadn't earned the right to them yet. The Lord's Prayer was repeated, the collection was taken, another anthem was sung by the choir.

Joe watched the choir stand up in the balcony in their black robes like dark columns. They were opening and closing their mouths, gazing intently at their music, their eyes flicking up now and then to glance at Augusta. Joe was envious of the way they stood so steadily, charged with life and vitality, while Claire in the front pew was huddled against Lorraine Bell, her sturdy health destroyed. Joe folded his arms and listened as Ed Bell rose to read the lesson.

> "They that wait upon the Lord shall renew their
> strength; they shall mount up with wings as eagles;
> they shall run, and not be weary, and they shall walk,
> and not faint."

It was time for the sermon. The congregation braced itself. It was now or never. Would the man pass muster? Politely they settled themselves to listen, their critical faculties astir as their new minister stood up once more and put on his glasses.

But as he cleared his throat and stared at his page of notes, there was a disturbance in the last of the box pews on the south side of the church. Joe Bold glanced up in surprise to see a large man in a brown suit throw himself against the door of the pew, snap the latch, and blunder up the aisle, shouting.

It was Howie Sawyer. Homer Kelly lunged after Howie and caught him just as he turned to the side and tried to wrench open the door of the pew where Charlie Fenster and his wife were sitting beside Carl and Betsy Bucky. The congregation sat transfixed, craning their necks, staring in horror as Homer and Charlie dragged Howie back along the aisle and through the vestibule and down the steps outside. Joan Sawyer followed them, her face blank with despair. So did Arthur Spinney, the local medical man. Ed Bell walked quickly down the pulpit steps and hurried out after them.

Soon Howie's meaningless cries faded. A shocked silence settled on the congregation, broken by a fit of coughing from George Tarkington, who suffered from emphysema. George got up too, and hurried out-of-doors.

It was an appalling interruption. Shaken, the members of Old West Church tried to calm themselves. As their minister gathered his wits and looked once again at the notes for his sermon, Homer Kelly came back in, pushed open the broken door of his pew, and sat down beside his wife. Charlie Fenster came in too, and took his place. As Joe cleared his throat, Ed Bell walked softly up the aisle to the pew where his daughter and his wife were sitting with Claire Bold.

Hunched over the pulpit, gripping it tightly, Joe began his sermon. He did not smile or make jokes. He was not learned like old Mr. Jennings. His sermon was not stuffed with quotations like raisins in a pudding. It was a homily upon the return of moral courage in a time of trouble, on the sources of renewal in moments of fear and doubt. As he finished and called for the last hymn, Joe wondered in what period of ebullience he had delivered the sermon for the first time, in which year of his Pittsburgh ministry? Yesterday he had picked it out of his file for only one reason.

Lorraine Bell guessed the reason. Sitting beside Joe's wife, helping to hold her erect, she recalled the text he had chosen from Isaiah: *They that wait upon the Lord shall renew their strength; they shall mount up with wings as eagles.* The sermon was for Claire. Joe had been addressing the needs of his wife rather than those of his eager and inquisitive congregation.

But they were obviously gratified. Glancing discreetly at each other in satisfaction, they swung into the hymn Augusta Gill had chosen for the end of the service. The verses were by Milton, the music was Handel's.

> *Let us with a gladsome mind*
> *Praise the Lord, for he is kind;*
> *For his mercies aye endure,*
> *Ever faithful, ever sure.*

It had been all right, decided Joe Bold, walking down the aisle. The board chairmen and college professors had begun to look less formidable. He was no longer intimidated. Turning around at the door, he lifted his hand for the benediction.

But then there was another calamity. Instead of a solemn blessing from their minister, the men and women of Old West heard only a gasp. Joe Bold was running up the aisle. His wife had slipped off the bench. She was lying on the floor, with Ed and Lorraine Bell kneeling over her.

Alarmed, the congregation stood uncertainly, then fumbled out of the pews into the aisles. The service was obviously over. Looking back over their shoulders in concern, they drifted toward the doors.

Only Maud Starr took pleasure in the dread events of the morning. Pulling on her buzzard coat, she stared at the new minister as he stooped over his fallen wife. Soaring over them at ceiling height, Maud circled lower and lower, beak and claws extended.

7

*While events of infinite importance have been of daily
occurrence . . . it could hardly be expected that even a
ladies' Missionary Sewing Circle could pursue its work
with accustomed interest and success.*

Annual report, 1861
Missionary Sewing Circle
First Parish Congregational Church, Lincoln

*O*n the steps of the church they
stood in knots and clusters, wondering what had gone wrong with
Howie Sawyer, asking each other about the illness that had so
plainly brought the minister's wife to death's door.

"What about the reception in the parish house?" said Geneva Jones, thinking about the tray of elegant tidbits waiting in
her car. "I suppose it will be called off."

"Oh, too bad," said Betsy Bucky, disappointed. Betsy had
brought a batch of her special coconut squares, and she was eager
to hear the little cries of pleasure as people bit into them.

Only Parker Upshaw knew what was the matter with Claire
Bold. "Cancer, naturally," he said grimly. "She's had two operations already. She's due for another mastectomy this week."

"Oh, the poor darling," said Imogene Gibby.

"Oh, I'm so sorry," said Geneva Jones.

Rosemary Hill said nothing, but she listened anxiously to
Parker Upshaw, then hurried home to lie down with a heating pad
over the place that hurt.

Deborah Shooky was distressed at the sight of her husband's
drawn face in the bright noonday light outside the church. "Phil,
dear, are you all right?"

"Oh, sure," said Phil. "Just sort of upset. It was terrible seeing Howie Sawyer like that. You know, out of his head like that."

Hilary Tarkington was surprised to find her husband lying in the back seat of their fourteen-year-old Chrysler. "Oh, George, dear, I should have come out sooner."

"It's all right," said George, pulling himself up. He sat in the back seat, wheezing, while Hilary drove home. Shifting the gears noisily, she told him about the minister's wife. "Oh, George, you didn't see her lying on the floor. Oh, the poor woman."

It had been a shattering morning. Eloise Baxter rushed away for a dialysis appointment at Mass. General Hospital. Bill Molyneux suspected a return of his own peculiar symptoms. Agatha Palmer felt distinctly unwell. Thad Boland went home in a fit of nervousness and made himself a sandwich, but he couldn't get it down. He took one bite and left the rest on his plate. The sickness in the church was catching. There was illness in the air.

Only a few parishioners were still gathered around the church door when Joe Bold and Ed Bell came out, carrying Claire between them on their crossed hands. Claire was sitting up with her arms around their shoulders, her face white and strained. But then Ed said something that made her laugh as they tucked her in the back seat of his car.

Homer and Mary Kelly hurried across the grass. "Is there anything we can do?" said Homer. "Mary knew Mrs. Bold at school."

Ed Bell was pleased. So was Joe Bold. Mary leaned down to the back window of the car and introduced herself. Claire's face brightened. She grasped Mary's hand. "Why don't you come with us?" said Joe. "I know it will do her good."

They took off quickly, the five of them in Ed Bell's car, accompanied by Peter Terry in his police cruiser. It was Ed who had called police headquarters in the Town Hall, and he was glad that the man on hand was his old friend Pete, even though it was Sunday, and you would think the chief of police would be home Sunday morning with his wife.

Pulling the cruiser away from the curb, Pete Terry turned on

4 4

his siren, thinking unhappily at the same time about his wife, Flo, and her crazy prophecies. Damn it, the woman was right again.

Arlene Pott was one of the last to leave the church. She was reluctant to go home. Not till everyone else had driven away did she walk around the green to her own car on Carlisle Road. Working her key into the lock, she felt the churchly aura of comfortable sanctity slip away, and all the excitement of the new minister's appearance, and the sensational confusion of the two interruptions. As soon as she opened the door of her car, she was enveloped once again in the poisonous atmosphere of home. Her fear gripped her as she drove down Lowell Road. Wally was probably carrying on with Josie Coil right now.

Arlene's suspicions were well grounded. No sooner had she driven off to church that morning than Josie had come running right over to be with Wally. Josie had known Wally was waiting for her. She knew how unhappy he was with Arlene. She knew his whole life had taken on new meaning since she had moved next door to take care of old Mrs. Hawk.

Wally Pott was a small-time insurance adjuster who spent his days arguing with the wrathful owners of wrecked automobiles and the survivors of accidents. Some of the survivors were damaged and crippled, some were not, but all were greedy and litigious. The work was infuriating, the pay was small. Wally's salary was only a tenth of Arlene's income, a monthly stipend left her by her father, who had been a wealthy contractor. Arlene's father's money had paid for their new house. His company had built it. Arlene never let Wally forget that the house was hers, and hers alone. "Take your feet off my sofa," she would say. "Don't walk on my grass."

It was a bitter standoff. The weeks and months had come to seem more and more unbearable to Wally until the day Josie Coil came to work next door. They had been attracted to each other right away. Josie respected him. Josie admired him. Wally swelled in his own estimation. The dimples in Josie's cheeks were invitations to a better life.

But this morning Josie was restive. "Look, Wally, how long

4 5

can we go on like this? Honest to God, I'm really sick of it. You know what I think I'll do? I'm going to take that job in the modeling agency in Watertown. This guy I met, this Victor, he says I can get a job easy. You know, doing ads for fingernail polish and panty hose." Josie waggled her fingers and pointed her toes.

"What guy?" said Wally uneasily.

"Oh, this big good-looking guy, I told you, his name's Victor. I could tell he fell for me in a big way. So what good does it do to wait around while you make up your mind? It's Arlene's money, right? This whole house, it's Arlene's daddy's money that built it? So if you divorce her, she gets the house and the alimony, right? So, listen, I'd have to go on working, wouldn't I? Nursing old ladies like Mrs. Hawk, the way I am now, right? Giving them baths in bed, emptying their bedpans? What good is that? Honestly, now, Wally."

Wally glowered at her. "Listen, you just forget this Victor guy, you hear me? I'll break his neck."

Josie laughed, showing her dimples. "Oh, Wally, no wonder you're jealous. You should see him. He's really good-looking. You know, big and strong, with these heavy eyebrows that meet in the middle and this big cleft chin. And he's really crazy about me, I can tell. So hurry up, okay, Wally? Do something. I mean, here I am"—Josie spread her arms and looked down at her plump breasts, her delicious tummy, her cozy thighs—"just withering on the vine."

Josie stayed too long in the Potts' pink-and-beige living room. Not until Arlene's car door slammed in the driveway did she jump up and scuttle out the back door.

Arlene was no fool. She saw the bushes shake, she saw the white trousers scramble through them. And she couldn't bear it. She was crushed.

But Arlene was tired of fighting with Wally. Walking across the grass, she unrolled the chicken-wire door of her vegetable garden and put her big purple pocketbook down at the end of the stretched white string that showed where she had planted her early peas. Squatting down on her high heels, she stared along the row, looking for some sign of life, tears running down her heavy cheeks.

Eleanor Bell and her mother were the last to get home from church that morning because they had to walk all the way. When they turned in to their driveway, Eleanor was astounded to see Bo Harris waiting for them on the front porch, looking at them anxiously. His bicycle was leaning against the porch steps.

"Mrs. Bell?" he said eagerly. "Did your husband tell you about me and my car? I mean, my name's Bo Harris. Did he say anything about me?"

"Why, no, he didn't," said Lorraine.

"Hello, Bo," said Eleanor, thrilled and excited.

Ignoring Eleanor, Bo followed her mother into the house, talking a blue streak. "It's this car I just bought—my mother won't let me fix it in our driveway. So Mr. Bell said maybe I could work on it in your back yard, if it's okay with you. I mean, my mother cuts the grass with a pair of scissors, I mean, you know, she's really fussy, but I noticed your grass isn't exactly—"

Lorraine laughed. "I'm insulted, but never mind." She sighed, picturing pieces of junk car littering the back yard. "Well, if Ed says it's all right, I won't say no."

"Gee, thanks, Mrs. Bell."

"Have something to eat, Bo?" said Eleanor, smiling eagerly, snatching off the cover of a chocolate cake her mother was saving for company. Eleanor's hair was a riot of golden curls. Her nose and cheeks were pink. This morning in church her mother's friends had gushed over her. "Oh, my dear, how precious." "Oh, Eleanor, dear, how charming." "Ah, youth! Darling Eleanor!"

But Bo Harris didn't seem to see her. "So I'll get my father to bring it over with the trailer hitch on his car. Okay with you, Mrs. Bell?"

8

I have been reflecting on the changes of life—its mutability and uncertainty.
James Lorin Chapin
Private Journal, Lincoln, 1849

*J*oe Bold sat in the waiting room of Emerson Hospital with Ed Bell and Homer and Mary Kelly, waiting for word from the doctor who had taken his wife in hand. Beyond the big windows of the waiting room, the white pines tossed their branches sorrowfully, as if they knew Joe's trouble. Claire's tragedy lay on the table with the magazines. It seeped out of the water fountain on the wall.

Down the corridor, the door to the examining room had stopped shuddering under the blows of Howie Sawyer's fists. Howie must have been given a sedative. The reverberation of his shouting died away.

"What was he saying?" said Mary, puzzled. "Something about brass beds?"

"It sounded like brass beds," said Homer, bewildered too.

"Howie buys furniture for a big chain of stores," explained Ed Bell. "Brass beds, upholstered chairs, dining-room tables—that kind of thing." Ed looked solemnly at the floor, suspecting that Howie Sawyer would no longer be ordering beds and chairs and tables, not ever again in his life.

Upstairs in Dr. Arthur Spinney's office, Joan Sawyer answered questions about her husband. "Have you noticed anything different about him lately?" asked Dr. Spinney, looking at her mournfully. "Lapses of memory, anything like that?"

Joan's eyes were dry. So was her throat. Her face felt dirty with haste and confusion. "Yes. Several times he's seemed disoriented. And one morning he fell asleep in the middle of breakfast."

"I expect it was a small stroke. He must have had another one, much more severe, this morning in church."

"Do you think—" Joan clenched her fingers and tried again. It was a tremendous question, the only question, the only one that mattered. "Do you think he'll come back to his senses?"

"I don't know," said Dr. Spinney gloomily. "At this point it looks an awful lot like multi-infarct dementia. I'm afraid—" Then Dr. Spinney shook his head and prevaricated. "It's too soon to tell." And he dismissed her with a sympathetic squeeze of the hand, too kind a squeeze, Joan knew, to accompany anything but the bitterest news.

Downstairs in the waiting room, Ed Bell, too, took Joan's hand. Mary and Homer Kelly asked her about Howie, and Ed introduced her to Joseph Bold. Joan looked curiously at the new minister, feeling an unhappy sense of connection between them, as though they were rats caught in the same trap. But they were not the same kind of rat. It was apparent that Joseph Bold was stricken with fear about his wife's illness. He wanted her well, he wanted her back—while Joan wanted her husband to die. *Let Howie die*, she had prayed to herself upstairs when Dr. Spinney had squeezed her hand. *Let him die, let him die.*

Appalled at herself, Joan shook hands with the minister and listened to his polite wishes for her husband's recovery. Then she said goodbye and walked out of the hospital, reflecting that the Reverend Bold's courteous words were merely professional good manners. Even so, they affected her powerfully. For a moment Joan Sawyer was swept far out to sea.

9

*Prayer is that Golden Key, which being oyled
with Tears, and turn'd with the hand of Faith,
will unlock the Cabinet of Promises. . . .*
                        Reverend Joseph Estabrook
                                Concord, 1705

*N*ext Sunday, Ed Bell sat beside
his wife and daughter at the front of the church and was surprised
to see that the sunlight was falling on the pews in the same way
as before. It was as if nothing had happened to threaten the
tranquillity of Old West Church. The red carpets still ran straight
up the aisles, the red cushions on the benches were still faded to
the same degree, the painted floor was the same remote and
faraway blue. As the church filled, Ed saw Joan Sawyer sit down
calmly beside Homer and Mary Kelly in the same place where she
had sat before, and Joan too seemed the same, although her life
had been wrenched out of shape and utterly changed. Even the
broken latch of the pew door had been mended. George Tarkington's work, guessed Ed.

In the rear pew on the south side, Mary Kelly talked softly
with Joan Sawyer, while Homer sat with folded arms watching
Geneva Jones thrust wands of forsythia into a jar in front of the
pulpit. Geneva was kneeling on a small stool, and it occurred to
Homer that she was the only person in the room whose knees
were sore. For a moment he missed the ritual kneeling of the
Catholic church in which he had spent so many reluctant hours
as a boy. Would anything drive these Protestants to fall on the

floor? What if God himself were to appear in the pulpit, God in glory with angels and seraphim, his countenance spreading its radiance into every corner of the chamber, would these good people prostrate themselves before him in awe and wonder? Well, no, they wouldn't, decided Homer. It would be too awkward. There wasn't room. They'd bump their heads on the backs of the pews in front of them. They'd have to wedge themselves sideways on the floor, and stick elbows in other people's eyes and beg each other's pardon. It wouldn't work at all, and God had better confine his appearances to churches with kneeling benches embroidered by the ladies of the altar guild.

Jerry Gibby, too, was a lapsed Catholic. But Jerry wasn't

thinking about the dark candlelit interior of the Somerville church where he had once been an altarboy. He was shifting nervously on the bench thinking about something called "shrink." Shrink was a decrease in store inventory for unknown reasons. *Shrink,* good God, it was going to destroy him. His customers were walking out with the entire contents of Gibby's General Grocery. They were dodging past the cash registers with their stolen goods, and nobody was paying any attention. Yesterday, glancing down from the window of his office high above the courtesy booth, Jerry had seen a man push a cart full of frozen turkeys into the florist department and disappear. Racing downstairs, Jerry had rushed out into the parking lot, but the man was nowhere to be seen.

How many times had that thieving bastard pulled that trick? And he wasn't the only one. The books showed a steady increase of unexplained outgo. There was pilferage at the front end, missing cartons of cigarettes, candy, chewing gum. "Shrink," mumbled Jerry aloud. "Jesus."

"Sh-h-h, dear," whispered Imogene. Then she smiled at the woman who was sitting down beside her, a portly woman with a drooping face and dyed red hair. "Good morning," murmured Imogene. "I'm Imogene Gibby. This is my husband, Jerry."

"Arlene Pott," said the woman. "Why, you must be the new people in my neighborhood. Aren't you in the house with the columns? How do you do!"

"Oh, here comes the minister," said Imogene, reaching out to squeeze Arlene's hand as Joseph Bold opened the door beside the pulpit and entered, his robe swirling in the draft from the cold hall.

Remembering his tragedy, his parishioners grew solemn. But Joe was bringing up the matter himself. Leaning over the reading desk, he spoke about his wife, explaining her latest surgery. "Claire will soon be well enough to have visitors. I know she'd love to become acquainted with the members of this church. But of course her strength mustn't be overtaxed. Mary Kelly has kindly offered to organize the visiting. Just call Mary, and she'll arrange it." Joe stared at his notes, and looked up again. "Mrs. Hill? You have an announcement?"

Rosemary Hill was a member of the parish committee on prison visiting. Standing up, Rosemary explained that a job and a temporary home were needed for a young inmate of the Concord Reformatory so that he could be discharged on early parole. She hoped someone in the congregation would provide either the job or the housing. Then Rosemary sat down, and the occupants of the pews around her sat silent, mulling it over, raising the question uneasily with themselves, trying to set it aside, not altogether succeeding. Ed Bell glanced at his wife and raised his eyebrows. Lorraine rolled her eyes and made a face, meaning, we'll talk about it later.

It was time for the first hymn, and everyone stood up. After the hymn they remained standing to recite the Lord's Prayer. For Ed Bell it was like talking to an old friend. "Our Father who art in heaven, hallowed be thy name."

"Thy kingdom come. Thy will be done," said Rosemary Hill, thinking timidly about her appointment with a specialist in Boston, two weeks away.

". . . on earth, as it is in heaven," said Betsy Bucky confidently, soaring upward, rollicking joyfully in the sky, while Carl stood silently beside her with sunken shoulders and gray face.

"Give us this day our daily bread," said Parker Upshaw, speaking loudly and clearly, providing leadership as always, thinking that his daily bread was something like two hundred dollars a day, not counting Libby's income. He smiled to himself, imagining how some rich old geezer in Biblical times would stare at his daily bread, if the old geezer could see it stacked up in gold Roman coins.

"And forgive us our debts, as we forgive our debtors," muttered Jerry Gibby, adding a silent parenthesis: *Oh, Jesus, Mother Mary, you hear that, God?*

"And lead us not into temptation," whispered Arlene Pott, thinking of Wally and Josie Coil, angrily transferring her prayer to her husband.

"... but deliver us from evil," mumbled Joe Bold in anguish. *Deliver my wife from her sickness. Spare her, O Lord.*

"For thine is the kingdom, and the power, and the glory, forever. Amen," murmured Joan Sawyer, for whom God was a once-powerful deity who had created the world and then turned his attention to other things.

10

Work, work, work has been my lot this day.
James Lorin Chapin
Private Journal, Lincoln, 1848

*T*hese days Homer's researches on the outward spread of the faith from Concord were taking him to the library of the town of Lincoln. Bundled up in a heavy sweater, Homer sat at a table in the marble chill of the vault in the basement, taking notes on the sermons of the Reverend William Lawrence. Lawrence's eighteenth-century handwriting was spidery and faded, his sermons dry and doctrinal. Before long, the dust of the ages began piling up around Homer's ankles, his knees, his waist, his throat. He was suffocating. Jumping to his feet, he put away the little volume of sermons, picked up his papers, and drove home for his midday meal.

Pulling up beside the house on Fairhaven Bay, Homer ran up the porch steps eagerly, remembering the words of the funeral eulogy for Reverend Lawrence's wife. "Hail, yokefellow!" he cried, throwing open the door. "O woman of stately mien and benign countenance, O wife of uncommon wisdom and prudence, what's for lunch?"

But Mary was on the phone, and Homer had to make his own sandwich. Slathering mayonnaise on bread, he listened resentfully while the women of the parish called, one after another, making appointments to see the minister's stricken wife.

Mary had become essential to Claire Bold. Claire had grasped at her old acquaintance, and she clung to Mary now as her only friend in a foreign land. Her desperate friendship was taking a lot of Mary's time. Luckily it was Homer's turn to teach the class on Civil War literary history at Memorial Hall in Cambridge. And now Mary was simply shelving her new study of the women of nineteenth-century Concord. All of them were dead and gone, after all, and here was a twentieth-century woman, alive and breathing (if only barely), who actually needed her. Every day Mary sat in Claire's hospital room, correcting midterm papers or reading aloud, while Claire struggled to gain enough strength to go home. Every day another visitor dropped in promptly at three o'clock.

Augusta Gill brought sprays of flowering cherry, Lorraine Bell long wands of peach blossom she had urged into bloom in jars of water. Imogene Gibby presented Claire with a pair of ruffled bedroom slippers, Barbara Fenster potted up a cutting from an enormous rubber plant that had come down in her family, Libby Upshaw gave Claire a thirty-dollar azalea, Betsy Bucky made her a bed jacket appliquéd with teddy bears, Rosemary Hill had forced a bowl of tulips on the cold steps under her bulkhead doors.

In spite of all this attention from her husband's parishioners, in spite of the care and concern of the nurses and doctors, Claire Bold made no progress toward getting well. There were tests and more tests. When a diseased bone was discovered in her shoulder, the surgeon called Joe into his office and tried to speak plainly. "Perhaps it doesn't make sense to put her through the ordeal another time."

But Joe refused to understand. "There's no alternative," he said desperately, flapping his hands. "Is there? Is there?"

"Well, I guess not," said the surgeon feebly.

"He can't let her go," said Mary, telling Homer about it afterward. "That's the trouble. It's his way of holding fast."

The case of Howie Sawyer seemed equally hopeless. Howie was in no danger of dying, but there was no expectation of mental recovery. "He could live for another twenty or thirty years," said the cardiologist, looking at Joan with pity, making no pretense that it was good news.

The nursing home cost a hundred dollars a day. It was too expensive. Joan had learned to her dismay that in the last few months before his attack in church, Howie's affairs had fallen into a disastrous state of confusion. He had ordered the same five thousand rolls of broadloom carpeting from a firm in Philadelphia nine separate times, apparently under the delusion that each time was the first. There were urgent phone calls from the proprietors of warehouses in Braintree, where the rolls were stacked in tens of thousands. Instead of a comfortable bank account, a portfolio of investments, and a prosperous business, Howie's estate was a disheveled mass of unpaid bills.

"I was wondering if I should say something to you," his lawyer confessed to Joan. "But generally it isn't good practice to talk to the wife behind the client's back. I must say, however, I was increasingly dismayed." The lawyer failed to ask Joan about her plans for dealing with her financial embarrassment. Sympathy was all very well, up to a point, but it was usually better not to get personally involved. Surely the woman had friends of her own.

Joan had friends, indeed, but there was little they could do for her. She had taken care of herself before Howie came along; she would take care of herself now. Without a pang she put the house on the market, found an apartment in Watertown, and went back to her old job in the office of a lumberyard in Waltham. She applied for Medicaid for Howie and visited him every day after work. She continued to come to church, driving over from Watertown, although she wished her fellow church members would not stop by to see Howie with the same dutifulness with which they called upon Claire Bold. Perhaps it would be better for them not to behold the spectacle of a man who had so entirely lost himself.

But on one Saturday morning Joan was glad to have the company of Mary Kelly at Juniper Terrace.

"It looks like a nice place," said Mary politely, inspecting the scalped yews beside the front steps. Juniper Terrace had a sleazy pomposity, a kind of cut-rate majesty, with tall columns of white-painted aluminum and a doorway ornamented with a skimpy pediment and urn.

"Well, it's not a nice place," said Joan.

The front hall matched the exterior. There was an upward-swooping staircase and a chandelier on a chain. At a desk in the curve of the stairway sat the receptionist. She had an ageless face and a complicated arrangement of fawn-blond hair. Gracefully she rose and hurried toward them, her tall heels wobbling on the marble floor. "Oh, Mrs. Sawyer, I'd like to speak to you here in the foyer after your visit, if it be convenient."

"Well, all right," said Joan, running ahead of Mary up the carpeted stairs.

Together they walked through the TV room, where rows of elderly children drooped in their wheelchairs. "It's just not a good place," murmured Joan angrily, breaking into a run in the corridor on the other side.

They were stopped by an obstruction in the shape of an old woman who was being wheeled out to her visiting relatives.

"Doesn't Mildred look a picture?" said the nurse, fluffing Mildred's white hair, patting her new housecoat.

"Aunt Mildred?" said one of the relatives loudly. "I brought you a present. Shall I open it for you?"

"Oh, Mildred," said the nurse, "look at that, a new pair of slippers. What's that, dear? Why, Mildred, what a naughty thing to say!"

Mary had been in nursing homes before, but now she was distressed all over again. At the next open door she hesitated and looked in at the specter on the bed. The old woman's face had fallen in. Her mouth was a hole. She was uttering hoarse cries. She stared at Mary and gestured with her hooked hand.

Two nurses were chatting in the hall. "Oh, please," said Mary, running up to them. They stopped talking and looked at her. "The woman in this room needs something, I think. She's crying."

One of the nurses abruptly turned away and walked briskly in the other direction. The other smiled. "Who, Shirley? Don't worry about Shirley. She's fine, just fine. Shirley always cries." Dodging around Mary, the nurse strode past the open door without looking in.

Shirley always cries. Mary stood uncertainly. She wanted to do something for Shirley. But Joan was waiting for her at the door of Howie's room. Mary gave up and hurried down the hall.

She met Phil Shooky in the doorway. Phil had been visiting Howie. He was shaken. His feet were uncertain on the polished floor. "It's so terrible to see him like this," he said to Joan. "Just terrible."

"I know," said Joan. "Thank you, Phil, for coming."

"Goodbye," said Phil, looking vaguely around, starting in the direction of the sun porch at the end of the corridor.

"Not that way, Philip," said Mary, taking his arms lightly and turning him around.

"Oh, I see," said Phil. But a moment later he was back, wandering helplessly, and she had to set him on course again.

They found Howie locked in a wheelchair. A tray was

clamped across his lap. When he saw Joan, he began thumping with his big hands on the tray. She stroked his arm and held his hand, and soon he stopped thumping and quieted down. His attention drifted away. When Joan released his hand, he seemed not to notice. When she said goodbye, he was still gazing at the flowered wallpaper.

Mary was as upset as Phil Shooky. Out in the corridor, walking down the hall again with Joan, she didn't know what to say. There were no nurses in sight. There was no sound but the heartbroken cries of the woman whose name was Shirley. *Don't worry about Shirley. Shirley always cries.* How many years had Shirley been crying?

"Oh, Mrs. Sawyer!" The woman at the desk in the lofty front hall hurried to the foot of the stairs as they came down, then drew Joan aside and spoke to her in a whisper. "I'm afraid you're going to have to move your husband to another facility."

"Move him?" Joan was astonished. "But why?"

"I'm afraid you didn't understand the terms upon which we accepted his application to reside here. We do not accept Medicaid patients at Juniper Terrace. This is a private facility. If he is to be paid for by Medicaid, you will have to find an alternate residence."

"Oh, no," said Joan. "I thought—"

Not a single fawn-blond hair stirred as the woman shook her head from side to side and closed her eyes. "I'm sorry. Medicaid payments are not acceptable. You told us your husband was to be a private guest."

"Well, that's what I thought at the time. But I can't pay that much anymore. You see," said Joan desperately, "I thought my situation was better than it is. I thought—"

"I'm sorry, Mrs. Sawyer. So could you please be ready to move Mr. Sawyer out as soon as possible? We have another guest waiting for his room. Oh, and Mrs. Sawyer?" The woman glanced at a paper in her hand. "There will be an extra charge of two hundred and fifty dollars for a broken window."

Rosemary Hill arrived promptly, to the minute, at Brigham and Women's Hospital for her appointment with the specialist.

But he was distressed that she had waited so long before coming to see him. "You should have done something about it sooner. A lot sooner. You see what's happened." He showed her the X-rays and shook his head. "The thing's out of control."

Timidly, Rosemary studied the white blobs on the dark negatives. "Yes," she said, "I see. Well, I know I should have done something about it last fall, but the pain went away for a while. I thought it didn't amount to anything. Listen"—she turned to the doctor swiftly and said what was on her mind—"when it gets bad, can I count on you to finish it quickly? You know, fix it so that I don't have to wait long?"

The doctor looked at her sorrowfully. "Look, Mrs. Hill, there are things we can do about the pain. You don't have to worry about that. But you can't ask anyone to do what you just said. I can't do that. I'm really sorry."

Dr. Spinney said the same thing when Rosemary made a special appointment to see him, just to talk about the problem of making a graceful exit by her own will rather than an awkward one at the brutal hand of nature.

"Rosemary, you don't know what you're asking. Listen, there was a case just last year in Tennessee. There was this doctor, a good man with a fine reputation. He obeyed the urgings of this old guy who was dying, and the pressure from his daughter and son-in-law. They all wanted the same thing. They were all pleading with the doctor to finish him off quickly. The old man didn't want to die in the hospital, he said. He didn't want to be a burden for another six months or a year. He didn't want all that anguish and mental suffering, and all that expense. What was the point? So the doctor relented and eased him out of his life painlessly and quickly. But then the son-in-law, the bastard, realized he knew something about the doctor that could be held against him, and he sued him for malpractice, for first-degree murder. He won the case and the physician lost his license and went to jail, and the insurance company paid seven million dollars to the daughter and son-in-law, and the cost of malpractice insurance doubled overnight in Tennessee. So I'm afraid the answer to your question"—Dr. Spinney took Rosemary's hand and looked at her kindly—"is no."

"But look at Claire Bold," said Rosemary, gazing at him intently. "How long must she go on suffering? She's had three operations. I understand there's to be another. Surely that's a mistake. Anybody can see there's no hope. And Howie Sawyer! He could live for years as a vegetable. Why doesn't somebody help him out of his misery?"

But Arthur Spinney was intractable.

"Well, all right," said Rosemary to herself, "I'll think of something. I'll take care of it myself. I'll find a way. But first I'll clean the attic. I can't leave the attic for the kids to clear out. I'll clean the attic and then I'll do something."

Somehow, some way, she would take care of it.

11

'Twas from the silver flood that VENUS rose.
Reverend Charles Stearns, Lincoln
The Ladies' Philosophy of Love, 1797

*E*leanor Bell lay in the tub. The water foamed around her in perfumed bubbles. Her breasts rose out of the bubbles, pale and freckled. They seemed miraculous to Eleanor, and important, terribly important, more important than anything else. And yet she couldn't talk about them out loud. She couldn't say proudly, "Look at me." Her mother had stopped short one day and stared at her and said, "Eleanor, darling, good gracious, you're developing a bust. We'll have to go to Marshall's and get you some brassières."

Climbing out of the tub, hot and pink, Eleanor put on an old shirt and a pair of ragged cutoff jeans torn to the hip socket. It was a nice day, but it was still only the middle of May. Eleanor shivered as she leaned against the sink and got to work on her face. She would have to change clothes again this afternoon for her job at the copy center, but this morning Bo Harris was coming over to start work on his car, and he was going to notice her this time. Just because he was a junior and she was a freshman, that didn't mean he didn't have eyes. Painstakingly Eleanor applied mascara to each separate fine hair of her lashes, then drew a line along her eyelid with a pointed brush. Consulting the latest issue of *Seventeen* for advice on the use of cover stick and cosmetic sponge, she dabbed at her nose and drew big dots under her eyes, then blended it all in, using outward strokes. Next she chose a blue eye shadow and highlighted it with silver. "Finally, for a perfect pout, add a touch of soft, nearly nude pink lip-gloss."

Eleanor occupied the bathroom for half an hour. When she came out at last, her mother was approaching with a pile of clean towels. Eleanor gave Lorraine Bell a brilliant anxious smile, then dodged into her own room and slammed the door.

Lorraine stared at the shivering door, astonished. But she held her tongue, remembering her own youth and a certain kidney-shaped dressing table in New Jersey, its glass top covered with creams and elixirs, powder puffs and curling irons and eyelash curlers. Adolescence hit a girl like an avalanche, and there was nothing anybody could do about it. No, it wasn't an avalanche; it was more like a cave, a labyrinth Eleanor would have to negotiate without a candle. It was a fraying rope across a bottomless abyss. Would she come out of it whole and unscathed? Lorraine and Ed Bell had watched and waited four times already, fearfully, while Eleanor's older brothers and sisters had collapsed under the fall of rock, and descended into the cave, and teetered along the rope across the chasm. Every one of those four kids had come out all right. Surely, worried Lorraine, Eleanor would too?

Of course Ed was making it harder, by inviting this boy Paul Dobbs to stay in the house, the boy on parole from the Concord prison. Lorraine had protested, but Ed had talked her into it. "Look, my dear, half the problem is already solved. Jerry Gibby's going to hire him to do shelving in his supermarket. I'll drive him to work and back. All the kid needs is a place to stay."

"But what about Eleanor?" protested Lorraine. "She's just the wrong age. She's so—you know, vulnerable right now."

"Ellabelle?" Ed laughed. "Eleanor's just a little girl. Paul won't pay any attention to Eleanor."

"Ed Bell, how can you be so blind? Have you *seen* Eleanor lately? Have you *looked* at her? She's come into puberty with a bang. She wears a size C brassière. She's a young woman. She spends every cent she earns at that copy center on makeup and clothes. The little girl you knew and loved is gone forever. I'm sorry, dear, but you're living in a fool's paradise."

When Bo's father pulled into the Bells' driveway with Bo's Chevy in tow, Eleanor danced around eagerly on the grass, tremendously excited. The coming of Bo's car was one of the great arrivals in the history of the Western world. She watched, overjoyed, as Bo hopped out of his father's Oldsmobile and began untying the three narrow tree trunks he had lashed to the roof of the Chevelle, while her father welcomed Fred Harris. Eleanor's legs and bare feet were blue with cold. She stood here, then there, as Bo and his father unhitched the Chevy. She waved to Mr. Harris as he drove away. She tried to help Bo erect a tripod of tree trunks, but most of the time she was in the way. When Bo opened the hood of the car to begin taking the engine apart, she was no use at all. She stood back and watched as he leaned over the fender with her father, staring at a rusted bolt.

"You need some penetrating oil," said Ed.

"What's that?" said Bo.

"Something I haven't got," said Ed. Together they struggled with wrenches, then worked at the jammed nut with a sledgehammer and a crowbar, while Eleanor took a freezing sunbath on the weedy grass, her bare legs stretched out, long and blue-white from hip to toe, her black beaded eyelashes closed in fringes on her Enchanted Orchid cheeks, her lips glossy pink in a perfect pout.

Poor Eleanor, she was on the wrong track. She was too much like Bo's three sisters. Back home in the immaculate house on Lowell Road, Bo Harris was overwhelmed, swamped, engulfed in adolescent females. The very air of the house was thickened by the heavy nervous breathing of pubescence. All three of his sisters were going through the same painful rites of passage that now tormented Eleanor. Bo's dignity, his privacy, his masculinity were continually assaulted by the powerful combined claim of Louise and Jennifer and Cindy on the attention of his parents, on space and time, on the hours of day and night, on the world at large, the sea and land, the sun and moon and stars. Their belongings filled the bathroom and crowded the rest of the second floor—their racks of drying panties and bras, their stuffed animals, their plastic jellies, their gold bangles, chains, and lockets, their tights and tutus, their panty hose, their lipstick and eye shadow and nail polish, their hair spray and deodorants, their moisturizers and hair conditioners, their breath fresheners and complexion creams. Bo's eldest sister was going to be married next year, and now the downstairs too was mostly off-limits, with its piles of shower presents, its lists of wedding guests, its samples of tulle and lace, and its bridesmaids' dresses in long white boxes.

Therefore the sanctified quiet of the Bells' back yard was a refuge. Bo came to it like a monk to a monastic cell, an ascetic seeking the peace that passeth understanding, a martyr to a haven of rest and contemplation.

But even in this tranquil cloister there was a disturbing presence. Eleanor Bell was always there in her mascara and eyeliner, Eleanor Bell in her dopey clothes, with her hair in a frizz and each of her toenails a different color. She jarred on his manly solitude. She was too much like Louise and Jennifer and Cindy. She gave him a pain.

12

If we speak of absolute perfection, there has been but one being in our world . . . who, possessing our mortal nature, and tempted as we are, was yet without sin.

Reverend Barzillai Frost
Concord, 1856

*A*rlene Pott had persuaded her husband, Wally, to come to church because it was her birthday. But on the whole Arlene could have done without another birthday. "I'm fifty-eight now," she told herself ruefully. "How old is Josie Coil? Not more than thirty-five, I'll bet. I can't compete. It isn't fair. Fifty-eight! How can I be fifty-eight?"

In the balcony, Augusta Gill played a sprightly prelude by Orlando Gibbons. Pausing as she flipped the page of her music, she held one note past its time. Downstairs, sitting in her customary pew beside Homer, Mary Kelly wished the note would last forever, that eternity would happen, that they would always remain seated on these benches with the sun slanting in on Parker Upshaw, glowing on his left ear; that Joe Bold would forever occupy the pulpit, crouching behind the reading desk with bowed head; that his wife, Claire, would remain alive, poised on the edge of the grave but never falling in.

Across the aisle, Betsy Bucky was not frolicking with the Virgin Mary in her habitual Sunday-morning state of holy transport. She was meditating profoundly just the same. Betsy was composing in her head a letter to Confidential Chat, a page of anonymous letters in the Boston *Globe.* Chatters wrote letters

about their personal problems, or they asked for recipes, and their letters were printed, and other Chatters replied. "Dear Chatters," Betsy's letter was going to say, "I have this problem with my husband, who is retired. He just mopes around the house and I can't have my friends over. When I try to clean, he's always in the way. Any suggestions, Chatters? Oh, I loved Bee-Zee-Q's recipe for Tomato Soup Cake! Anybody want directions for a darling knitted bolero? Yours, Oatmeal Cooky." (Oatmeal Cooky was Betsy's *nom de plume*.)

Of course Betsy didn't really need to write the letter at all. She was taking care of her husband problem every day in her own successful way. As a result, Carl Bucky was feeling distinctly ill this morning, even worse than usual. Sitting beside Betsy, Carl felt his heart bump in his chest. Before coming to church this morning, he had really overstrained himself. Betsy had suddenly decided she wanted the big TV upstairs, and she wouldn't take no for an answer.

Carl had tried to reason with her. "Oh, Jesus, Betsy, that TV isn't what you'd call portable. It must weigh a hundred fifty, two hundred pounds."

"Now, Carl," Betsy teased, "a big strong man like you! Look at those muscles! Don't tell me you're not my big strong hubby anymore?"

"Honest, Betsy, I just don't think—"

"Carl Bucky, I'm ashamed of you!" And then Betsy had rushed into the den and put her little scrawny arms around the television set and heaved at it as if she were going to drag it upstairs all by herself.

What could he do? "Oh, hell, Betsy," Carl had said. "Wait a minute. Here, get out of the way." And then he had lugged the damn thing upstairs for Betsy, shoving it up from step to step, gasping, "My God, oh my God, oh, Jesus Christ, oh, God almighty."

Joe Bold sat behind the pulpit, waiting for the service to begin, looking out the window at the trees tossing in the sunshine. The new leaves were just spreading themselves open, responding to their first breezes, lifting and poising and falling, their delicate tissues sensitive to the lightest airs like the sails of ships at sea. It was surprising the way the sun always shone on Sundays, the rain confining itself to the other days of the week. It meant nothing, of course, that it should be so. There was no special blessing on the Sabbath, no singling out of one charmed and holy day of the week.

But to Parker Upshaw, sitting smack in the way of the sunlight, the sun did indeed seem to have a pedantic purpose in flinging itself ninety-three million miles through the darkness and cold of outer space to illuminate his own particular face. *Is it really you, Parker W. Upshaw, upon whom I have the honor to shine?* The heat warmed his ear, his scalp, his lean jaw, the pimple he had bloodied with a razor that morning. Singled out as a chosen vessel, Parker basked in the sunlight as the service worked its way from opening hymn to the recitation of the covenant, to the offering, to the prayer, to the lesson from Scripture. To one in his exalted state, the lesson really struck home. It was a verse from the Gospel of Matthew: *Therefore be ye perfect, even as your Father in heaven is perfect,* one of the trickier passages in the New Testament. What would Joe Bold make of it, Parker wondered. But then, stroking his sunlit ear and pondering the notion of perfection as a philosophical ideal, he stopped listening to the words from the pulpit and drifted off into contemplation. Perfection! There were of course any number of kinds and categories. On the one hand, there was physical perfection, to be achieved by continuous exercise, by sprinting down the road every day for a mile, two miles, five miles, just a little farther every day. Parker was already an accomplished jogger. He congratulated himself that every time his feet hit the ground his cardiovascular system was strengthening, his lungs were inhaling more deeply, his legs and arms were putting on more muscle.

And as for moral and spiritual perfection, that too was attainable. One could move from perfection to perfection. All it took was the will and drive to achieve a more perfect life-style.

After all, Parker had been lucky so far. He had been born to the right parents. (Parker's father was an ophthalmologist in New Haven.) He had gone to the right institutions of higher learning. He had married the head of college government at Vassar. His son and daughter were enrolled in the most costly private schools in Concord, their teeth were being straightened by the most expensive orthodontists in Boston. And Parker's job at General Grocery was a rung on the ladder of infinite future advancement. Just last week he had accomplished a coup by getting rid of that idiot Will Daly. Sooner or later, Parker W. Upshaw would occupy a spacious office in the tall glassy high-rise on State Street, along with the rest of General Grocery's top management. Parker closed his eyes and pictured his new office, longing for it as John Bunyan's pilgrim had hungered for the Celestial City.

Joe Bold was preaching on and on. Dreamily, Parker turned his attention away from his own little orgasms of the ego to stare out the window at the perfect trees. No, the trees were not perfect this morning, after all. Gypsy-moth caterpillars were spinning webs from branch to branch. The perfection of the created universe left something to be desired, compared with the upward progress of one truly dedicated human being.

Once again Imogene and Jerry Gibby had been seated by the usher next to Parker and Libby Upshaw. It made Jerry uncomfortable, but Imogene didn't care where she sat. There were new friends all over the church, Arlene Pott and Betsy Bucky and Ethel Harris and Lorraine Bell and Rosemary Hill and Geneva Jones. The quilting group was going to meet at Imogene's house this week, and Imogene was on the nooning committee. The Gibbys had been asked to usher next Sunday. Poor Jerry, he was being a little grumpy about ushering. He didn't want to do it. Poor darling boy, he worried so. Why didn't he leave his problems at work? That was what Imogene always said.

But Jerry couldn't leave his problems at work. Jerry's problems had come right into the church with him in the shape of Parker W. Upshaw. Last Wednesday, Will Daly had passed along the bad news.

They had been lunching together at the Colonial Inn, an old building on Monument Square in Concord, one of the places where Henry Thoreau had lived. Jerry Gibby didn't care about Thoreau, and neither did Will Daly. Leaning forward over their Boston scrod and chopped beefsteak, they talked intently about matters of grim importance.

Will had started the conversation by dropping a bombshell. He told Jerry he had just been fired.

Jerry had stared at him in horror. "Oh, Jesus, Will, I'm

sorry." Then it hit him. "Oh, Lord, if you're not there, who'll be in charge of my franchise from now on?"

Will looked back at him morosely. "Guy named Upshaw."

"Upshaw?" Jerry choked. "Oh, no. Oh, God, no. Not Parker W. Upshaw? Oh, my God, Will, say it isn't so."

"It's so, all right. It's Upshaw. Up-the-Ladder Upshaw." Will was seething with outraged innocence. "I'll tell you what happened. He moved in on me. I mean, I could tell from the start he was bad news, as soon as he came into the office last spring and took over Benjie's job. Remember Benjie Shapiro? The next thing I knew, Archie Pendelton was out. Then it was Henry Garber. Pretty soon I could feel Up-the-Ladder's hot breath on my own neck, you know?" With angry playfulness Will put his hand on the back of his collar. "Well, he got a little too close. They fired me last Tuesday."

Jerry had lost his appetite. He put down his fork and looked at Will, his eyes hollow. "I know Upshaw. He wears these J. Press suits, right?"

"Right, that's Upshaw. What he did to me was, he went to the big boss, told him I'm letting some of my accounts go overtime on their monthly payments. You know, like yours, Jerry." Will took another mouthful of chopped beefsteak and chewed slowly, looking meaningfully at Jerry.

"But, my God, Will, I'm going to pay up soon, doesn't he know that? I mean, I can't go wrong, can I? People have to eat."

Will waved his knife. "That's what I told him. Breakfast, lunch, supper, every day of the year, three hundred million people gobble, gobble, gobble, every single day, they all got to eat. But Upshaw, he was thinking about the interest on the loans. That money belongs to General Grocery, he says, only those franchise guys are hanging on to it, so we can't invest it and get interest on it, so we lose big, he says. And the big boss on State Street agrees with him. State Street! He went over everybody's head to State Street! That's Up-the-Ladder for you. The only thing higher than State Street is the board of directors. Maybe he'll try the board of directors next. No, even Upshaw wouldn't have the gall to do that. Anyway, can you feature a creep like that?

The bottom line is, I got fired, and they moved Up-the-Ladder into my spot on the chart, plus a bunch of other spots. The dirty, rotten rat." Vengefully, Will chased his last piece of beefsteak around his plate and plunged his fork into it. "That's what I get for being Mr. Nice Guy."

Jerry turned white and pushed his plate away as the implications of Will's story sank into his digestive tract. "But, my God, Will, that means he's going to be after me to pay up. Christ, Will, I can't pay now. I'm overextended. There's no way I can catch up until I've had a year in the store. Oh, God, Will, it's going to be all right. You know it'll be all right, if I can just have a little more time. You should see the way people pour in there and fill up their carts with ninety, a hundred dollars' worth of stuff, and then in three or four days they're back for twenty or thirty more, and they just came in for a loaf of bread. It's going good, Will, honest. I mean, people have got to—" Jerry clutched at a straw. "We go to the same church. Maybe as a fellow church member he'll give me a few months of—what do you call it, grace?"

"Upshaw goes to church, does he?" Will guffawed bitterly. "He ain't no Christian, believe me. They don't teach theology at the Harvard Business School." Will's eyes brightened as he turned metaphysical. "Well, maybe, sure, yes, they do, only their god is Money. And the angels, flap, flap"—Will flapped his arms like wings, and a waitress had to skip out of the way with her carafe of coffee—"they're certified public accountants, and the prophets are these big important stockholders and trustees. And the Bible!—the Bible is this big account book with everybody's credits on one side and debits on the other, and, you know, like they keep track of your sins up there in the sky. And heaven is this big, gigantic"—Will made a vast embracing gesture with both arms, and a busboy had to dodge backward, nearly dropping his tray of glassware—"multinational syndicate, and St. Peter is chairman of the board, and they don't let you in the pearly gates without you've got this big roll of bills. And hell is—hell is—"

"Okay, okay," said Jerry. "I get the message."

"Dessert?" said a waitress, whipping out her notebook. "Indian pudding? Apple pie à la mode?"

"Oh, no, thanks," said Jerry, putting his hand pathetically on his churning stomach.

Joe Bold's sermon was coming to an end. Jerry hadn't heard a word. He stood up with the rest and moved his lips while Augusta Gill played a canon by Thomas Tallis and the congregation sang about the guardianship of almighty God:

> *He shall with all-protecting care*
> *Preserve thee from the fowler's snare;*
> *When fearful plagues around prevail,*
> *No fatal stroke shall thee assail.*

Show me, thought Jerry Gibby, caught like a trapped bird in the fowler's net. Go ahead and show me.

13

. . . the same old pain remains in my head.
James Lorin Chapin
Private Journal, Lincoln, 1849

*I*t was the hundred-and-fiftieth year since Ralph Waldo Emerson had stood up in Divinity Hall at Harvard and delivered his famous address to the seniors in the Divinity School. The address had deeply offended the professors, but time had assuaged their dismay, and once again there was theological chic in the transports and raptures of the transcendentalists. The Harvard Divinity School now wished to celebrate the sesquicentennial of the famous address. The central ornament of the celebration was to be a lecture by the Reverend Joseph Bold. Joe was to speak in the same chamber in Divinity Hall to the current members of the senior class.

He dreaded it. He had accepted the invitation more than a year ago, before Claire had become so ill. Now it was all he could do to frame an adequate speech. But when the day arrived, a rainy Saturday morning in June, he urged himself into his car and drove to Cambridge to do his duty.

He knew why the organizers of the celebration had chosen him. Among his colleagues he had acquired a reputation as a sort of late-twentieth-century incarnation of Emersonian eloquence. He was famous in a small way as a transcendentalist of the same stripe. Driving down Oxford Street, looking for a parking space,

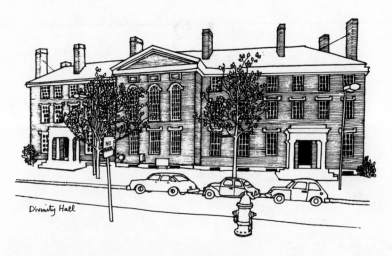

Divinity Hall

Joe wondered how long he would be able to preserve the esteem his Pittsburgh preaching had won him. Now with each passing week in the Nashoba church, as Claire faltered closer and closer to a spaded trench in the lawn of the cemetery on Carlisle Street, his Sunday-morning sermons were more hesitant, more lame, more untruthful. Why, then, did the drowned visions beyond his windshield continue to press in on him, distracting his attention, forcing him to wonder at the rain falling in misty sheets and at the three-deckers and apartment buildings and science classrooms rising thickly on either side? He saw the classrooms crowded with students, and in the houses mothers spooning food into the open mouths of children, and men staring out the window at the rain. Out of sight to the south, beyond Memorial Hall and the Yard, lay the Charles River winding in a gray loop. He could almost smell the fresh muddy damp of the water-soaked shore. Even the vast bulk of the Museum of Comparative Zoology, that familiar place where he had spent so many hours cataloguing blowfish, attracted him with its monumental grip on the ground. Even the pattern of the chain-link fence around the parking lot at Andover Hall gave his vulnerable eyes no rest, even the raindrops beaded on the polished hoods of cars.

To Joe's surprise, he found an empty slot, and pulled in. Turning off his engine, he looked at his watch. He was more than an hour early. He didn't want to walk into Divinity Hall too soon. What should he do now?

The rain fell, too, on Joan Sawyer as she moved her husband into the County Hospital in Waltham. For Joan, the rain provided no visual stimulus. It merely added to the grimness of her errand.

But the hospital was not as bad as she had feared. The staff members were tough and friendly, the head nurse massive and competent, armored like a knight in a stout foundation garment. Beneath her white uniform, her rigid bearing was obviously sustained by buckles, zippers, and grommets, a mighty girdle with a great fan of laces across the rear. Corseted thus, the woman inspired confidence.

Yet the place itself was more depressing than Juniper Terrace. The patients were an even sadder lot, and the ward, while clean and airy, was pockmarked and battered as though the blood of battle were hosed down every day.

The head nurse introduced Joan and Howie to the other patients, Miss Stein, Mr. Canopus, Mrs. Beddoes, Mr. O'Doyle, Mr. Keizer. All of them were suffering from the same sort of affliction that had destroyed Howie. They stared languidly at Joan—all except Miss Stein, who kept her eyes shut. Joan shook hands with them, then cried out as something hit her painfully in the shoulder. "No, no, Mr. O'Doyle," raged the head nurse, snatching up his ball. "What did I tell you? No, you can't have it back, not today."

"I don't mind," said Joan, rubbing her shoulder. Then she said goodbye to Howie, afraid that he would cling to her and refuse to stay. But he hardly seemed to notice he was in a different place. Joan left him in the care of the head nurse and drove away, grateful that the transfer had been uneventful, wondering which was worse, her life before or after her husband's mental disintegration.

Before Howie's stroke, Joan had lived in a condition of fierce hypocrisy, clothing her unhappiness in a perpetual pretense of contentment. It had been a ceaseless muscular effort of will, like lifting weights or balancing plates on sticks above her head. Her decision to marry Howie had been a rational act, an attempt to improve her life, to exchange her dreary apartment in Somerville for Howie's handsome house in the suburbs, and her dull job for perfect freedom. She would be alone all day, Joan had thought, she would take walks in the woods, she would make new friends and entertain.

It had been a mistake. Whenever she ventured into the wooded valley behind the house, it was only to discover that Howie's name was emblazoned on every tree, stamped on every leaf. And the dinner parties dominated by Howie's loud voice had been the keenest torture. A few weeks ago she had thought life would never ask more of her in the way of bitter courage than those cheerful goodbyes to clusters of pitying guests.

But now her daily visits to Howie had become another kind of torment, sharpened by something new, her raging sense of error. The reasoning part of her mind knew that Howie's condition was purely a physical breakdown. The unreasoning parts of her body, her heart, lungs, and liver, told her that if she had truly loved him, he would not now be a puzzled beast locked in a bullpen. Joan was torn apart by the shattering disparity between her genuine concern for his welfare and her passionate desire that he should die.

It was still raining. At the end of the hospital driveway she impulsively urged her car left instead of right. With the rain battering the windshield, she couldn't face the thought of her dark apartment. She felt wretched and careless. Driving mindlessly along Trapelo Road, she beheld the shape of her own bitterness as if from some calm zenith. It was not some nameless woe, but a precise and particular despair. Knowing so clearly what was happening to her, she abhorred it. Her pity and scorn for Howie had flowed over into a contempt for everything else, that was the trouble. All the other men in the world had begun to seem pitiful too, inadequate and fallible. She had cut herself off from human affection. The punishment for her failure to love Howie was the inability to love anyone or anything else. The world had become drab. The sky was no longer blue. The stars were merely flecks of chalk on a smeared blackboard.

In Cambridge, Joan parked on Sacramento Street, then

walked along Oxford to the Museum of Comparative Zoology to try the tonic effect on her condition of stuffed zoological specimens in glass cases. She hadn't visited the museum since she had come with her father on Sunday afternoons long ago to see the hummingbirds and the whale bones and the bird that puffed out its throat like a red balloon. Would they still be there, twenty years later?

Yes, yes, the bones were there. Joan grinned with pleasure at the whale still hanging gigantically from the ceiling, its vast baleen bristling like a comb. And the place still smelled of embalming fluid and mothballs and feathers and varnish and leather and the shells of giant Galápagos turtles collected a hundred years ago. The hummingbirds were there too, scores of them, poised with their long bills tipped up, their wings outstretched, gazing at Joan as if she were a colossal flower. They were dustier than she remembered. They had been in the case a long time. Joan could imagine the bright skins arriving in tiny parcels from Burma and Ceylon, from Brazil and Chile, from California and Oregon.

Cheered by the hummingbirds, she stopped to admire the small hippo and the warthog, then made her way to the glass cases in which the great cats stalked, caught in mid-pace, their glass eyes staring. Someone else was looking at the lions. It was Joseph Bold.

Joe glanced at her without making any sign of recognition, then began to speak as if he were continuing a monologue. "You see," he said, gesturing at the lioness, "those claws are retractable, like a house cat's. She can fold them down, then lift them up to claw at something whenever she feels like it."

"Yes," said Joan, staring at the claws. "So she can."

"It's what Darwin said," Joe went on, waving a forlorn hand. "He said this terrible thing."

"He did?" said Joan.

"He said . . ." Joe paused and turned to her as if to unburden himself of some ghastly secret. "He said that a devil's chaplain could write a book about the horrible blundering cruelty of nature. That's what he said."

"Oh, yes," said Joan. "I guess I read that somewhere myself."

"Well, that's it." Joe turned and waved feebly at the other glass cases. "It's all like that." Without saying goodbye, he walked away, his shoulders sagging, his hollow coat flapping. Then he looked back at her and released another appalling confidence. "You know what else he said whenever anybody asked him if he was the one who wrote the *Origin of Species*? He said it was like confessing to a murder." With this hideous disclosure, Joe wandered away and disappeared in the direction of the gibbons and chimpanzees.

Joan turned away too, and wandered in the other direction, looking for the bird that puffed out its chest like a balloon. She found it with the peacocks, the frigate bird. The taxidermist had

the PELECANIDAE

the FREGATIDAE

stuffed its bare red breast with wads of padding. "Female frigate birds," said the legend on the card, "are attracted to the male during the mating season by this extraordinary ability of the male to extend its breast."

Joan stared at the frigate bird, realizing to her astonishment that she had been snatched completely out of herself by her encounter with Joseph Bold. His drooping coat and melancholy face were working upon her in the same way that the breast of the male frigate bird compelled the attention of the female. They were like the glorious cantilevered tail feathers of the peacock, or the rosy bottom of the baboon. As a trick of wily Mother Nature, this particular arousal of her interest was destined for failure. It would not end in reproductive success. Her excitement was merely a part of an immense extravagance that tossed hundreds of seeds to the wind from a single milkweed pod, or deposited thousands of eggs in a mass of jelly from a single frog.

Closing her eyes beside the frigate bird's case, Joan dwelt on the glance of Joe's hazel eye, his expression of pensive doubt, the cracked texture of his light voice, the swing of his loose coat. Then she descended the steps of the museum, feeling pleased with herself, as if she had taken a spoonful of medicine, a specific for her condition. For her outward life, the prescription was meaningless and could work no cure. For her inner wretchedness, it was a wholesome tonic.

She walked back to her car feeling better.

14

*. . . the love of a wife (such as I have got) grows stronger
and stronger every day, and cannot be bought for any
money.*

James Lorin Chapin
Private Journal, Lincoln, 1849

"*L*ook at it rain!" said Betsy Bucky to Carl. "Oh, Carl, you know what I'm going to do this afternoon? I'm going to start that bedspread. I'm not going to wait another minute." Betsy hopped up from her chair, dragged it over to the refrigerator, climbed up on it, and reached for her pattern books, which were lying in a heap on top.

Then she gave a little shriek. "Oh, Carl, I dropped it. I dropped the instructions behind the refrigerator. You've got to pull the fridge away from the wall. I can't make my pretty new bedspread without the instructions."

Carl looked up from his lunch and stared at his wife in horror. "Listen, Betsy, I can't move the refrigerator."

"Don't be silly, honeybun." Betsy hopped down from her chair and ran over to the stove. "Here, have another plate of spaghetti to build up your strength. Then you can do it. I just know you can."

Rosemary Hill had risen that rainy morning more tired than when she went to bed. After breakfast she had gone back upstairs to take a nap, but she still hadn't been able to sleep. Now she sat in her bathrobe at the telephone table in her front hall, talking to Ed Bell, letting it all out in a flood.

But Ed interrupted, obviously stricken. "Oh, Rosemary, I'm so sorry. Have you been to another doctor? Are you sure?"

"Oh, yes," said Rosemary. "I'm sure. But that's not the point. The point is—listen, Ed, dear."

And Ed listened while Rosemary went on and on, faltering, explaining. In the end, he said why didn't they get together at his house and talk the whole thing over. And Rosemary said what about Thad Boland, he'd be interested, and so would George Tarkington, whose emphysema was so bad, and Rosemary had heard a rumor about Eloise Baxter.

"Well, certainly," said Ed. "Let's all get together. What about three o'clock this afternoon at my house?"

And then Ed hung up and set his mind to the new task. It looked very hard. Rosemary and Thad and George and Eloise would come into his living room at three o'clock, and they would all sit down and look at each other, and then somehow they would have to begin to talk. The moment would present itself, and he would have to face it. Ed had no fear that he would not be able to say something. The right words would float into his mouth, his tongue would shape them, his ears would hear them coming out of his lips. He had only to wait for them and expect them, and they would be there.

By midafternoon the sky had cleared. On Lowell Road, Arlene Pott had spent the rainy morning fighting with her husband. Then she had tried to make up by preparing his favorite lunch of tacos and beans.

"Wally?" said Arlene, knocking on the door of his den. "Lunch is ready."

"I'm not hungry," growled Wally through the door. Arlene could tell by his voice he had been sleeping on the couch.

She went back to the kitchen, slapped the tacos into the garbage disposal, crashed the dishes into the sink, and wept a little. Then as the sun came out, she collected herself and decided to spend the afternoon in her vegetable garden. Putting on her old slacks and galoshes and a pair of gloves, she went outdoors.

Immediately she felt better. She was pleased to see all the

yellow flowers on her tomato plants. Her zucchinis were rioting all over the ground. Arlene tore out the old pea stalks and staked her beans. How amazing, she thought reverently, that all this lush greenery should have come from a few tiny seeds. She weeded everything, kneeling on the wet ground, getting her slacks dirty. Her garden was going to be a showplace. It was already a solid comfort, a solace for her bruised soul.

The Kellys, too, had a vegetable garden, a ratty-looking plot rescued from the forest underbrush on Fairhaven Bay. When the rain stopped, Mary went out in her rubber boots, pushing through the drenched weeds to find the ingredients for a rata-touille, half a dozen baby zucchinis, some summer squash and green beans, an eggplant, a green pepper. The tomatoes were still a month away. She would have to buy some at Jerry's super-market.

Mary had spent the morning with Claire Bold, and now Joe Bold was coming to supper. To be so much in company with the wife's courage on the one hand and the husband's anguish on the other was a peculiar kind of burden, a strange hiatus in the normal progress of Mary's days. It was as though she had been shunted into a waiting room in some abandoned train station, an old railroad depot with a littered floor. There she sat with Claire in the half-light, waiting interminably for a train that never came, that would pull in at last to stop for Claire, then move away slowly, its iron wheels grating and screaming on the rusted track. She could wait forever, thought Mary, among the broken benches and empty gum machines and dirty windows, and pray that the train would never come.

The meeting at Ed Bell's house, the one inspired by Rose-mary Hill's urgent problem, began tentatively, in a mood of self-conscious embarrassment.

"Well, here we are," said George Tarkington, sitting back in his small chair, looking around at everybody, his hands on his knees. "Here we are."

"I just thought we should all get together," said Rosemary.

Reaching into her sewing bag, she jerked out a rag and began jabbing it with pins.

Then Thad Boland started on a rambling story about his septic tank, a saga that had no point and no relation to anything they had come together to talk about. The rest of them listened patiently, as though they too were unable to confront the thing that sat invisibly among them in the center of the braided rug.

When Thad's story finally petered out, they all sat silently staring at the rug until Ed spoke up and took the creature by the throat.

"Look," he said, "we're all going to die someday. Some of us just happen to know more or less when it's going to happen. That's bad in some ways, but maybe it's good in others. It gives us control over circumstances. It means we can get ready for it. We can help each other through it. Perhaps we can even do more than that."

"More than that?" said Eloise Baxter, trembling.

"More than that, right!" exclaimed Rosemary. Clashing her scissors in the air, she slashed at the rag in her hand. "If anybody thinks I'm going to die in the hospital with tubes going in and out of me, and losing control of my bladder, and going in and out of comas, they've got another think coming." Fiercely she ripped her ragged piece of cloth down the middle.

"Oh, I see," said Eloise, putting pale fingers to her mouth.

"Yes, yes," said George. "I know what you mean. I worry about it all the time."

When all of them had had their say, Ed ended the meeting by reading the twenty-third Psalm. They all joined in, murmuring the well-known phrases about green pastures and still waters and the valley of the shadow of death, and the words penetrated very deep, and Eloise wept, and they all embraced and said goodbye and went home.

As the meeting at Ed's house broke up, the dinner guest at the Kellys' house was just arriving. Joe Bold drove down Fairhaven Road, took a wrong turn, drove back, took another wrong turn, tried again, then arrived at last at the steep descent beside the river. Cautiously he inched his car down the slope and pulled up beside the house, then climbed out to say hello to Homer and Mary as they came running down their porch steps to greet him.

He had arrived early, and therefore supper was early. And after supper there was still so much light that Homer said, "Look, let's go to the hospital by the river."

Mary and Homer pulled the canoe down among the pickerel weed, and Homer climbed in. Then Mary hung on to one end while Joe got in awkwardly after putting one shiny shoe deep in the mud.

"It's a good thing Homer's paddling has improved," Mary said, giving the canoe a big shove. "You should have seen him in the old days. Remember, Homer, the time we had to paddle with a lunchbox? Goodbye, you two."

"I remember the snapping turtle," growled Homer. "See that?" He showed Joe his scarred thumb. "She thought it was funny. She laughed fit to kill." Picking up his paddle, Homer turned the canoe silently in the shallow water and headed into the slow current. The mosquitoes pursued them. It was the night of the full moon. As the sun set downstream, the moon's pale shield rose over the low hills behind them. Pulling out into the middle of the river, they rested their paddles and drifted, gazing at the ripples under the aluminum prow, at the fireflies flickering in a sloping field, at the jet trail high in the failing light, turning from rose to gray, at Venus, a spark above the sunset.

Homer glanced over his shoulder at the moon. "There was a certain moment Thoreau used to watch for, the moment when the light of the rising moon took over from the setting sun. He tried to catch it, that little interval of time when night began. It's too early right now, I guess." Homer paddled steadily, lifting his blade straight out of the water, making purling seams that curled away behind them, while Joe talked about his day at the Divinity School.

"The students were interested in something they call the life of the spirit," he said bitterly. "The life of the spirit is really big there now. Of course it's a good thing. I mean, when I was a student it was all rationalism and the social mission, and I was sort of odd man out. But now it's spirituality they want. I don't know, Homer, somehow it left me cold. They were all so radiant." Joe's paddle splashed and clanked against the metal side of the canoe. "I confess I felt more and more disgruntled."

The hospital loomed in front of them, its windows alight. "Well, maybe you're on the right track," said Homer. "Maybe disgruntlement is the correct attitude toward the universe."

Joe shook his head vigorously. "No, no, it's not. I know the correct attitude. It's plain as the nose on your face. The right attitude is Ed Bell's. He comes into the hospital to see Claire and tell her funny stories and make her laugh, and once in a while he says something about the good Lord. He has this nice simple faith. He trusts in God in the most natural way, as though his good Lord were one of the family. Well, I believe in his God, but only for Ed, not for me. As soon as Ed leaves, his good Lord goes with him." Joe dipped his paddle savagely, turning the canoe toward the shore. "The church would be a lot better off if I resigned and Ed Bell took over."

"That's ridiculous," said Homer, looking around at Joe in astonishment. "Besides"—Homer gesticulated excitedly with his paddle—"Ed Bell probably doesn't know Leviticus from Exodus. He doesn't know Noah from Nicodemus. He doesn't know the Archbishop of Canterbury from the Patriarch of Jerusalem. He doesn't know the Defenestration of Prague from the Donation of Constantine. He doesn't know—"

"Look, Homer," said Joe, gazing up at the sky, which had darkened to a deep greenish-blue around the high walls of the hospital. "It's now, right now."

"So it is," said Homer softly. "The moon's in charge from now on."

15

. . . these tabernacles of flesh are to be rent in pieces, these houses of clay are to be broken down by the hand of death. . . .

Reverend Paul Litchfield
first minister of Carlisle, 1781–1827

When in doubt, throw it out. Rosemary Hill was cleaning the attic. She had spent days and days under the roof in the sweltering heat, bowed over on a low stool, sorting through papers and memorabilia, taking small respites downstairs in bed, then coming back up. Ruthlessly she tossed things into the wastebasket. What possible use to Jeffry and Amanda were her life-drawings from art school, thirty years back? Why would they care about these old yellowed copies of the Nashoba *Bee?* Out with them all, out, out.

But Rosemary couldn't throw away the cheap school photographs of Jeffry in the third grade, or the notes on parish visiting at the Concord Reformatory. Jeffry would want the pictures and the church might want the notes. Rosemary stacked them beside the attic stairs, then gazed around the attic.

There was still such an awful lot of stuff. How much longer would she have the strength to keep on? How many weeks or months? She looked at her watch. She would have to stop in a little while for the second meeting of the group at Ed Bell's house at three o'clock. There was time for just one more box. Undoing the string on a carton of old linens, Rosemary pulled out a dresser scarf. Would Amanda like a dresser scarf? Amanda's own great-grandmother had made it, and nowadays this sort of thing was coming back in style.

At the Bells' house, on Acton Road, Ed was getting ready for his afternoon meeting, looking critically at the living room. It seemed comfortable enough, a little frowsy from the battering it had taken from five children and any number of dogs. But the chairs were too far apart. For a gathering like this one, people really needed to be closer together. He pushed one of the big upholstered chairs closer to the sofa and dragged the other one across the rug on its two back legs. His wife looked in as he crowded the desk chair against the coffee table.

"Another one of those meetings?" said Lorraine. "Honestly, Ed, dear, it's the craziest thing I ever heard of." Lorraine had her pocketbook in her hand. "Illegal, immoral, and I don't know what else."

"We just talk, that's all we do," said Ed. "You're going for Ellabelle?"

"Yes, and I'm late."

But late as she was at the copy center, Lorraine was still too early for Eleanor, who always found it hard to stop working. Eleanor had turned her job into a dance. Now she grinned at her mother, snatched the next customer's sheet of paper, whirled around, tossed up the cover of the copy machine, slipped in the paper, snicked the cover down again, punched a row of buttons with quick dabs of her fingers, whirled again with tossing hair, to seize the ringing telephone and tuck it between ear and shoulder and josh with the boy in the office upstairs while she gathered up the copies from the bin, smacked them smartly into a pile, twirled to put the phone down, beamed at the customer and dropped his copies in front of him, all complete.

Lorraine stood waiting, lost in admiration. What a girl that Eleanor was! She could do anything she set her mind to. In school she was a responsible student. In her modern-dance class she was nimble and quick: she could turn around in midair, she could stand on one leg and bring the other one up beside her ear. On the basketball court she could sink a ball in the basket every time she tried. She could swim fifty laps in the school swimming pool, she could run like a deer. Therefore it was all the more pitiful to see what was happening to her at home, snarled as she was in the toils of love. Lorraine watched her daughter and waited, gripping her pocketbook.

This afternoon Bo Harris would be coming over again to work on his old car. And the new boy, Paul, would be arriving, moving into Stanton's room. Eleanor, Bo, and Paul—how would the three of them get along? Darling Ed, he had taken Bo aside and asked him to encourage Paul to help with the replacement of the engine block. Eleanor would be mooning around the edges, abject, eager, trying to help, getting in the way. Poor Eleanor! She had thrown herself so passionately into Bo's great enterprise. His resolute seriousness was hers as well. She was making a heroic effort to understand the workings of a gasoline engine. She was an authority on pistons, on the fatal delay of the spark. But it was all book-learning. She didn't have the mechanical know-how Bo Harris seemed to have been born with.

Dropping Eleanor off at home, Lorraine drove off to ransack Gibby's General Grocery. Thus, when Eleanor came running downstairs in full cosmetic regalia, it was her father who took her outside and introduced her to Paul Dobbs, and Paul to Bo Harris.

Paul was a cheerful-looking sinewy boy with a bruised face. "Well, hey, there," he said, grinning at Eleanor, whistling in admiration. Eleanor had washed her hair and blown it dry so that it streamed forward around her face and then back at the tips as if the wind had changed direction in a hurricane.

Eleanor said hi, then turned to glance at Bo, but he was looking at his car, which stood among them like a monument. Above it like a canopy rose the tree-trunk tripod and the new block and tackle. Eleanor's father had paid for the block and tackle. He had always, he said, wanted a block and tackle.

Then Bo turned to Paul and looked at him soberly. "You want to help me install the clutch? It's a two-man job. It's really tricky to line up the spline with the clutch plate."

Paul looked vaguely at the tripod and the block and tackle and the car. "You should see my brother's Jag." Leaning against the porch railing, Paul bragged about the Jag and about a couple of Suzukis and BMW bikes he had ridden in the past. Then he talked freely about his four brothers. Two were rich. The other two were locked up in houses of correction.

Bo made another try. "Here, you want to grab the back end of the transmission?"

But Paul had other things to do. He turned away importantly. "I got to go to Winthrop. My brother, he's going to pick me up. He's got this place right on the water."

So Bo had to fall back on Eleanor. "This shaft goes into that hole, see? You got it?"

"Got it," said Eleanor, and she took a firm hold. But she wasn't strong enough. They couldn't get the shaft lined up. Bo cursed and fumed. At last, in desperation, he poked around in the house until he found a broom in the kitchen. Then, bumping down the cellar stairs, he looked for a workbench with tools.

There were two large obstructions in the cellar, a monstrous object with iron doors into which coal had once been shoveled and a modern oil-fired furnace. Mr. Bell's workbench occupied an enclosed space behind the new furnace—the old coal bin, guessed Bo. He took Mr. Bell's saw off the wall above the workbench and carried it outdoors with the broom. Resting the broom on the top step of the back porch, he braced it with his knee and sawed off a length of handle.

It worked fine. It lined things up just right. Satisfied, Bo ate half a dozen of Eleanor's fudge brownies, mounted his bicycle, and rode away.

Eleanor stood in the driveway, gazing after his bare back as he coasted onto Acton Road. Then she had to move out of the way because Mr. Tarkington's car was turning in to the driveway. It was rusty and dented. It looked almost as bad as Bo's. And another car was slowing down. Eleanor recognized Mrs. Baxter at the wheel.

What were all these people doing here? Eleanor held the screen door open for Mr. Boland, who came hurrying up from across the street. Then she looked for her father, to tell him he had company.

She found him clattering glasses onto a tray in the kitchen. "What are all these people here for?" said Eleanor.

"Oh, it's just a meeting," said her father, smiling at her.

"What kind of a meeting?"

Ed took a pitcher of lemonade from the refrigerator. "Just a friendly support group, Ellabelle."

"A support group? For what?"

"For each other." Ed Bell winked at his daughter, put the pitcher on the tray with the glasses, pushed open the swinging door, and carried the tray into the hall to greet his guests.

The last arrival was Rosemary Hill. Eleanor saw Mrs. Hill climb the porch steps, holding her purse against her side in a queer sort of way. In a moment Mrs. Hill was in the living room with the others. Eleanor stood in the hall, staring at them, wanting to know what was going on, until her father winked at her and pulled at the heavy sliding doors. The doors rumbled together across the floor and shut off Eleanor's view of the meeting. Shrugging her shoulders, she went upstairs to her room.

When Lorraine Bell came back from her shopping expedition, the meeting was over. There were no other cars in the driveway, except of course Bo's old wreck under the tripod.

Ed helped his wife carry the groceries indoors. "Oh," said Lorraine, stopping with a bag in her arms, gazing at the mutilated broom on the grass beside the back steps. "Look at that. What happened?"

Ed's new hacksaw lay on the driveway beside Bo's Chevy. Ed picked it up. "Oh, careless youth," he said, wiping the blade on his sleeve.

16

*But, let me not forget to mention the worthy deeds of
the* fair *sex of this town. . . . Ladies, you have
done* virtuously, *and have* excelled.

Dr. Ezra Ripley
First Parish, Concord, 1792

*N*ext Sunday the morning ser-
vice was to be followed by a nooning, the annual church picnic.

"Do I have to come?" groaned Homer Kelly, who sometimes
wearied of his studious preoccupation with Old West Church, his
Sunday mornings of sermons and hymn singing, his sleepy afternoons deciphering the handwriting of pious country parsons.

Mary was frying chicken, turning it expertly with a pair of
tongs. "Of course you have to come. Listen, Homer, it will be like
those old noonings in the nineteenth century, those picnics between the two Sunday sermons when everybody visited with everybody else while they ate from their picnic baskets. It will give
you a better understanding of the old days in the church. And
anyway this is what it's all about."

"What do you mean, what it's all about?"

"Getting together, being all in one place at the same time.
Oh, of course they were all together inside the church, listening
to the sermons, but then they had to be quiet and not talk to each
other. At the nooning they could gossip and find out how people
were, and learn about each other's needs and minister to each
other."

"Oh, right, right—well, all right," said Homer grudgingly.

9 4

So once more the pickup ground its way up the bluff beside the river, out onto Route 2, through the center of Concord and along Lowell Road to Nashoba, to the parish house of Old West Church, the clumsy building of green-painted shingles that had once housed the Unitarians.

The nooning had taken over the huge gymnasium-like room in the front of the parish house. The pews had long since been removed, but the organ was still there, enclosed in paneling, and the homely stained glass still glowed green and yellow high in the wall. The acoustics were bad. In the clapboarded building to the west, it was sunlight that rebounded from walls and ceiling, but here it was noise, recoiling, reverberating, colliding, smearing together the voices of the picnickers as they scraped their folding chairs across the floor and hurried back and forth to the kitchen and talked across the tables. Children's high staccato voices echoed and re-echoed.

Battered by discord, Homer stood in the doorway, wondering if the building could have been constructed at a more terrible moment in the architectural history of the nation. In the year 1882, only the mightiest intellects had manipulated the ponderous style with an understanding for the requirements of its massive proportions. The parish house was large without grandeur, its ornamentation graceless and sparse. Homer couldn't help comparing it with the church down the street where they all met on Sunday mornings, the little edifice the dissenting Congregationalists had built for themselves in 1836. They had merely thrown it together like a barn. The result was perfection.

Homer's wife, Mary, pulled out a chair and sat down at a table where there were two empty places between Carl Bucky and Joe Bold. Homer took the seat beside her, accepted a heaped-up paper plate, and lifted a chicken leg to his mouth.

But Mary was jogging his arm, whispering, "Wait, Homer."

"What for?" said Homer loudly.

"Shut up, you ninny. They're saying grace."

"Oh, sorry." Homer lowered his chicken leg, and the noise in the hall died away, except for the clatter in the kitchen, where Betsy Bucky and Mollie Pine were still shouting gaily at each other. Then they, too, abruptly stopped, and Joe said grace; there was a little pause, and then the noise rose again to full volume, and hands that had paused in mid-gesture went on unpacking baskets of food and handing out bowls of potato salad and plates of sandwiches.

Betsy Bucky flew out of the kitchen to unveil her own contribution. For Betsy, the nooning was an opportunity for showing off. It was a platform for the display of her culinary genius. This morning she had loaded Carl down with two heavy baskets. Now she opened them and brought out her pinnacle achievement, a platter of her famous sausage fritters, fried in deep fat. There were cries of "Oooh, Betsy," and groans of wonder as the fritters were passed around and tasted. Betsy's sausage fritters were her specialty, something she had invented herself. They were flaky and delicate, seeming to have no relation to the slaughterhouse in Fall River where the original hogs had been knocked on the head, boiled, flayed, and ground into sausage. Out of Betsy's baskets came more fritters, then half a dozen butterscotch pies.

Lorraine Bell had prepared a simpler meal, bean salad and thin slices of roast beef. "I brought extra," she said to Joe Bold, piling some of it on his empty plate.

"Have some of our cherry tomatoes?" said Mary Kelly, filling in the gaps. "A piece of chicken?"

"Oh, thank you, thank you," said Joe in confusion as Maud Starr piled a mountain of marinated mushrooms on top of everything else. Then Maud squeezed her chair in close and leaned sideways, engaging Joe in a huddle of serious talk. Mary watched, thinking about Joe's wife, Claire, remembering Claire as she had been at school. Compared to Claire Bold as she had once been, Maud Starr was nothing. She wasn't in the game at all. But that was before the rules had radically changed, before Claire's cards had fallen to the floor. Now any fool could play against her, any bitch who was alive and well, whose breasts and bones were whole, whose body was not riddled with disease. Mary cringed as she thought of yesterday, when Maud had come running into the hospital to visit Claire. Maud had chuckled a greeting at the pallid face on the pillow. "Oh," she had squealed, "what a darling bed jacket," and then she had dashed away with a flick of her scrawny skirt. Now the damned woman was deep in sympathetic conversation with Claire's husband about his wife's condition. It gave Mary a pain.

She was glad when all conversation was interrupted by Ed Bell. Strolling out on the platform that stretched across one end of the room, he called for quiet. Ed was inaugurating the annual church canvass. As usual, he was the chairman of the money-raising committee, because nobody else could bring in pledges the way Ed could. Ed had a way of teasing people into emptying their pockets. He cajoled them, he inspired them, he pestered them into it; he didn't let them go. And nobody minded, because Ed Bell, after all, was Ed Bell.

This time he had made up a song, *"A tisket, a tasket, put your money in the basket."* It was a terrible song, but it brought down the house, as Ed pretended to tap-dance, shuffling his feet and flourishing a cane and waving a straw hat. He kept tipping the hat and

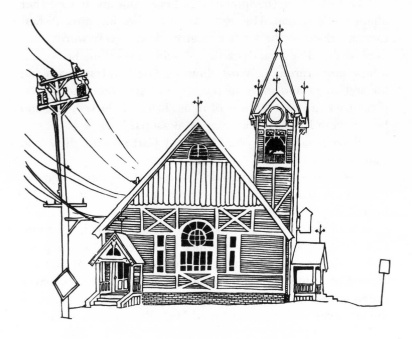

putting it on and taking it off and waggling it comically in his hand while everybody shrieked with rapture. Then Ed called for his canvass captains, Charlie Fenster and Julie Smith and Hilary Tarkington. He made them line up in a row and do the same kind of buck-and-wing, right there in front of everybody, without any practice. Charlie and Julie and Hilary were good sports, and did their best, and they were even funnier than Ed.

The entertainment was over. It was time for dessert. "Weren't they a scream?" said Betsy Bucky, cutting a huge slab of her own butterscotch pie for her husband, Carl.

Carl couldn't reply. He was choking. A crumb of sausage fritter was stuck in his throat. Struggling to his feet, trying to breathe, he tipped the table up on two legs. Homer Kelly's plate slid into his lap. Dr. Spinney raced across the room, took hold of Carl from the rear, and jerked until the crumb came up. Carl sagged, coughing, breathing again. The table joggled back into place. Mopping his chin, his face blazing red, Carl sat down, rescued his plate, then pushed it away.

In the kitchen, Dr. Spinney took Betsy aside and lectured her about her husband. Homer Kelly was collecting dirty dishes, carrying them to the kitchen, and he heard every word. "See here, Betsy, don't you think Carl should be watching his weight a little more carefully? What about feeding him less starch and fat and sugar and more in the way of vegetables and low-fat protein? You know the sort of thing, fish and chicken, rice and beans, fresh fruit? And go easy on desserts?"

Betsy laughed merrily. "Who, my Carl go on a diet? You think I haven't tried?"

"Well, see what you can do," warned Dr. Spinney. "I mean it, Betsy. A man in his condition needs to put less strain on his heart."

Betsy chuckled and nodded as if she understood, but a moment later Dr. Spinney was horrified to see her plop a huge piece of butterscotch pie in front of her husband and spoon over it a mound of whipped cream. Fascinated, he watched from across the room as she hovered over Carl, unscrewing a thermos, pouring him a cup of dark brown liquid. Well, that was better. At least

she was making sure he got decaffeinated coffee instead of the strong brewed stuff from the church kitchen.

Carl drank his coffee, then offered the thermos around the table as Homer sat down again to eat a piece of Betsy's pie. "Anybody want some of my decaf?" said Carl. "Here, try some. It's really good."

"Why, thank you," said Homer, holding out his cup. "Don't mind if I do."

Carl poured it out, and Homer lifted the cup to his lips, then gasped. The black stuff in his cup was the strongest, bitterest brew he had ever tasted.

"Good, right?" said Carl.

"Oh, right," said Homer, putting down the cup.

Betsy was back, pinching Carl's arm. "Come on, honeybun, time to go."

"Oh, okay, ooof," said Carl, struggling up from his chair.

"But first you've got to take the tables down cellar."

"Oh, no, Betsy, my God. I can't do it. I ate too much."

"Carl Bucky," said Betsy, shocked and sorrowful, "whose fault, may I ask, is that?"

The nooning was over. Homer and Mary Kelly went home. Mary had things to do. She got out her oil paints and began painting a map of the river on the wall of the front room. But Homer was restless. He couldn't settle down to anything. He couldn't get Carl Bucky out of his mind.

"That poor man, Carl Bucky," he said. "His wife is a scheming woman. She's destroying him. She's feeding him to death."

Mary dipped her brush in black paint and began painting a row of turtles on a log. She laughed. "Well, Betsy's not alone. I imagine a lot of wives are doing the same thing. Me, too. I mean, we can't help it. We were brought up to cook like that. Our own mothers taught us to make all those rich delicious things. Cooking delicious things was the way to win your family's affection. Then when the health-food people came along and told us not to do it, it was too late. It was ingrained in our whole pattern of married life. Betsy's not the only one."

"Maybe not, but she's worse. Homicidally worse. There was something really menacing about the way she shoved the stuff at Carl, the way she stood over him while he lugged all those heavy tables and wouldn't let me lend a hand. Did you see her come after me when I tried to help him? We had quite a little tussle there in the middle of the floor. I thought she was going to put my eye out. And the coffee—did I tell you about the coffee?" Homer turned and put his hand decisively on the knob of the front door. "Listen, remember those sausage thingummies of hers? You want the recipe, right?"

"The recipe?" Mary made a smudge with her brush, and looked at Homer in surprise. "*I* want the recipe?"

"I'm going over there right now and get the recipe. I want to see that poor guy at home. I want to tell him. I want to warn him. I want to save his life."

"Oh, I see. The recipe is just an excuse. Well, listen, Homer, here's what I really want from Betsy Bucky." Mary looked at her husband slyly. "I want to know how she gets her layer cake to come out horizontal like that. I mean, mine always slopes down-hill. And her pie dough, does she chill it first? I mean, us murder-ing wives, we need to share our little secrets. See here, dear, what do you want for supper?"

Homer clutched his stomach. "Oh, Lord, as a matter of fact, I don't think I'm going to be especially hungry for supper."

"Well, I may not be here anyway when you get back. I prom-ised Joe I'd spend some time with Claire."

When Homer pulled into the Buckys' driveway, he saw at once that Carl was still in mortal trouble. He was mowing the sloping lawn, lunging after the huge lawnmower, heaving it around at the end of each swath, panting after it. The machine made an enormous racket.

As Homer strode long-legged up the hill, Carl paused, turned down the throttle, and leaned against the shuddering control bar. He wiped his forehead on his sleeve. He was beet-red. The lawnmower trembled and backfired.

"Listen, Carl," said Homer, "why don't you wait till the sun moves to the west a little? An hour from now this whole hillside will be in shadow."

Carl shook his head. "Betsy's in a hurry. She's got these girls coming over, wants everything spruced up."

"Well, let's sit down a while anyway," said Homer, setting a good example, lowering himself to the grass.

"Sure, why not?" sighed Carl. Turning off the lawnmower, he sank down and lay back with his arms over his face, panting, his big stomach rising and falling.

But it was no use. Betsy heard the silence. She shrieked from the doorway, "Carl? They'll be here any minute. Can't you finish the front lawn? Homer Kelly, is that you? Come on up here and have a glass of iced tea."

Homer and Carl stood up slowly. Carl put his foot on the lawnmower and grasped the starter rope.

"Don't do it, Carl," said Homer. "You shouldn't be pushing that big machine. Honest to God, you look terrible."

"Carl?" cried Betsy. "How about it, honeybun?"

Carl shrugged at Homer and jerked on the rope. It didn't

catch. Walking reluctantly up to the house, Homer heard the gasoline engine sputter and die, sputter and die, sputter and die. He looked over his shoulder as it caught at last, and watched Carl guide the thundering machine across the slope. It kept tugging at him, trying to run downhill. Carl had to keep hauling at it, pushing down on the handle to aim it uphill again.

"Say, Betsy," said Homer, "do you really think Carl ought to be out there working so hard in the hot sun?"

"Who, Carl?" Betsy tittered. "Oh, Carl's all right. He's just fine. He just loves working outdoors. And it's good for him to get a little exercise." With a bright wink, Betsy patted her skinny midriff. "Good for that big belly of his." And then Betsy laughed merrily as if Homer's cautionary remark were the funniest thing she had ever heard.

17

*Have attended church today and listened to two discourses
from Mr. Jackson—one from the text "Be not high minded"
and the other I cannot now recall to mind.*
                                    James Lorin Chapin
                                    Private Journal, Lincoln, 1848

*T*he church services followed
one another relentlessly, Sunday after Sunday. Somehow Joseph
Bold managed to find an hour or two every week when he could
separate himself from his wife's calamity long enough to scratch
together a sermon. Some of his efforts were less adequate than
others. The congregation listened calmly and made no public
complaint.

But Parker Upshaw protested privately to his wife. "This sort
of thing, any kid fresh out of seminary could do it. We don't have
to pay an experienced minister to deliver a sermon like that. Oh,
granted, the poor guy is going through a hard time, but lots of
us go through hard times and still manage to do our job. Is this
what we were looking for when we traveled around the country,
all last year, a minister like this? That sermon this morning was
terrible."

"Oh, Parker," said Libby, "be charitable. You know he's just
upset right now. And anyway I didn't think it was so bad."

Every six weeks the service included communion, a custom
handed down from the Congregational side of Old West Church.
As a former Catholic, Jerry Gibby was astonished when one of the
deacons handed him a tiny glass of purple liquid and a basket

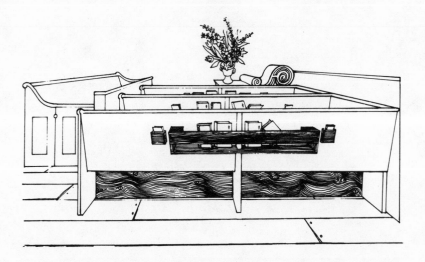

containing a loaf of bread. Awkwardly he tore off a morsel of the bread and swallowed the liquid. The bread went down his gullet easily, but when he tasted what was in the glass, he spluttered and almost laughed aloud. It wasn't wine, it was grape juice. Imogene glanced at him and made a soft shushing expression with her mouth.

For Joe Bold, too, the communion service was a new experience. Like Jerry, he wondered why this freethinking community celebrated it at all. Somehow it seemed strange that all these computer engineers, Wellesley graduates, building contractors, supermarket owners, middle-management men, doctors and lawyers, librarians and teachers, mathematicians and bankers should sit together dwelling on the mystery of the transformation of King Arthur flour and Welch's grape juice into the body and blood of a young Hebrew prophet who had wandered around Palestine two thousand years ago. Of course nobody pretended there was any actual miraculous transubstantiation, not in this Protestant church. Nor did the partakers come forward to kneel and take the sacrament from the hands of their pastor. Instead the deacons passed the bread and the gleaming silver trays of little glasses, and the parishioners sat firmly on the red cushions in the pews and chewed the bread and swallowed the grape juice, then set their glasses in the hymnbook racks, in the round holes especially drilled for them by George Tarkington. In this case, thought Joe, communion was a metaphor for self-sacrifice and spiritual dedication, that was all, just as so much else in the service was a metaphor. Swallowing his grape juice, feeling it trickle down his throat, Joe sat with bowed head, reflecting that the church itself had almost become a figure of speech. He forced himself to concentrate on the teachings of Jesus that had always moved him most profoundly, *Come unto me all ye that labor and are heavy laden, and I will give you rest. Except ye turn and become as little children, ye shall not enter the kingdom of heaven. Inasmuch as ye have done it unto the least of these, ye have done it unto me. Love your enemies, bless them that curse you. Take my yoke upon you and learn of me.* Then Joe thought of the parables of the treasure in the field and the pearl of great price, and at once the other metaphors faded and only the fact remained that his treasure was being taken away from him, his precious pearl.

Grimly he stood up and brought the service to a close, and everyone drifted out of the building, except for Barbara Fenster, who folded the white tablecloth so that she could take it home to be laundered, and the head deacon, Bob Ott, who collected all the little glasses from the pews, and Julie Smith and Geneva Jones, who washed and dried them in the church kitchen.

Metaphor or no metaphor, the communion service was a lot of work.

18

. . . the invalid . . . hopes to be better in a short time . . . to hope at all is to show the frailty of the human mind.

James Lorin Chapin
Private Journal, Lincoln, 1849

*C*laire's spoon rattled on the hospital tray. "I know I should try," she said to Mary Kelly, "but I just can't."

"Well, never mind." Mary picked up the new Travis McGee novel and began reading aloud where she had left off. Every now and then she dipped Claire's spoon into the applesauce, then slipped it into Claire's mouth as if another spoonful were part of the story, as if building up Claire's strength were not a matter of supreme importance.

Out in the corridor, Joe Bold was persuading the surgeon to make one final try. "I don't know," said the surgeon, shaking his head. "If it were my wife, I don't think—"

"It's not your wife," said Joe, choking. "It's mine."

The surgeon said nothing. For a moment they both stood staring out the window at the river winding in the direction of Fairhaven Bay. Below them a crow ended its swooping flight on the top of a white pine tree, and the branch dipped under its weight. From far away they could see its beak open, they could hear the faint squawk. The surgeon rubbed his tired face, and Joe couldn't help perceiving that the gold hairs on the backs of the surgeon's hands were arranged in spiral patterns. To Joe it seemed a bitter fact that while his nightmare blundered on from one dread event to another, the figures it cast upon his senses were still majestic with color and light.

At the County Hospital, Joan Sawyer continued to visit Howie every day. Sometimes she wondered why she bothered to be so diligent. Howie rarely seemed to notice her. If she didn't come, he wouldn't miss her. She was only trying to impress the head nurse, decided Joan cynically, by demonstrating her wifely loyalty. But the head nurse must guess her true feelings. The head nurse was no fool.

The other regular visitor to Howie in the County Hospital was Ed Bell. Joan knew about Ed's visits and she often thanked him for them, although she had never happened to be in Howie's ward when Ed was there. But one Saturday afternoon their visits coincided. As Joan approached the locked door, she could hear singing on the other side.

The head nurse let her in, her face wreathed in smiles, and tipped her head in the direction of the bizarre barbershop quartet at the other end of the ward. Ed Bell, Rosemary Hill, Howie Sawyer, and Mr. Canopus were standing arm in arm, their heads thrown back, singing "Jingle Bells." Mr. Canopus wasn't actually singing, but he had a clutch on Ed, and his head was nodding, his mouth was working. Howie was lost in the song, carried away. He had the words just right. In front of them Mr. O'Doyle tossed his ball excitedly, and caught it, and tossed it again.

Even Mrs. Beddoes was singing, sitting in her chair. Mrs. Beddoes was a sweet-looking old woman who had been reduced by senile dementia to the level of a two-year-old child. One afternoon Joan had met Mr. Beddoes sitting beside his wife, holding her hand. "You'd never think it to look at her now," he told Joan, "but Franny used to be in charge of a whole office. I mean, she had forty people under her." He shook his head sadly, then jumped up as his wife rose in her chair and began to cry wildly, "I got to go, I got to go." "Okay, honey," Mr. Beddoes said, releasing her to the head nurse. "Come on, dear," said the nurse, bustling away with Mrs. Beddoes.

Now Mrs. Beddoes was singing softly, "Oh, what fun it is to ride in a one-horse open sleigh." Even in her shattered memory the familiar tune brought the words along with it.

"Jingle Bells" was over. Ed winked at Joan and started a new song, "Row, Row, Row Your Boat." It, too, was a big success. The head nurse plucked Joan's arm and nodded again, this time at Miss Stein. "She's smiling," whispered the head nurse.

It was true. Crouched in her chair with her eyes shut, little Miss Stein was smiling. Her eyes had been shut ever since Joan had first brought Howie into the ward. Now Joan could see that the thousand wrinkles around her mouth and eyes had been made in the first place by smiling. For once, her face looked right. Miss Stein had been a biologist, a teacher, a specialist in tidal life, until something terrible had happened to her. Now she kept her eyes tightly shut, and whispered the fragments of her dreams. The tide washed in and out, and in and out, and Miss Stein remained asleep.

The singing was finished. Rosemary Hill picked up her purse, shook hands with Howie and Ed, and came over to say hello and goodbye to Joan.

Rosemary felt terrible about Miss Stein. "It's so sad. You can see what she was before, somebody really admirable."

"I know," said Joan.

"It would have been better if she had died," said Rosemary, looking directly at Joan.

"Yes," agreed Joan, and she knew Rosemary meant it for Howie too. It would have been better, far better, if Howie had died.

"And what about Claire Bold?" said Rosemary fearlessly. "I understand she may have to undergo more surgery. I just wonder if it might not be better if they just let nature take—"

"I know," said Joan again, nodding and nodding. "I know."

Rosemary went home and went to work once again in her attic. She spent the afternoon working on financial records, old canceled checks from ten years back, tax receipts and dusty bank statements. There was no earthly use in cluttering up the children's lives with this kind of thing. Ruthlessly, Rosemary chucked them out.

At the County Hospital, Ed Bell, too, was ready to go home. He said goodbye to Miss Stein and Mrs. Beddoes and Mr. Canopus and Mr. O'Doyle and Mr. Keizer and Howie Sawyer, and accompanied Joan to the parking lot. "You know, Joan," he said, coming to the point without preamble, "there's no reason why you should always be married to Howie."

Joan stumbled, and Ed had to grab her arm to keep her from falling.

"You could get a divorce," he went on. "Why not?"

Joan stopped beside her car and fumbled for the key. "But I thought—" *I thought people like you would be shocked if I did such a thing.* "Oh, Ed, I couldn't do that." *Could I? Could I?*

"Why not?"

Joan opened the door of her car and tossed her pocketbook inside and began to cry.

"You could still be responsible for him financially," said Ed. "You could still visit him faithfully, just as you're doing now. You could work it out with a lawyer. Me, for instance. But you don't need to be tied to him in a formal way, a way that has no meaning any longer. You don't need to ruin your own life because his has been destroyed." Ed waited for her to stop crying. He looked around the parking lot, a dreary stretch of asphalt full of potholes.

Joan took a tissue out of her pocketbook and mopped her eyes. "Thank you, Ed," she said. "I'll think about it."

"Good for you," he said, and left her.

19

Consider; your present state is deplorable, and
if continued in will be irremediable. . . . Findest
thou no relentings, O sinner, no movings of the
heart?

Reverend Daniel Bliss
Concord, 1755

*T*he basement room where the
precious documents belonging to the Nashoba public library
were kept was colder, if anything, than the vaults of the Lincoln
and Concord libraries. Homer had forgotten to bring his heavy
sweater. He was wearing only a thin shirt and a pair of shorts.
When Flo Terry, the reference librarian, brought him an afghan
she was knitting during her lunch hour, he wrapped it around
himself gratefully, knitting needles and all.

But Flo had tribute to exact. "How's your new minister?" she
said, looking at Homer shrewdly. "Getting along all right, is he?"

"Why, sure, I guess so," said Homer, feeling sheepish in the
fierce glare of Flo's inquisitive eye.

"What about his wife?" said Flo. "Mrs. Bold, how's she
doing?"

"Well, a little better, I guess, last I heard," said Homer
uncomfortably.

"And the congregation?" Flo towered over Homer like Jeremiah or Ezekiel. She was threatening and monumental at the
same time. "All those parishioners are bearing up okay?"

Stubborn resentment rose in Homer's breast. Flo wanted

him to tell her that Old West Church was breaking down, it was
a valley of dry bones, it was afflicted with famine and pestilence.
"Why, certainly! They're fine, they're just fine." Then Homer
yelped in anguish as one of Flo's knitting needles pierced his
thigh.

*   *   *

1 1 1

For Jerry Gibby, too, the morning was taking on an Old Testament character. In Jerry's case it was about to become a day of judgment.

From the window of his office high above the courtesy booth in Gibby's General Grocery, Jerry could see the inspector poking around his store. It was a new franchise inspector, not good old Gabby Fritz. Whenever Gabby came to Jerry's store on an inspection tour, he always began by climbing the stairs to Jerry's office to pass the time of day, and then he would look around a while and before long he'd come up and clap Jerry on the back and go away again. What the hell had happened to poor old Gabby? Jerry suspected Parker Upshaw had been at work once more. Gabby was probably out on his ear.

Jerry squirmed in his chair uneasily, and watched the inspector move up and down the aisles, peering at the refrigerated shelves of cheese and margarine, the packaged baloney and boiled ham, the bread and rolls. He was scribbling in his notebook. It was apparent by the severity of his expression that something was wrong.

"The pull dates," said the inspector, standing beside Jerry's desk, staring down at him angrily. "Nobody's paid any attention to the pull dates. Half the stuff has been on the shelf too long."

"But that can't be," said Jerry indignantly. "Business has been terrific. People are grabbing everything off the shelves. I can't get 'em restocked fast enough."

"It must be your stock boys," said the inspector. "They're not moving the old stuff to the front and putting the new stuff in back. By tomorrow morning you've got to have every single item off the shelf that's past its pull date. You hear me? Or I'll close the store and take away your license."

"Show me," said Jerry grimly. For the next half hour, he followed the inspector around the store, examining the frozen chicken pies and the cereal and the hot-dog rolls and the yogurt. And it was true. There were weevils in the boxes of Cap'n Crunch, skims of white mold on the olives. "Look at that," said the inspector, tearing off the wrapper of an expensive coffee cake. "Stiff as a board. That's bad."

"It's bad, all right," said Jerry.

When the inspector left, Jerry looked around for the stock boys. He was perishing to bawl them out. The only one he could find was Paul Dobbs. Paul wasn't exactly on the job. He was leaning against the wall beside the shipping door, smoking a cigarette.

Accused, he merely shrugged his shoulders and said it wasn't his fault. *He* always put the old stuff in front. But when Jerry demanded that Paul show him how he did it, Paul didn't know how to read the pull dates. Jerry gave him hell. He took him by the shirt and threw him back against the wall. "Overtime, I'll have to pay overtime to get this stuff off the shelf. A couple thousand dollars it'll cost me, all on account of one lazy kid."

"Why don't you sue me," said Paul, rubbing the back of his head, and then he ambled away to the front of the store to bag groceries and flirt with the checkout girls.

Steaming with rage, Jerry went back upstairs to make a sign,

CLOSED SATURDAY FOR INVENTORY. He found Jeanie, from the basement office, putting a letter on his desk.

The letter was from Parker Upshaw.

> Dear Mr. Gibby,
>
> It has come to my attention that the monthly payments on your franchise are three months in arrears.
>
> Unless the account is made fully current by the end of September, the entire loan will fall due, as per the original agreement.
>
> Yours truly,
> Parker W. Upshaw

Jerry let the letter drop from his fingers, and tore at his thinning hair. What was he going to do now? He had bled his relatives dry. His credit was stretched to the limit. Why in God's name had he bought a car and built a house when he was trying to start his own business? The house, Jesus! It would break Imogene's heart if they had to sell the house. Well, at least he could do something about the car. Jerry walked out to the parking lot and looked glumly at his Coupe de Ville. It was a beautiful automobile, the car of Jerry's dreams—pure white, with classy little windows cut out of the vinyl beside the back seat.

"Well, the hell with it," said Jerry, getting in and slamming the door. The Coupe de Ville came from Genial Jack's, a glossy showroom on Route 9. Maybe Jack still had Jerry's old car. Maybe Jerry could trade this one in and get his money and his old car back, even-steven.

At Genial Jack's Cadillac-Oldsmobile dealership, Jerry parked his car in front of the showroom, then walked around the lot, looking for his old Chevy. Yes, there it was, way around in the rear. They hadn't even fixed the dent in the trunk where Imogene had backed into a tree. Jerry picked up his courage and walked into the showroom.

Genial Jack was there in person, striding forward to meet him, his hand out. "Hi, there. You want another one for the wife, ha-ha, isn't that right?"

"No," said Jerry abruptly. "I want to turn mine in. You've still got my old Chevy out there. I want it back. I just want to reverse the deal, okay?"

"You want to do what?" Genial Jack couldn't believe his ears. His jaw dropped. His mouth hardened. "Listen, friend, this isn't a secondhand store. That model we sold you, we sold it in good faith. You said you wanted the best. It was our premier model, the top car in the showroom. We ordered it special, the white. You want to turn it in secondhand? You must be kidding."

"Look," said Jerry nervously, trying not to let himself be pushed around, "I know it won't be as much money. You'll have to take off a couple of hundred, maybe. But it's still in perfect condition. Not a scratch on it. Only been a few hundred miles. It's just like a brand-new car."

"A couple of hundred?" Genial Jack had never heard anything so ridiculous in his life. "A couple of hundred? Listen, friend, I don't bother with stuff like this. Talk to my assistant." Whirling around, Genial Jack marched across the showroom to a desk in a far corner, where a young goon in a three-piece suit was standing up, staring at Jerry.

On the way home in his old car, Jerry reflected grimly on the new life he and Imogene had begun only a few months ago. They had felt reborn, like those people on the radio on Sunday morning who fell on their knees and shouted "Hallelujah." Redemption—that was what they called it. Christ's sacrifice on the cross had redeemed them, they had been born again. Well, this rebirth wasn't coming off. The transformation of the Gibbys hadn't worked. The new Jerry and the new Imogene were shriveling and dying in their bassinets.

When Jerry got home, Imogene was working in the front yard with a bucket of soapy water. She was scrubbing the birdbath, wearing her old slacks. There was a bright new kerchief on her hair. Imogene looked up in amazement as she recognized Jerry's old car.

"Bastard took off a thousand," said Jerry. "Only six hundred miles on it, not a speck, not a single chip off the paint, clean as a whistle, and he took off a thousand."

"But, Jerry, what for? What's happened?"

Jerry stamped ahead of Imogene into the house, his head forward, his shoulders slumped. "Upshaw, he wants to call the loan on the store."

"Call the loan?" shrieked Imogene. "But he can't do that, can he, Jerry? Can he?"

"He can," said Jerry, turning to her, his eyes red. "And he will."

20

How the days pass! They fly like clouds before the wind. . . .
James Lorin Chapin
Private Journal, Lincoln, 1848

*E*d Bell's retirement had been an active one from the beginning, but now he was busier than he had been in the old days when he went off to work every morning. In Boston there were more board meetings than ever, and the church canvass was taking a lot of his time, because whenever he called on Old West parishioners at home, they were always so sociable and welcoming he usually had to stay a while and pass the time of day.

And then there was Rosemary's group of people in various kinds of desperate physical trouble. They had started meeting at Ed's house regularly every Sunday afternoon, and the whole thing was taking on more consequence all the time, more investment in the way of cogitation in the middle of the night. The group had expanded, and the formidable problems and perplexities of its members were more heavily on Ed's mind with every passing week. Charter member Rosemary Hill was suffering from inoperable stomach cancer, Thad Boland had a similar sort of growth in his colon, Eloise Baxter's kidneys were failing, and Agatha Palmer had been stricken by leukemia. George Tarkington was another charter member, but his emphysema often kept him home in bed or cooped up in the hospital attached to a respirator. A new member was Philip Shooky, with his threatening heart condition.

At first Ed had felt out of place, an impostor, since he alone was perfectly healthy, not terminally ill like the others. But as time went on he almost forgot that he was well. More and more he began to feel like one of them, as if he too were under sentence of death. He was not alarmed by this sensation. In fact, it gave a pure beauty to every common thing, as though he were beholding it for the last time—the curved back of a chair, the rough bark of the maple tree, the mounded shape of Farrar's Hill, the comfortable outline of his wife in middle age, the awkward loveliness of his daughter.

With Phil Shooky's appearance in the group, the meetings changed their character, becoming more gravely purposeful. As a veterinarian, Phil knew things that might be immensely helpful to all of them in their assorted plights. It was true he was getting pretty vague about a lot of things—everybody knew Phil was terrified of having another stroke and losing his mind entirely—but about the details of good medical practice he was as sharp as ever.

Rosemary and Thad and Eloise and Agatha listened gravely as Ed explained the breadth and usefulness of Phil's medical and pharmaceutical understanding.

"That's right," said Phil earnestly, nodding his head. "I mean, I may not know everything about human diseases, but in some ways humans and animals are just alike. I mean, you know, at certain times you could do the same thing for humans that you do for animals, if you see what I mean."

Then Thad Boland told a long story about the time his angora cat had been put to sleep, and they all grew more and more depressed, and afterward Ed had to kid them back into good humor. He passed around a plate of peculiar cookies he had made himself, because Lorraine had washed her hands of the whole thing.

But Rosemary, Thad, Eloise, Agatha, Phil, and George were not the only members of the parish who were the victims of hopeless disorders. Claire Bold and Howie Sawyer were two more. In fact, it had been the terrible spectacle of Howie Sawyer's stroke, that day in church, and Claire's interminable dying that were the double inspiration for the existence of the group in the first place.

And Ed had Howie's wife and Claire's husband on his hands as well. Joan Sawyer's tightlipped poise was extremely fragile, and Joe Bold was nearly prostrate. Ed had to keep picking Joe up off the floor and propping him against the wall, only to discover that he had slipped down again the next day into total despair.

Still, with Ed's help, Joe managed to give at least an appearance of doing his job. In his office in the parish house he was present most of the time, Tuesdays through Fridays, keeping Felicia Davenport, his secretary, fairly busy. He attended regular meetings with the church-school director, the religious-education committee, the Parish Committee, the canvass committee, and the prison-visiting committee, but the Bible-study class was getting along without him, dutifully working its way through the Old Testament. Leaderless as they were, the members of the class were mired down at the moment in the Book of Ecclesiastes, becoming more and more dejected in the face of its suicidal cynicism. Wasn't Bible study supposed to improve your moral fiber and tone up your spiritual life? Well, this time it wasn't working. At the last meeting Deborah Shooky had burst into tears over the passage, *What gain has he that toiled for the wind, and spent all his days in darkness and grief?*

Even if Joe Bold had been able to summon the strength to join the Bible-study class on Thursday nights, it's doubtful that he would have been useful to them in keeping their courage up. He was too sunken in gloom himself. But at the Parish Committee meetings on Tuesday evenings, under the jurisdiction of Ed Bell, Joe did his best to shape up. When new member Joan Sawyer offered to oversee the sexton and keep track of problems having to do with the physical plant, Joe promised to show her the rotten place in the eaves of the church. And he was there in his office, as agreed, on the morning she came to have a look.

But when Joan arrived at the parish house and walked into Felicia Davenport's office to say hello, Felicia looked at her darkly, and nodded her head balefully in the direction of her boss's ministerial study. "You can't go in yet. *She's* in there."

"She?"

"Maud Starr. Claimed it was an emergency. Stuck her nose in here and giggled at me and romped down the hall. What could I do? She's been in there for an hour. Oh, watch it, here she comes." Felicia turned back to stare at the sheet of paper in her typewriter, but both she and Joan were listening to Maud's jolly farewells. Now Maud was popping into Felicia's office, grinning at the two of them, girlish in overalls and high-heeled sandals. To Joan, Maud didn't look like a woman caught in the desperate grip of trouble, but of course one couldn't really tell. Some people's laughter was the same as other people's tears.

"Honestly," gushed Maud, "isn't he just great? I mean, I brought him my little problem, and we got down to the nitty-gritty right away. Oh, Felicia, he's having supper with me tonight, so just put that on his calendar, okay?" Chuckling and nodding, Maud pattered to the door, her bag swinging jauntily from her shoulder, her hands in her pockets, her buzzard wings folded, her red wattles trembling.

Felicia was deeply shocked. "How can he?" she whispered to Joan. "With his wife in the hospital, deathly ill?"

But Joan Sawyer wasn't shocked. She didn't care. It was no concern of hers. Gratefully she approached Joe's office, smiling, looking forward to a conversation about rotten wood and carpenter ants, because talking to Joe was medicine, the best kind of medicine. She would swallow it greedily, every drop, knowing it was doing her good.

21

But scarce the maid to thirteen summers lives;
Ere with soft joys her ripening bosom heaves,
The brilliant moisture sparkles from her eyes,
And o'er her cheek the bloomy colours rise. . . .

But not in all the progress is the same,
Some youths, till twenty scarce discern the flame.
Reverend Charles Stearns, Lincoln
The Ladies' Philosophy of Love, 1797

*N*ext Sunday morning the sun rose bright and clear once again and hurled down radiant bolts of light through the windows of Old West Church. They sparkled on rings and bracelets and the wristbands of watches; they glittered on the metal frame of the wheelchair belonging to Claire Bold, who was home from the hospital at last. But today the sun had summoned the full force of its heat and light to illuminate young Eleanor Bell. It was Eleanor's turn to be shone upon. Sitting between her mother and father, she was directly in the path of a blazing shaft.

Eleanor had come to church of her own free will, but Bo Harris, sitting across the aisle, was there only because his mother had put her foot down. "Once in a while, that's all I ask," Mrs. Harris had said, standing over his bed. "Once in a blue moon your royal highness can condescend."

Yet now, sitting next to him, Mrs. Harris felt unconnected to her son. Bo was so large, he was such a huge and complex piece of protoplasm, such a great chunk of flesh! His destiny would work itself out long after she was dead. Ethel Harris was astonished to think she had once brought him into the world, a helpless, bawling newborn babe.

Lorraine Bell, too, was thinking sorrowfully about her off-spring. She was uncomfortably aware that Eleanor at this instant had reached some kind of dizzy pinnacle. The sunlight was suffusing her shoulders, touching her slightly parted lips. Every separate strand of her bright hair glistened along its length. Sitting there so quietly in the path of the sunlight, Eleanor was soaking up its warmth and sending it out again in waves of longing. Lorraine could feel the assault from her daughter's flushed cheeks. It was thrusting against her, rolling past her to fill the church; it was pressing against the doors and billowing outside to batter the windows of cars passing on Farrar Road. Eleanor was in full bloom; she was a flower with the last petal opening. Lorraine wanted to stand up and shake her fist at nature's plot to continue the race. It was too soon. Eleanor wasn't ready. She was too young. Why couldn't the savage process be delayed until the poor child could handle it? Gently, Lorraine patted Eleanor's knee. It felt warm to her touch. No, Eleanor wasn't a flower, she was something more insistent, more intense. She was a bonfire, she was burning like a torch. Oh, it was too soon, it was much too soon.

Lorraine glanced at Ed, sitting so serenely on the other side of Eleanor. Did he know what was happening to his daughter?

Probably not, and that was odd, because most of the time Ed was so clever about people. Lorraine shifted uneasily on the pew cushion, praying that Bo Harris would not notice the miracle that was happening on his account across the aisle, that he would stay stupid—the idiot!—at least for a while.

It was time for the first hymn. Ethel Harris poked her elbow into Bo, reminding him to stand up. Obediently he stood and fumbled in the hymnbook, looking for the right page as the organ sounded loud and everyone around him began to sing:

> Turn back, O man, forswear thy foolish ways.
> Old now is earth, and none may count her days;
> Yet thou, her child, whose head is crowned with flame,
> Still wilt not hear thine inner God proclaim:
> "Turn back, O man, forswear thy foolish ways!"

Bo mouthed the words, aware that something was pressing at his attention across the aisle, something hot and pink in a flare of sunshine. But instead of glancing at Eleanor, Bo turned his mind to the Chevy. His rebuilt engine wasn't turning over. Maybe he had the generator hooked up wrong. Either the wiring was defective or the timing was out of sync. Maybe he had the wires from the regulator mixed up. Maybe Mr. Bell could help him out. So far Mr. Bell had been a really good sport. He really understood what Bo was trying to do. "This is a mighty project you've undertaken here, Bo," he had said yesterday. "Like Lewis and Clark going up the Missouri, or the Curies isolating radium from pitchblende. We've got to see you through." And Mr. Bell was really great about coming up with ideas whenever Bo got stuck. Maybe he'd know what to do about the wiring. Oh, God, the wiring! The wiring was really giving Bo a lot of grief. Unseeing, he stared at the hymnbook, while around him the congregation went on singing:

> Earth might be fair and all men glad and wise.
> Age after age their tragic empires rise,
> Built while they dream, and in that dreaming weep;

*Would man but wake from out his haunted
sleep. . . .*

Haunted sleep, thought Lorraine Bell; that was putting it
mildly. The trouble with people wasn't their vague dreams, it was
their obsessions. Oh, it wasn't just Eleanor and Bo, it was everybody in the congregation. They were all being dragged in one
direction or another by some fierce sense of destiny. Here they
sat so quietly, yet life was going on passionately inside them, love
and dread, cruelty and kindness, envy and ambition. They were
juggernauts, all of them, barreling down the road. The church
was full of juggernauts, grinding forward headlong on collision
courses. Sooner or later their paths would intersect and there
would be terrible splinterings and shiverings asunder.

On the other side of the church, two of the juggernauts sat
next to each other, Parker Upshaw and Jerry Gibby. Once again
the usher had seated them side by side, although Jerry had
wanted to catch Barbara Fenster's arm and whisper, "Not there."
But Imogene had already slipped into the pew and settled her
purse with flutterings and beamings and exchanges of whispers
with Betsy Bucky in the pew behind her. Upshaw had turned a
frigid glance upon Jerry, a severe look that said, "Well?" from
under his dark brows. Now Jerry sat staring at the pulpit, his face
red, his collar choking him, telling himself that in this building
he was supposed to love his enemy. Well, he didn't; he hated him.
Upshaw was screwing him. Yesterday the bastard had walked into
the store and repeated his ultimatum in a loud voice right there
among the cantaloupes, humiliating Jerry in front of the bag boys
and checkout girls. Jesus, where was Jerry going to come up with
forty-seven thousand dollars before October? And the landscaping company was demanding payment for all those rocks and
rhododendrons. Jesus, the rocks! A thousand dollars for a bunch
of rocks! Jerry sat glowering beside Imogene as she peeked gaily
around the church. He hadn't yet told all this to his wife. She had
no idea they were in hopeless trouble. Poor Imogene, she was
upset enough already about the car. Christ, that bastard Upshaw.
Holy *Jesus.*

It was time for the sermon. Joseph Bold stood up and shuffled the papers on the reading desk. This morning he had pulled an old set of notes out of his file at the last minute. It was a sermon he had delivered to his Pittsburgh congregation last year. How easily it had come to him that morning! Now, reading the same words aloud, it was as though he had never seen them before. Joe stumbled over sentences, puzzled by his own logic. When he came to a stop at last, the congregation heaved small sighs of relief. They stood up and adjusted the frames of their glasses and felt the tension go out of their bunched shoulders.

Homer Kelly couldn't find the right hymn. The pages of his hymnbook stuck together. It fell to the floor with a slam, and he cursed under his breath.

"Here, dear," said Mary, holding her own book open in front of him.

At the organ, Augusta Gill was seized with regret. Why hadn't someone told her Claire Bold would be back in church today? Oh, God, the hymn was a ghastly mistake. Augusta plowed through it courageously, wincing as the verses were sung, inexorably succeeding one another.

> *In heav'nly love abiding,*
> *No change my heart shall fear,*
> *And safe is such confiding,*
> *For nothing changes here. . . .*

> *Green pastures are before me,*
> *Which yet I have not seen;*
> *Bright skies will soon be o'er me,*
> *Where darkest clouds have been. . . .*

At this point Joe Bold nearly broke down. Stubbornly the congregation struggled through to the end, careful not to look at their minister or at the shining wheelchair where his wife sat gazing down at the hymnbook in her lap. But George Tarkington was so affected he began to cough violently, and his wife had to hurry him out of the church.

The trouble with hymns, thought Mary Kelly, wasn't just the verses, it was the tunes. Singing the old successions of notes for years and years gave the words an emotional authority that had nothing to do with the understanding. Notes and words welled up together from some place more profound than the mind. The musical phrases carried a burden of feeling in which the words had become embedded. No matter how silly the text might be, it caught you by the throat. The rhyming lines might have been written by superstitious parsons or sentimental dowagers with primitive beliefs, yet, set to music, they shook the foundations.

The service was over. Mary and Homer were the first to escape outside. There they found Hilary Tarkington looking anxiously at her husband, George, who was leaning against his old station wagon, wheezing and coughing.

"Good heavens, George," said Homer. "Are you all right?"

"Oh, it's nothing," gasped George, grinning, his face purple with the effort to breathe. Pulling himself together, he opened the door of his old car for Hilary.

"Nice old Chrysler," said Homer, looking at the car fondly. "Reminds me of one I used to own. My God, George, how do you pass inspection?"

"Oh, I go to this special place, other side of Waltham," wheezed George amiably, getting in behind the wheel. "No problem. They're not so damn fussy as the guys around here. They've got some respect for an old car. I get away with murder."

"Honestly, George, dear," objected Hilary, and then she waved at Mary and Homer as the Chrysler moved away from the curb, its rusted skirts trembling.

When Parker Upshaw burst out-of-doors, he was in a passion of sanctimonious anger, eager for conspiratorial wheeling and dealing. He was in his element. In church he had gloated over Joe's faltering sermon with a pouncing consciousness of outrage, and hugged his fury to himself. Now, here on the lawn in the open air, darkly joyful, he took Ed Bell aside.

"Somebody's got to do something. We can't go on this way, Sunday after Sunday. The man's got to do better. I must say, it's a sad chapter in the life of the church."

Ed didn't seem to understand. He smiled at Parker and shook his head. "But you've got it all wrong. It isn't a sad chapter at all. It's a rare time for us, a real opportunity, a time for us to *be* a church. Here's a need, a real need, and we can all throw ourselves into it and help out."

Parker stared at Ed blankly, astonished. It was obvious he had come to the wrong man. He turned away and tested his pique on Homer and Mary Kelly. They too seemed surprised, just like Ed. They muttered and demurred. It wasn't until Parker waylaid a couple of the younger parishioners that he awakened any sympathy for his complaint against Joe Bold. Donald Meadow and Jonathan Sinclair responded immediately with melancholy dignity, and the three of them were soon deep in grim resolve and hypocritical betrayal.

But before long Parker had to tear himself away. His perfection principle was still dominating his life, driving him to new peaks of performance, urging him to find new ways to succeed at General Grocery, demanding that he run five miles a day instead of four, insisting that he learn French in his spare time (French!) and read a little Plato (Plato!). This morning Parker had a tennis date with Fred Harris. He was determined to polish up his serve. He drove home in a hurry and changed into his tennis whites and whizzed in the direction of the town courts.

He found Fred an easy victim. The poor guy didn't seem to take the game seriously. All he wanted to do was lob the ball lazily back and forth across the net. But Parker W. Upshaw was in the game to win. Slashing and smashing, he raced up and down the court, slamming the ball into the corner farthest from Fred, racking up a top-heavy score. Afterward he shook hands and went home in a roaring mood of self-satisfaction.

But there he found things in a less exalted state. Libby was grumpy, the children were whining. Sunday dinner was cold chicken legs.

"I'm sorry, Parker," Libby said, slapping down the platter on the kitchen table. "I just don't have *time.*"

"Well, why don't you hire somebody?" said Parker, trying to keep his temper. "Get a woman in by the day, or something."

"Oh, you think I'm not managing well enough by myself, is that it?" said Libby, tearing off her apron. And then they were at it, hammer and tongs, and Parker's enjoyment of his own consummate excellence was blighted by the failings of his less than perfect wife.

Arlene Pott had been in church, too, that morning, and as usual her absence had given her husband a chance to alert his neighbor Josie Coil.

But today, for the first time, Josie failed to answer the call. The truth was, Josie was trying to get her life figured out, and she was no longer sure Wally Pott should be part of it. One thing was sure: Josie was sick and tired of caring for old Mrs. Hawk. She wanted to quit. And it was beginning to appear that Wally was a dead-end street.

So when Mrs. Hawk's daughter swooped her car into the driveway to take over for Josie on her day off, Josie was ready. She had taken a bath. She had put on a sleeveless dress with a low neckline that showed a lot of plump shoulder and bosom and back, and now she hurried out to her car and unlocked the door.

Instantly, Wally jumped at her out of the shrubbery.

Josie shrieked. "Oh, Wally, don't do that. You really gave me a turn."

"Listen," said Wally roughly, "where have you been? I put the damned cactus in the window and you never showed up."

"Oh, you know, Wally, sometimes I just can't get away."

"Well, how about now? You're off duty, right? And Arlene's in church."

"Oh, honestly, Wally, I can't—not right now." Josie swung open the door of her car, then turned on him with a look of chubby determination. "You want to know why? I've got a date with Victor, that's why."

"A date with Victor?" Clammy fingers gripped Wally's heart. "So that's why you're all gussied up. I should've known."

"Listen, Wally, it's no good, you and me. Where's it going to get me? You're not going to divorce Arlene, and I want to settle down. I mean, I need somebody to lean on. All this hiding in the bushes, I'm sick of it." Josie looked at her little gold wristwatch. "Listen, I'll be late. Victor doesn't like me to be late."

Enraged, Wally lunged at Josie, but she plumped herself into the car, and slammed the door, then revved the engine and zoomed backward out of the driveway.

"Oh, God almighty," sobbed Wally. Running out onto Lowell Road, he watched Josie speed away in the direction of Watertown. Victor loomed in the dusty pavement, in the distant mailboxes, in the far trees. Victor was stealing Josie away from him, and Josie was all Wally cared about in the whole world.

22

This day is the beginning of sorrow.
James Lorin Chapin
Private Journal, Lincoln, 1848

*C*arl Bucky died on a warm Saturday night in September, while the fan droned in the bedroom window and the faded stars above the Buckys' house withdrew behind damp blankets of heat. Snuggled against her husband, Betsy woke next morning to find his body cold.

Instantly she shrank away with a little cry. Then she sat up and stared at the man she had been married to for forty-seven years. Carl's eyes were open. So was his mouth. His chest was not rising and falling. Betsy put her hand on his soft belly. It was flabby and chill. The blood heat was gone. Putting her head down on Carl's chest, she could detect no heartbeat.

Exultant, hardly able to believe it, Betsy bounced out of bed and put on her robe and slippers, congratulating herself. It was the pie! The lemon-chiffon pie! The pie had done the trick! Last night she had mounded Carl's plate three times with spaghetti, and then she had forced on him second and third helpings of lemon-chiffon pie for dessert. Carl had begged her to stop. "Gosh, Betsy, I'm really stuffed. I can't eat another bite." But he had finished it all, somehow or other, and then he had downed two mugs of Betsy's special coffee. No wonder he had passed away, the greedy pig! It was his own fault!

Betsy had looked forward to this moment a thousand times, and planned what to do. But it had never occurred to her it might be a Sunday morning. Too bad! Betsy hated to miss church. She loved singing the hymns in her piercing soprano; she loved leaning over one way to hear what Mollie Pine and Mabel Smock were up to, and the other way to get the latest news from Priscilla Worthy. Was it true the minister's wife was back in the hospital? Had Arlene Pott really walked out on Wally? Betsy stared at her dead husband and regretted the necessity of missing church. What a shame! Her fresh-baked pan of cinnamon swirls would go to waste. She had made them last night while Carl was watching TV, so she could pass them around during the after-church coffee hour while everybody oohed and aahed. And there was her new idea for the Christmas Fair, crocheted ruffles you could tie around candlesticks. They'd sell like hotcakes, Betsy was sure of it, and she wanted to tell Mollie and Priscilla. But here was Carl, passed away in bed! It was just like him, even now, to be in the way.

Then it occurred to Betsy that she could just leave Carl right here on the bed and go off to church anyway. Why couldn't she call Dr. Spinney when she got home? She could say Carl had wanted to sleep late because he wasn't feeling well, so she had gone to church without him, and then when she got back she had found him like this. Why not?

So Betsy Bucky went to church on the morning after her husband's death, and enjoyed every minute of it. She soared with the Virgin Mary and gossiped with Mabel Smock and learned that Wally Pott was indeed living in that big fancy house all by himself and didn't know where Arlene had gone, and then after the service she passed around her cinnamon swirls in the common room downstairs, and everybody said, "Scrumptious!" and "Delicious!" and Agatha Palmer said, "Betsy Bucky, is there anything you can't do?" and Betsy tittered in joyous high spirits, "No, not a single thing!"

Ed and Lorraine Bell were helping out in the common room too, making small talk with other members of the congregation in the company of Joseph Bold. This necessary parish duty of

Sunday-morning sociability had become almost intolerable to Joe. But when Ed Bell said, "Say, Joe, did you hear Bob Ott hit that high note? Bob, you ought to be in grand opera, right, Joe?" the task was easier.

So the Bells were late getting home after the service on the day Carl Bucky died. In fact they were still changing into their old clothes when they heard a car speeding past the house, whanging into a pothole with a suspension-busting jolt. "Good heavens, who's that?" said Lorraine, running to the window.

Ed looked out too, just in time to see the doctor's little VW careen around the bend. "It's Arthur Spinney. I wonder where he's going in such a hurry?"

But the VW wasn't the first car to pull into Betsy Bucky's driveway. Betsy had also called the police. While the doctor was racing past Ed Bell's house, the emergency medical technician from the Nashoba police department was already tumbling out of the ambulance.

But as soon as he took a look at Carl Bucky, he put down his equipment. "How long has he been like this?" he asked Betsy.

"Well, the truth is," said Betsy, thinking quickly, anxious to protect herself, "I left him sleeping when I got up this morning, and I didn't check on him before I went to church."

When Dr. Spinney ran up the stairs into the bedroom, he too could see at a glance that it was too late. He made an examination anyway. Then he straightened up and looked sadly at Betsy, and told her he was sorry.

"Cremation," said Betsy firmly, leading the way downstairs. "That's what Carl always wanted. He told me so, jillions of times." Betsy had figured out this part long ago. A container of ashes wouldn't require an expensive cemetery plot. It wouldn't need a big stone monument. Betsy would put Carl's ashes in a nice jar she had inherited from her mother, a really dignified and handsome sort of cooky jar, with shepherds and shepherdesses on it, and lords and ladies in white wigs. She would seal the jar with hot paraffin, the way she did with her preserve jars, and bury it under the shrine to the Virgin Mary in the front yard and surround it next summer with red salvia and orange marigolds.

23

I saw nothing . . . this afternoon but a train of ladies . . . each armed with four knitting needles, busy with their fingers and as busy with their tongues.

James Lorin Chapin
Private Journal, Lincoln, 1849

*J*oe Bold had never visited the Buckys' house before. When he got out of his car, the shrine took him by surprise. Beside it a garden fork had been thrust into the grass next to a deep hole and a pile of dirt. There was a shovel in the hole.

The shrine was unexpected, but the noises from the house were even more startling, screams of laughter and gales of high-pitched giggles. When Joe rang the bell, the laughter stopped in mid-shriek. There was a throbbing silence, then the squeal of a chair being scraped back and hurrying footsteps. Someone was running to the door, throwing it open.

"Well, Reverend, hi, there," cried Betsy. "You just come right in. Some of the girls are here. We're just planning the service."

Joe didn't know what to say. He had come to console the bereaved widow, but consolation didn't seem to be what was wanted. And he had called at the wrong time. When Betsy led him into her dining room, he found a luncheon party in full swing. Priscilla Worthy and Mabel Smock and Mollie Pine were sitting at Betsy's table, looking up at him, their mouths respectfully pursed. The table was laden with provender. There were orange baskets filled with sherbet, canned pears coated with halved grapes to look like clusters on the vine, a great pile of Betsy's special sausage fritters, and slices of checkerboard cake fanned out on a platter. The food was as yet untouched, but the bottle of sherry was empty. The sherry was inside Betsy and Mabel and Mollie and Priscilla. Before long it dispelled their false dignity. Once again hilarity bubbled to the surface.

"We've planned everything except the flowers, Reverend," said Betsy proudly, giggling.

It was true. The service for Carl Bucky was all in order. The advice of Betsy's pastor was not required. Mollie Pine's sister from Quincy was going to sing Gounod's "Ave Maria," because it was Betsy's dearest wish. Heavy decisions had been made about after-the-service snacks. There would be no burial at the cemetery, because Betsy was going to lay her husband's ashes to rest all by herself. Joe goggled at the cooky jar on the sideboard and blushed, as though Carl had been listening, as though he had heard the laughter.

For ten tormented minutes, Joe sat quietly, while the four women talked at full tilt. Then he made his excuses and started for the door.

Betsy accompanied him, jabbering at his elbow. As they made their way through the living room, Joe saw the big lounge chair that had obviously been Carl's. The hollows in the plastic upholstery were all that remained of the big gloomy man who had come to church regularly, who always sat in the same pew, totally obscured by the energetic little woman who had dominated him so completely, who had killed him, Homer Kelly said, with savage and homicidal kindness.

"Don't let me keep you," said Joe at the door, but Betsy insisted on following him outside to show him the shrine. Together they stood in front of it. Tenderly the Virgin Mary spread her blue robe and gazed into the hole that gaped for Carl's ashes. Joe murmured his sympathy and went away, unutterably depressed.

24

*. . . the time is short;—life is precarious;—
opportunities swiftly pass away;—and
the final judgment is rapidly approaching!*
Reverend Ezra Ripley
Concord, 1809

*T*he day after Carl Bucky's fu-
neral, Claire Bold was scheduled for more surgery. But at the last
minute the surgeon changed his mind. Claire had been made
ready for him, she had been brought into the preparation room
deep in the lower levels of the hospital, where the sharp secret
work of the surgeons was carried on. The anesthetist was already
checking his dials. But Claire's doctor was shocked at the sight
of his patient's increased fragility, and he called the whole thing
off. The woman was surely too weak to endure another invasion
with his keen-edged tools. When he leaned over Claire and told
her his decision, she burst into tears. It was a cruel letdown, after
she had worked herself up to endure yet one more ordeal.

The surgeon found it even more difficult to inform the patient's husband.

Waiting upstairs, Joe saw the doctor walking toward him
along the corridor, too soon, much too soon. He stood up
shakily, his heart beating, to learn that the operation was not to
be performed after all. "But what does it mean?" he said, staring
wildly at the surgeon.

The doctor found it hard to explain. It's no use, he wanted
to say, but he knew Joe couldn't bear it, so instead he said, "Let's

go on building up her strength first. Your friend Mrs. Kelly is doing a good job, getting sustenance into her. Let's work on it some more. Then we'll see."

Once again the world presented itself to Joe in tragic but astonishing shapes. This time there were extraordinary patterns on the green operating tunic of the surgeon, imprinted by hot water in a boiling vat and the scorching heat of a dryer. Joe gazed fixedly at the wrinkled tunic. "May I take her home?" he said.

"Of course."

From that moment on, Joe made no pretense of fulfilling his duty to Old West Church. He took his wife back to the parsonage and set up a bed for her in the front room and handled the morphine syringe himself. Mary Kelly and Lorraine Bell took turns at mealtimes, spooning mashed vegetables into Claire, reading aloud from *The Mill on the Floss.* Mary had almost forgotten the days when she had had time for herself. She had stopped working on her teaching syllabus altogether. Homer would take over this fall and do all her teaching for her. Fortunately he saw the need and didn't grumble. As for Claire, she was obedient, opening her mouth for her supper like an infant bird. Joe was effusively grateful.

He was grateful to Ed Bell, too, because Ed was doing his best to make up for Joe's absence from the church. All at once Ed was in action everywhere, keeping the whole parish running in its ordinary groove. When Felicia, the church secretary, complained that nobody was telling her what to do, Ed kidded her into standing on her own two feet and making decisions by herself. When a pair of sudden crises appeared on the agenda of the Parish Committee, Ed handled them with diplomacy and tact.

The first was a problem with the sexton. He was falling down on the job. Should he be fired? Ed turned the question over to a subcommittee of one, Joan Sawyer, and Joan took care of it swiftly. Sitting down with the sexton, she learned he was working at two jobs, sixteen hours a day, like some nineteenth-century wage slave in a dark satanic mill. Soon the Parish Committee was surprised to find itself doubling his salary. The sexton promptly quit his other job, and the problem was solved.

The second crisis was more serious. It was a letter from Parker Upshaw, Donald Meadow, and Jonathan Sinclair, a formal request to the Parish Committee to consider the dismissal of Joseph Bold. "The needs of the parish are not being served," declared the letter.

Ed sat at the scratched table in the Sunday-school room that was the meeting place for the committee and led the discussion. "We've got to rally around the man," he said persuasively, "not kick him out because he happens to be enduring the severest trial that can happen in anyone's life. What's a church for, anyway?"

What *was* a church for? The phrase had worked before. It worked again. But it had been a near thing. If Ed hadn't posed the question, Parker Upshaw's opinion that *The needs of the parish are not being served* might have won the day easily. As a rallying cry against Joe Bold, it was dangerously plausible. And its swift defeat in the Parish Committee did not mean it had gone away for good. It was still seething in Upshaw's breast, Ed knew that. It would turn up again, sooner or later.

And there were other urgencies to occupy Ed's attention. Filling the pulpit was one, on those Sunday mornings when Joe couldn't bear to leave his wife's bedside. Lay ministry, Ed called it. Suspecting that every parishioner had at least one sermon to deliver, he called on them one by one. Charlie Fenster was glad to oblige. Homer Kelly was waiting his turn. Agatha Palmer worked up her courage to present her recollections of Junior Endeavor, a youth group that was part of the program at Old West, back in the twenties. Even Parker Upshaw was flattered to be asked by the wily Ed Bell to address his fellow church members. Parker got to work and slaved over his sermon, a lengthy homily on aspiration, on man's need to set himself lofty goals, to achieve the most soaring heights.

The crisis would last only as long as Claire Bold remained alive. "The poor woman is fading away," whispered Lorraine Bell to her husband in the privacy of their bedroom. "She can't last much longer. How is Joe going to stand it?"

"I don't know," said Ed. "Are you sure she's in such a bad way? Joe's promised to be in church next week."

But next Sunday Joe wasn't there, after all. At the last minute he called in desperation and begged off. "I can't," he said. "I just can't. Not this morning."

And therefore Ed walked jauntily up the pulpit steps himself and delivered a sermon off the cuff. It wasn't a sermon, it was an informal monologue about the last thirty years in Old West Church. Ed dwelt on the lighter moments, remembering disasters like the time the boiler blew up. He ended with a prayer for the minister and his wife, fervent but calm.

But of course that was not the end of Ed's duties. The secret Sunday-afternoon meetings were still taking place in his house. Percy Donlevy was a new member, and so was Bill Molyneux. Bill suffered from multiple sclerosis. He was younger than the rest. Percy Donlevy was far gone with Parkinson's disease.

Lorraine Bell was still staying strictly away from Ed's Sunday-afternoon gatherings in the living room. "I don't want to know anything about it," she told him firmly, more than once. "It's not my affair." But sometimes Lorraine couldn't help noticing mysterious things. Why, for example, was Rosemary Hill so solemn, one day after church, when she told Ed she had finished cleaning the attic? Why had Ed embraced her so affectionately? And why did Phil Shooky always bring his toolbox when he came to the house on Sundays? Lorraine suspected it contained something other than tools, but she reminded herself severely that it was none of her business. Still, she couldn't help wondering.

Deborah Shooky wondered about the meetings too. One day she asked Lorraine about them point-blank. "Phil's always so anxious to get over to your house every Sunday. What goes on there anyway?"

"What does Phil say about it himself?" said Lorraine guardedly.

"Oh, church stuff of some kind," said Deborah vaguely. "At first I thought it was the deacons all getting together, because Phil's a deacon. But Rosemary Hill goes to the meetings too, and Rosemary isn't a deacon."

"Well, I'm sorry, but I don't know," said Lorraine. "I'm always busy doing something else on Sunday afternoon."

Homer Kelly was curious about the meetings too. He stumbled into one of them without warning.

Lorraine tried to block his way. "Did you want to talk to Ed?" she said, standing nervously in front of the closed living-room doors, wishing he would go home.

"Well, it's about this sermon he wants me to deliver next

week," said Homer. "I mean, I never expected to find myself in such an embarrassing position. I just want to know what gyrations Ed wants me to go through up there in front of the congregation. What does he expect in the way of prayers, readings, genuflections, supplications, sacraments, hosannas, libations, burnt offerings, and human sacrifices? That sort of thing, you know?"

"Well, I don't think you can see him now, Homer," said Lorraine, glancing over her shoulder at the living-room doors. "They've just begun. Maybe you should come back later."

Homer looked curiously at the sliding doors. On the other side he could hear a soft murmur of voices. "I'll just pop in and ask when he can see me," he said to Lorraine, and then, before she could stop him, he flung the doors wide open.

"Hey, Ed," cried Homer, and then he stopped short and backed away in confusion from the circle of people who were standing with bowed heads and linked hands in front of the fireplace. "Oh, whoops, excuse me," said Homer, mortified. Slamming the doors together with a bang, he looked at Lorraine, abashed.

"Really, Homer," said Lorraine in honest dismay.

Next day he came back by careful appointment and sat down with Ed and accosted him inquisitively about the nature of the meeting he had barged into the day before. "Some kind of prayer meeting, was that it, Ed?"

"Prayer meeting?" Ed grinned. "Well, yes, of course, that's just what it was, a prayer meeting."

"Okay if I join? Become a member?"

"Sorry, Homer, I think we'd blackball you."

"Not pious enough, right? Old reprobate, right?"

"Right. That's it exactly. That's right."

25

Betsy, never allow Daniel to go into the
pulpit until he has had his rum.
                        Mrs. Charles Stearns
                        Lincoln, ca. 1800

*N*ext Sunday, Homer ascended
the pulpit steps and regaled the congregation with an oration on
the abolition movement in nineteenth-century Boston. He was
charming, outrageous, informative, and learned. Mary grinned at
him from her pew in the back of the church, and Homer was
relieved, because sometimes Mary didn't grin, she just looked
sorrowfully at her lap. As a temporary substitute for Joseph Bold,
Homer was a big success, and Ed Bell congratulated him warmly.

But that afternoon Ed's private meeting behind the sliding
doors of his living room was a disaster, because of the boy Paul
Dobbs. In the middle of the meeting there was a tumultuous
uproar from outside. It was Paul on a motorcycle, a big shiny
Mitsubishi belonging to one of his brothers. Once, twice, Paul
thundered around the house, and then he tore out onto Acton
Road and pounded away down the hill.

Five minutes later, the people assembled in Ed's living room
heard the phone ring in the hall, and then Eleanor Bell threw
open the closed doors and cried out to her father, "It's Paul. He's
had an accident."

The meeting broke up in disorder. Ed rushed away with Bill
Molyneux, Rosemary went home with Eloise Baxter, George

Tarkington drove away in his noisy old car with Phil Shooky, and Thad Boland and Agatha Palmer and Percy Donlevy walked home, highly agitated, in different directions.

But as it turned out, Paul wasn't badly hurt. He was merely mauled by the rasping scrape of his side against the pavement after the motorcycle collapsed when he leaned over too far, making a U turn in front of the Town Hall.

The motorcycle itself was totaled, slamming out of control into a stone wall. Afterward Paul's parole officer told Ed it was stolen property. The parole officer wasn't happy. He wanted Paul back in the Concord Reformatory.

Ed put up a fight. "The boy didn't know his brother stole it. And he's got a job. He's learned his lesson. We're happy to have him living with us. Why can't he go right on doing what he's doing?"

"Well, all right," said the parole officer. "But you're asking for trouble. Don't say I didn't warn you."

Lorraine agreed privately with the parole officer. "I don't know," she told Ed. "Really, dear, I just feel so uneasy."

"But you thought at first he was going to rape Eleanor, didn't you, now?" said Ed, smiling at her. "You'll have to admit you were wrong. They hardly even see each other."

"Oh, I know," said Lorraine. "She's only got eyes for Bo Harris. Still, I worry about it."

Lorraine didn't tell Ed about the teaching session she had overheard one afternoon on the back porch. Eleanor had suddenly taken it into her head to teach Paul to read and write. She had set up a card table on the porch. Lorraine was stuffing a chicken at the kitchen sink. She couldn't help hearing the voices outside. And she wanted to interfere, to protest, to tell Eleanor she was going too fast. Poor Paul couldn't keep up.

"Who cares about the alphabet?" said Paul shrewdly. "Listen, how you spell 'I love you'?"

"Oh, Paul, don't be dumb." Eleanor was angry.

"I am dumb," said Paul. "How you spell 'fuck'?"

Lorraine didn't tell Ed what she had heard. The poor man

had too much on his mind. Trying to keep the church going and attend his usual board meetings and help Bo Harris fix his car and drive Paul Dobbs back and forth to work—it was more than any one person should be expected to do. "It's too much," she complained to him. "Really, dear, you've got to slow down."

But instead of slowing down, Ed took on more and more of Joe Bold's neglected duties. Parish visiting was one of them. Ed was a natural at parish visiting. He was already an old friend of the head nurse in Howie Sawyer's ward at the County Hospital. Now he called on the eldest Ott boy, who was recovering from an appendectomy at Emerson Hospital. And then he drove into Boston to see Geneva Jones at Mass. General.

"Damn it, Ed," said Geneva, "my face-lift was supposed to be a secret. What are you doing here?" But then Geneva clasped Ed's hand and held it tightly. Going through the whole thing alone had been harder than Geneva expected.

It took a good deal of nerve to stop in at Wally Pott's house to ask about Wally's wife, but Ed had plenty of nerve. And he was worried about Arlene's continued absence. There were rumors afloat that Arlene had fled, that Wally was a wife-beater. There were counter-rumors that Arlene wouldn't run away, no matter what, that she would have thrown Wally out instead, because the house belonged to her, not Wally. Arlene's neighbor Ethel Harris was upset about Arlene's disappearance.

"Wally must have some idea where she is," Ethel told Ed. "I wonder if she's with her sister Beverly?"

But Wally claimed complete ignorance. When Ed knocked on the door and inquired politely about Arlene and asked how he could get in touch with her sister, Wally shifted his bare feet on the hall carpet and said, "I don't know where the hell Beverly lives. Someplace down South."

"May I come in?" said Ed, beaming at Wally.

"Well, I'm pretty busy," said Wally.

But Ed was already inside, exclaiming at the elegance of Arlene's living room, the glass coffee table, the split matched marble of the fireplace.

Wally gave up and waved him to the beige sofa. "She left me for good, that's the truth of it. She just walked out, and I don't know where the devil she's gone."

"Might there be letters from her sister? A Christmas card with her return address?"

Involuntarily, Wally Pott glanced at the tall desk against the farther wall. It was an expensive-looking dusty piece of furniture. The hinged front was closed, but Ed could see that a press of papers behind it had pushed it partly open.

"Oh, I don't think there's any letters." Wally looked carefully back at Ed, keeping his eyes away from the desk.

If Ed Bell had been Homer Kelly, he would have jumped up, crossed the room in two strides, and poked in Arlene Pott's papers, then snatched up the sheaf of unopened letters from Arlene's anxious sister in Abilene, Texas, and shaken them under Wally's nose. But Ed was not Homer Kelly, he was himself, and he didn't think it courteous to doubt Wally's word.

He made a polite suggestion. "Do you think perhaps you should call the police?"

"Oh, heck, no, not yet. She left me once before—came back in three, four weeks. I don't want to make, you know, a big fuss."

26

Went to church in the morning and heard Mr. Jackson preach upon the total depravity of human nature.

James Lorin Chapin
Private Journal, Lincoln, 1849

*P*aul Dobbs was still working at Gibby's General Grocery. When he came limping back on the job after his motorcycle accident, the manager of the grocery department ordered him to unload huge pallets of canned goods from a tractor-trailer at the back door. Paul's chest was still strapped with elastic bandages, still sore, and he felt aggrieved. He walked upstairs to Jerry Gibby's office to complain, to ask for something else to do instead.

At that moment Jerry Gibby was on the phone, shouting at Bill Pope, the senior financial officer of General Grocery. "It's Upshaw, right? Upshaw got you on my back? Listen, you better watch out for that guy Upshaw. You're next in line, what do you want to bet? He'll have your job next." Slamming down the phone, Jerry looked around wildly at Paul. He was about to burst into angry sobs, and he didn't want to do it in front of a stock boy. He yelled at Paul, "Get out of here! Go on, get the hell out!"

The truck driver at the receiving door was mad too. He had unloaded the whole order of canned goods himself, and it wasn't the sort of thing he was paid to do. "Hey, kid, come on, take this up to Gibby. He's got to sign the invoice. Hurry up. I got to be in Rome, New York, by noontime."

"Nothing doing," said Paul. "I'm not going up those stairs no more. No way."

"Well, somebody's got to sign it," said the driver testily. "Here, why don't you sign it yourself?" He thrust the invoice at Paul. "See? Right here where it says thirty-eight cartons? Here's a pen."

Paul stared at the piece of paper, which was covered with rows of meaningless hieroglyphs. "Sign it?" he said doubtfully.

"Sure, why not? Right there where it says X." The driver pointed with his big thumb.

"Well, okay." Carelessly, Paul took the pen and made a meaningless scrawl.

"Thanks," said the truck driver, snatching back pen and paper.

The next truck was a huge trailer from Pinecraft Paper Products, loaded with unwieldy boxes of toilet paper, paper towels, paper diapers, and paper napkins. The boxes weren't heavy; they were just awkward. Paul lugged twenty or thirty off the truck, then stopped for a smoke.

"Hey," said the Pinecraft driver, "get a move on."

Paul merely grinned at him and dropped ashes on the floor.

But instead of getting mad, the driver walked back to the cab of his big truck and returned with a cigarette in one hand and a can of Pepsi in the other. Squatting down beside Paul, he looked up at the scraped raw face and the black eye. "High-school kid?" he said.

Paul laughed. "High school? Hey, I got no time for high school. My brother, he works in City Hall in Boston. I'm just filling in around here for a couple weeks, you know?"

The Pinecraft driver was interested. "Hey," he said, "I got a suggestion."

"No kidding," said Paul. With mounting interest he listened to the truck driver's suggestion and grinned in agreement, then unloaded no more boxes that day. When the driver produced the invoice, Paul made another scrawl across it and accepted five twenty-dollar bills.

The grocery-department manager didn't show up in the receiving area until after lunch. Looking around, he was surprised to see the small number of cartons from Pinecraft. "Is that all? They usually fill up the whole end of the room here."

"Oh, sure," said Paul. "That's all. Jeez, it nearly broke my back."

"Who signed the invoice?"

"Mr. Gibby," said Paul smoothly.

"Well, okay, then." Taking out his case cutter, the grocery manager ripped open a carton of paper napkins.

27

Oh! the horrors of carelessness!
James Lorin Chapin
Private Journal, Lincoln, 1849

"*W*here is my sister?" The voice on the line was insistent. It was Arlene Pott's sister Beverly, calling Ethel Harris from Abilene, Texas. Beverly had met Arlene's neighbors, the Harrises, last year during her vacation trip to Massachusetts. "I keep calling Wally, and he keeps saying he hasn't heard anything from her. But really and truly, Ethel, my sister wouldn't just go off somewhere without letting me know."

"I'm worried about her too," said Ethel. "You know, Beverly, I hate to tell you this, but it's plain as the nose on your face Wally is carrying on with another woman. There's this practical nurse next door."

The upshot of the telephone conversation between Ethel Harris and Arlene's sister Beverly was that Ethel ran over to the Gibbys' to talk to Imogene, and then Imogene Gibby called Homer Kelly, because it was common knowledge Homer had been a famous detective in days gone by.

Homer was sympathetic but cautious. "Have you called Peter Terry?"

"Who?" said Imogene.

"The police chief, Peter Terry."

"Oh, Homer, Arlene wouldn't want us to do that. Maybe

she's just lying low so Wally won't find her. You know what he does sometimes—he's a wife-beater. I think she's afraid of him. Really, Homer, some men!"

"Well, that's possible, I suppose. You know, Imogene, a lot of wealthy women who disappear turn up later on, looking like movie stars. They've spent a couple of months at some health and beauty spa or some expensive ranch for alcoholics, and they come back all dried out and tucked up and bleached and dyed and curled and massaged and vitaminized, ready for a glorious new life, until the whole effect wears off and they're overweight again or sozzled into another stupor. Alas for their bright dreams! Alas for womankind! Alas for all our hopes for regeneration, rebirth, redemption, transcendence, exaltation, glory! Doomed, that's what we are, Imogene, doomed to the sordid grind, the ghastly plodding life of every day, the dismal windswept darkling plain, *the grating roar of pebbles which the waves draw back, and fling, at their return, up the high strand. . . ."*

"Homer? Are you all right?"

"Oh, sorry, Imogene. Well, of course, I'll see what I can do. I'll go talk to Wally, if you like, and see if I can find out anything at all. Ed Bell told me he didn't have much luck."

"Oh, thank you, Homer," said Imogene. "You're a dear." And Imogene hung up and ran next door, and then Ethel Harris and Imogene stared out the window at Wally Pott's house. "The cactus," said Ethel. "He used to put this big prickly cactus in the window whenever he wanted Josie to come over. But now it's there all the time."

Homer didn't notice the cactus when he walked up to Wally's house the next day, after parking his car in the woods a few hundred yards away. To his astonishment, he found the front door wide open, banging against the wallpaper in the front hall, tugged and released by gusts of early-September air.

Staring into the house, Homer rang the doorbell and listened to the chime. No one came. Wally didn't seem to be home.

The temptation to walk in was very strong. Homer gave in at once.

As soon as his foot crossed the threshold, he was aware of the general sense of carelessness, of disarray. In the living room the flower arrangements were dead. Tumblers and empty bottles stood on the glass coffee table, which was littered with crumbs and sticky with rings. A sheet of newspaper blew aimlessly around the room in the draft from the open front door. It caught on a lampshade, then fluttered against a figurine on the mantelpiece. The figurine fell to the floor with a crash.

"Don't blame me," murmured Homer, feeling guilty just the same, staring around the room greedily, taking in the silk blouse on the back of a chair, the pink lipstick on the rim of a glass. To whom did blouse and lipstick belong? The platinum-blond nurse next door, the one Imogene Gibby had told him about?

Shrugging his shoulders, Homer walked up the carpeted steps in the stone tower and poked his nose into the four corner bedrooms. Three were neat and untouched, looking like flossy ads for expensive bedroom suites. The fourth was a mess. The lavender sheets on the bed were churned up. A baby-doll nightie lay on the floor. It didn't look like a garment belonging to Mrs. Arlene Pott.

But the décor was obviously Arlene's. Everything was lavender, the layers of draperies at the windows, the bedspread dragging on the floor, the boudoir chairs, the rug. Homer examined the objects on the dresser, the artificial flowers, the porcelain birds, the hand mirror. There was a jewel box overflowing with junk beads and bracelets. There was a plastic case wrapped around with an electric cord. Hot curlers, decided Homer, remembering a temporary aberration of his wife's. The curlers were the secret of Arlene's frizzy hair. If it was true that she had run out on Wally, why hadn't she taken them with her?

Homer opened a drawer. It was jammed with lavender underwear, tightly packed. Closing the drawer, he had to stuff in the hems of slips. Abandoning the dresser, he turned to the closets.

There were two of them, his and hers. Like her drawers, Arlene's closet was crammed with clothing. Her taste ran to polyester dresses in big flowery patterns. The floor was littered with her shoes, two pairs deep. Wedged into a corner were three sleek lavender suitcases and a matching cosmetic case. If Arlene had gone away, why hadn't she used her luggage? Then Homer thrust his big face into the perfumed silky mass of Arlene's dresses and pushed his arms through to the wall at the rear. Instantly he found what he was looking for, her collection of pocketbooks, hanging on hooks at the back. Dragging them through the dresses, he laid them on the bureau for inspection. There were six of them.

1. A black patent-leather pouch with a gold chain, empty.
2. A brown leather-like receptacle with silver clasps, empty.
3. A big straw satchel, empty.
4. A beige monster with buckles, zippers, and straps, empty.
5. A heavy canvas bag with zipper pockets, empty.
6. A half-size purple briefcase with wooden handles, bulging.

Eagerly, Homer unstrapped the purple briefcase, and Arlene Pott herself swelled up from the interior, unfolding in the spreading scent of her perfume. Chiffon scarves and a linen handkerchief with a crocheted border billowed out of the bag.

Homer dumped everything out on the dresser, then examined the tumbled pile. There was a lipstick, a powder compact spilling lavender powder, a blue pearl earring, a container of pills (*One tablet three times a day for depression*—oh, poor Arlene), a bangle, a bent spoon, a collection of supermarket coupons, a pocket hair spray, a hairbrush, a comb with two missing teeth, a card case with credit cards and a driver's license (photograph of a lugubrious Arlene), a glasses case with gold-rimmed bifocals, a packet of tissues, a ballpoint pen, a broken pencil, a lottery ticket, a wallet with twenty-seven dollars in it, a change purse with three pennies and a button, a pamphlet on *The Power of Prayer,* and another pamphlet, *Taurus: What to Expect in August.* Inquisitively, Homer flipped open the astrological pamphlet to August first, the day Arlene Pott was supposed to have walked out on home and husband and gone off into the world alone. On August first all the men and women under the broad overarching protection of the constellation Taurus had been urged, "Stay at home, avoid long journeys, cherish your loved ones."

Homer dropped the pamphlet on the pile of Arlene's belongings, and stared at the litter on the dresser. If the woman had gone away to Reno or Honolulu or Los Angeles or Phoenix of her own free will, then she must have taken with her an identical collection of possessions in another bag—another driver's license, another Visa card, another pair of glasses, another container of pills, another wallet. It seemed highly unlikely that she would possess duplicates of all these things. Homer clicked his tongue in pious disbelief.

Then he cocked his doggy head and listened sharply as a crash shook the house. Good God, what was that? Moving cautiously to the window, Homer peered down through the layers of curtains. A car had run into a corner of the garage. Curses boiled up. A woman laughed. Then she got out of the car. She had bright blond hair and white trousers. It was Mrs. Hawk's nurse from the neighboring house. Wally Pott got out of the car too and walked ahead of her, carrying a paper bag.

If they found Homer inside, it would be a clear case of breaking and entering, even though he had merely walked in the open front door. Clumsily, Homer scrambled Arlene's things into her pocketbook, then thrust the whole collection back through the slippery soft dresses in her closet.

Downstairs there were fumblings, bangings, the woman's tipsy laughter. Loud talk drifted up the stairs from the direction of the kitchen. They had run out of bourbon, decided Homer. They had driven away on an errand so urgent they hadn't even bothered to close the front door.

Softly he made his way out of the bedroom and examined the stairway. The stair carpet was thick. The house was new. There would be no telltale squeakings of treads or shiftings of supporting joists, even though Homer's six feet six inches were fleshy with middle age. Creeping downstairs, he was grateful for the hilarity in the kitchen. "Whoops," screeched the woman. There was a tinkling crash, then screams of laughter and loud guffaws.

Poor Wally, thought Homer sympathetically, slipping out the front door, poor grieving abandoned husband, sucking his lonesome claws in solitude forlorn.

So far, so good. Now it was merely a matter of ducking under the kitchen window and dodging past the vegetable garden into the safety of the hemlock grove.

Homer's wife, Mary, was often distressed by her husband's rude habit of staring, by his manner of swinging his big head from side to side to sweep his surroundings with a prying eye. Homer had a truly embarrassing inquisitiveness, a nosy way of sticking his finger in the hole where the stuffing was coming out of the sofa, or the kapok from some wretched person's pride. Now, as he crouched past the vegetable garden, his attention was caught by the thick growth of weeds. Tsk, tsk, thought Homer, comparing Arlene's garden with Mary's vegetable patch at home. Mary's was weedy too, but not like this. Here were bushes six feet tall springing up around the poles of the bean vines. Homer paused in his flight and leaned over the chicken-wire fence. It was clear that someone had cared for this garden in the beginning and then had stopped caring for it. Surely it was the missing Arlene who had planted the green peppers and the sprawling squash, who had so carefully tied up the now shriveled beans, who had sown the seeds of the late-summer lettuce, bolted now into bitter towers.

How could the woman run away from a garden into which she had poured such devotion? Arlene should have stayed at home to harvest the zucchini before it grew so monstrous, she should have plucked the tender young lettuce, she should have picked the ripe tomatoes—if there were any tomatoes, only Homer couldn't see any. It struck him as odd that there were no tomatoes, and he craned his neck, looking for them, then moved cautiously around the chicken-wire enclosure.

How could anybody grow vegetables without growing tomatoes? Great juicy beefsteak tomatoes, delicious mouthfuls of cherry tomatoes, tomatoes for spaghetti sauce, tomatoes for sandwiches, tomatoes for— Ah, there they were, on the other side of the garden. But what had happened to them? Arlene Pott's tomato plants were wizened and drooping. They were dying. Most of them were dead. They looked as though their young lives had been interrupted, as though they had all perished suddenly in the midst of a hearty prime.

Homer glanced up at the house. From here he could see the open casement windows of the kitchen and hear the blare of the stereo. But the garden was to the north of the house and the kitchen windows looked out on the woods to the east. Unless Wally and his girlfriend moved their festivities into the living room, they would not catch a glimpse of the interloper bumbling around in the garden. Boldly, Homer stepped over the fence and trampled across the weed-engulfed squash vines to the rows of pole beans. Jerking a tall pole out of the ground, he carried it to the tomato bed, poked it gently into the dry earth, then shoved it straight down.

The pole stopped. Something was obstructing its thrust. Then, sickeningly, the obstruction gave way. Up through the pole a shuddering certainty transmitted itself to Homer's fingers. Slowly he withdrew the pole and looked at it. Fifteen inches of it were grimy with dirt, but the end was sticky with some other substance. Homer sniffed the end, then turned his head away and closed his eyes in sorrow, his stomach heaving.

Arlene Pott had not gone to Reno or Phoenix or Honolulu. She was not being transformed into a new woman at a beauty spa. She was right here at home, decomposing beneath her own vegetable garden. Her husband had murdered her, and then he had dug up the tomatoes and laid her down in the dirt and covered her over and replanted the tomatoes right on top of her, only he didn't know how to plant tomatoes, so they had all died. Poor Arlene. How had he killed her? With a gun, with a knife, with a hatchet?

Merriment was still issuing from the kitchen window, horselaughs from Wally Pott, soprano convulsions from the nurse with the mop of platinum curls. Filled with pity for the woman with the flowery dresses and the sad eyes, the woman who had felt the need of prayer, who had sought the blessings of Taurus, who had not lived to bring her tender seedlings to fruitful maturity, Homer carried the bean pole through the woods to his car. Opening the trunk, he laid the pole carefully across the spare tire. Then he drove slowly in the direction of the Nashoba police station, in the Town Hall.

The man was stupid, that was his problem. Careless and stupid. Too stupid to get rid of his wife's pocketbook, too dumb to throw out her suitcases, too feebleminded to know how to transplant a tomato. Homer didn't know which was more horrifying, Wally's brutal murder of his wife or his slipshod failure to cover up the crime.

An hour later, they were all together in the kitchen, Wally Pott and Josie Coil, Homer Kelly and Peter Terry, along with a couple of young guys from the department who doubled as firemen when the need arose. The young guys had already dug Arlene's strangled body out of the vegetable garden and wrapped it in one of her lavender sheets and laid it in the back of the police van.

"Don't look at me," cried Josie, backed up against the sink, her voice shrill in the accusing silence. "It's got nothing to do with me."

Wally Pott was beside himself. Addled by the sudden fall of the thunderbolt, he stared at Josie and whimpered, "But you said I had to do something. Soon, you said. This guy Victor, you said—" Wally could still see Victor in his mind's eye, looming up as threateningly as ever, Victor at the modeling agency, Victor with his cleft chin, Victor with his eyebrows that met in the middle.

"Victor?" cried Josie harshly. "Who's Victor? I don't know any Victor. It's all in your own mind, Wally Pott." She screamed at him, "You're crazy. You're just incredibly insane. It's got nothing to do with me."

Wally did not come peaceably. He was still shouting and struggling when they dragged him out of the van and pulled him into the police station. In the firehouse across the street, one of the volunteers was hosing down the hook-and-ladder truck. He dropped the hose and lent a hand.

28

Truly, sir, it is to me a wonder that the earth
swallows not up such wretches, or that fire comes
not down from heaven to consume them!
Reverend Peter Bulkeley
Concord, 1650

*T*he discovery of Arlene Pott's
dead body and the simultaneous arrest of her husband on suspicion of murder produced a sensation in the town of Nashoba.
There was shock and disbelief, pity for Arlene and revulsion for
Wally. Not until Wally's arraignment and imprisonment without
bail, not until the first scandalized excitement had died down, was
the day chosen for Arlene's memorial service.

It turned out to be a brilliant afternoon in early October,
when up and down Estabrook Road the undergrowth was decked
with berries and seed heads in bright reds and pinks, and the
foliage was spotted and flecked in hues for which there were no
names. Blood Street was lined with wild sumac as red as its name,
with towering cherry-colored cones rising above the blood-
soaked leaves. In the belfry of Old West, the barn owl drowsed
on a crossbeam, its offspring long since flown. Below the belfry
in the sunny open spaces of the church, Joe Bold sat waiting
behind the pulpit, ready to do his best to give the poor woman
a dignified farewell. The place was packed.

Peter Terry came in with Flo and sat down beside the Kellys,
and instantly Flo Terry transfixed Homer with her gelid eye.
Doom, that eye implied, had come at last upon the parish of Old
West Church, just as she, Flo Terry, had foretold.

Homer shifted uneasily on the bench, wedged between Mary's solid thigh and Flo's massive prophetic haunch. It was a good thing Flo didn't know about Betsy Bucky, another Old West parishioner every bit as homicidal as Wally Pott. Homer sought out Betsy in the congregation. There she was in the front row. The sun in its erratic favoritism had chosen her today for glory. Her eager little wiry frame was bathed in light. She was staring around the room, atwitter with excitement, obviously intoxicated by the lurid circumstances of Arlene's death. Was she comparing herself to Wally Pott as a fellow killer, a more capable assassin? Surely not, decided Homer. Betsy was one of those innocents who never caught themselves in the act. She was a ruthless natural killer, but as far as she was concerned Carl's death had happened by itself. Although she had slain her husband with a malicious violence equal to that with which Wally Pott had strangled his wife, she would never be brought to trial. Even Betsy's closest friends probably still thought of her as Carl Bucky's spunky little wife, although they had seen her kill him with her brutal coffeepot, her deadly deep-fat fryer, her lethal bread pans, her murdering eggbeater, her fatal cake tins. Look at the woman preen herself in the front row!

Then Homer dropped his gaze to his own slightly swollen midriff, remembering the French toast Mary had offered him at breakfast. Trustingly, like a lamb to the slaughter, he had eaten two slices and accepted two more. What if Mary Kelly were another Betsy Bucky? Homer glared suspiciously at his wife, but Mary was flipping the pages of her hymnbook, nudging him to stand up, holding the open pages under his nose.

Time, like an ever-rolling stream,
Bears all its sons away,

growled Homer, staring in horror at the words by Isaac Watts.

They fly forgotten, as a dream
Dies at the opening day.

It was true. How grim. Death was just around the corner, waiting for them all the time. They were here today and gone tomorrow. Like a fibrillating pulse, they vibrated for a moment on the earthly scene, then disappeared forever. The entire population of the globe was moribund. All those billions of people—black, white, brown, yellow, red—they were merely advancing toward the giant scythe that swept in its vast arc, ready to cut them down. Row after advancing row, they bowed their heads like the grass and fell before the inevitable blade.

> *O God, our help in ages past,*
> *Our hope for years to come,*

groaned Homer, sorrowing for Arlene Pott and Carl Bucky and all the other nameless doomed fellow human beings in the world, but especially for himself,

> *Be thou our guard while troubles last,*
> *And our eternal home.*

In the succeeding weeks, Homer's gloom about human mortality was fatefully underscored, at least in the parish of Nashoba's Old West Church, because, as it turned out, the deaths of Carl Bucky and Arlene Pott were only the beginning. From that moment on, the funerals in the church came thick and fast.

Philip Shooky's was the first. Ed Bell was with Phil when he died. Together they sat on the ground at the summit of a little knoll, leaning against a big white pine tree, looking out over a blaze of swamp maples. It was a place where Phil had always loved to take his dogs.

"Where's Deborah?" said Ed softly.

"Visiting the kids. She'll be back this evening."

"Oh, I see."

"Go ahead," said Phil, stiffening his back against the pine tree.

"No, wait, let's talk a little more." Ed put his arm around Phil's shoulders.

"No, we've talked enough." Phil rolled up his sleeve. "Do it now. I'm ready."

Ed removed his arm from Phil's shoulders and picked up the Bible and leafed through it, looking for the twenty-third Psalm. Phil recited it with him, muttering in a low voice, looking not at the book but at the dogs gamboling in the amber-colored grass in the field that lay between the swamp maples and the summit of the hill. . . .

It wasn't until four hours later that Deborah Shooky found her husband stretched out under his favorite tree as if he were asleep. Even in the midst of her grief, she assumed he had died of the stroke they had both been dreading.

But the post-mortem examination revealed that Phil's heart had simply stopped beating. He had not died of a brain hemorrhage or an embolism or a stroke. And there were some puzzling needle marks on his arm.

"Did he have a blood test recently?" Dr. Spinney asked Deborah. "Did he go to any other doctor besides me?"

"No," said Deborah. "Just the podiatrist."

"Oh, I doubt the podiatrist would have taken a blood sample."

"You know, Arthur," said Deborah, giving voice to her suspicions, "Phil was terribly afraid of losing his mental capacity like Howie Sawyer. He was just terrified of ending up like Howie."

"Yes," said Arthur Spinney, shaking his head dolefully. "He often expressed those fears to me."

"I just can't help but wonder if he didn't take his own life in some way. Those needle marks on his arm—"

"But there was no syringe beside his body. How did he get rid of the hypodermic?"

"I don't know," said Deborah, bewildered.

Together they examined the laboratory where Phil had taken care of an occasional dog or cat, even in his retirement. They found no used needles, only new ones still wrapped in sealed paper packages.

But Dr. Spinney shared Deborah's suspicions. As a veterinarian, Phil Shooky had been acquainted with all the latest systems for the painless dispatch of sick and unwanted animals. Sodium pentothal and scopolamine were handy on his shelves. And surely he had known about that simple chemical, potassium, undetectable by any pathologist because it came flooding out of the cells at the moment of death. Dr. Spinney looked for potassium chloride among Phil's collection of pharmaceuticals, but did not find it. Perhaps it was not Phil but someone else who had administered the fatal dose.

"I wonder if some other veterinarian, some friend of his, might have done it for him?" suggested Dr. Spinney.

"Well, I don't know who it would be," said Deborah, gazing sadly into space.

"Well, never mind." Shrugging his shoulders helplessly, Dr. Spinney signed the requisite piece of paper with a good conscience, *Cause of death: cardiac arrest,* grateful that Phil had asked no more of him.

Lorraine Bell was even more suspicious than Deborah Shooky. She confronted her husband in angry protest. "It was your group, wasn't it? Phil wanted to die, and you helped him. Oh, Ed, dear, be careful. I'm so afraid. You could get yourself into terrible trouble."

In church they said Phil's death was a blessing. "He knew his mind was going," said Charlie Fenster to Homer and Mary Kelly at Phil's funeral. "This way he won't have to suffer years of affliction like Howie Sawyer."

Homer assented, and Mary nodded sadly, and then all three of them glanced across the church at the bench under the window where Joan Sawyer was sitting by herself, gazing dreamily at the door through which the minister was about to enter, along with Deborah Shooky and all the younger Shookys.

"A blessing," said Charlie again. "Really a mercy."

It was a mercy too when Thad Boland died in bed. Thad's daughter found him when she came to pick up her widowed father's laundry.

"His heart simply stopped," said Dr. Spinney, calling Thad's daughter from the hospital after the autopsy.

"Oh, poor Daddy," wept Thad's daughter.

"And they found something strange. There was a hard mass in his abdomen, something pretty unpleasant. Your father wasn't my patient. Do you know who his doctor was?"

But Thad's daughter didn't know.

"Well, I just wonder if he knew he was in real trouble. Maybe his death was a blessing."

It was what everyone else said too, once again. Thad's death was a blessing in disguise. And they all thought of Claire Bold, who was not being granted the same blessing, who was lingering on hopelessly, dying slowly of the same disease that would have tormented Thad if he had not been mercifully released ahead of time.

Rosemary Hill's decease was a tidy suicide. Rosemary had finished sorting the stuff in the attic, and then she had turned her attention to the rest of the house. She cleaned it from top to bottom. She waxed the floors and washed the windows. She emptied the refrigerator and scrubbed it inside and out. She pickled the last of her green tomatoes. She straightened her cupboards, sent most of her clothes to the Morgan Memorial, threw away her old underwear, polished the silver, paid all the bills, mounded compost around her rosebushes, and raked the leaves. It was as though she were expecting an honored visitor for whom everything had to be spic-and-span. Then Rosemary wrote letters to each of her children and left them on her desk with her last will and testament and the keys to her safe-deposit box at the bank.

On the last day of her life, Rosemary washed her hair and took a bubble bath, then went out to lunch with her old friends Jill and Marigold. On the way home she mailed a letter to Dr. Spinney, then parked her car in her garage, left the key on the desk, climbed the stairs to her bedroom, put on her best nightgown, got into bed with her bottles of sleeping pills and a big glass of water, lay back on the pillow, gazed for a moment at the south windows of her bedroom through which the light of afternoon was flooding, took a deep breath, and began swallowing the pills.

Dr. Spinney didn't get his letter till next day. As soon as he read it, he rushed over, but of course he was too late. He called her son, Jeffry, in Cambridge, and Jeffry notified Amanda in Schenectady, and soon Rosemary's children and grandchildren were gathered in her house to arrange everything and plan the funeral.

As funerals go, it was a grand occasion, a celebration of Rosemary's generous life. Two of the grandchildren played the flute and the French horn in the balcony, accompanied on the organ by Augusta Gill. Joe Bold conducted the service. Ed Bell read a eulogy that was an affectionate summation of all that Rosemary's life had meant to her friends and her church and the town in which she had lived so long.

Arthur Spinney was grumpy about it. "For an honest woman, she was pretty crafty," he complained to Homer Kelly. "She lied to me about those sleeping tablets, claimed they were all gone, persuaded me to give her some more." But even Dr. Spinney admitted that for Rosemary it had been a civilized goodbye. "She might have had another six months of pain. I suppose it was a mercy."

29

*Their souls . . . are not . . . hurried away by insulting
Devils down to the infernal regions, but are convoyed
by kind and guardian angels into climes of bliss. . . .*
                    Reverend Paul Litchfield
                first minister of Carlisle, 1781–1827

*I*t was as though Phil Shooky had
set a fashion. While Claire Bold hung on to her fragile life by a
nearly invisible thread, her husband's parishioners began falling
out of sight like an eager crowd shouldering its way through a
dark door.

Agatha Palmer and Percy Donlevy and Bill Molyneux followed hard on the heels of Rosemary Hill. Their deaths were
skewed and off center, like Phil's and Thad's and Rosemary's.
None of them died in a way that might have been expected.
Agatha had been suffering from leukemia, but she hadn't been
desperately ill. One morning her cleaning lady, bumping the
vacuum cleaner through the door of the living room first thing
in the morning, was stunned to find Agatha lying peacefully on
the sofa with an open Bible on her lap. She seemed to have died
in her sleep.

Percy Donlevy's death was anything but peaceful. Percy
suffered from Parkinson's disease, but he died when his car
plunged down Arlington hill on Route 2 and struck a bridge
abutment head on.

As for Bill Molyneux, it was true that his multiple sclerosis
had flared up again, but the disorder was still a long way from

finishing him off. Bill died on a camping trip to Baxter State Park. The ranger found him in his little dome tent still curled up in his sleeping bag in the heat of a late-October noonday.

Bill's death was the last straw for Lorraine Bell. She raged at her husband and beat her fists against his chest. "That's where you were last Tuesday when you wouldn't tell me where you were going. You went up to Baxter State Park to meet Bill Molyneux."

Ed took her hands and held them gently. "But somebody had to help him. He couldn't do it alone."

"Well, why did it have to be you? Oh, Ed, you know what they'll call it if they find out. Murder, first-degree murder." Lorraine burst into tears.

Rosemary Hill's house

Eleanor heard her mother's sobs and appeared in the doorway of the bedroom, looking frightened. "What's the matter with Mom?"

"She's all right," said her father comfortingly, holding his wife in his arms, stroking her hair.

But Eleanor knew her mother wasn't crying about nothing. To see her in tears cast a shadow on the afternoon. Slowly, Eleanor went back to her room, walking carefully, as though a crack had opened in the solid floor. She lay down on her bed with her book and tried to pick up where she had left off.

It was a big book, a big thick book, a heavy indigestible masterpiece, *The Magic Mountain*. At this moment in Eleanor's fifteenth year, only massive volumes of proven literary genius were good enough. She had finished *War and Peace* and *Tess of the D'Urbervilles* and *David Copperfield*. Waiting in line were *The Last Chronicle of Barset* and *The Brothers Karamazov* and *One Hundred Years of Solitude*. Eleanor didn't worry about difficult words and bewildering paragraphs. Her eyes merely glided over them. And yet passages like "your peregrinations in this metropolis" (Mr. Micawber) or "something nebulous, preoccupied, vague, in his bearing" (Angel Clare) left a vivid stain upon her mind.

Blindly now, she turned the page. Oh, why was her mother weeping?

But of course Lorraine had a very strong reason for her despairing tears. And she wasn't the only member of Old West's congregation to be seriously troubled by the death of Bill Molyneux. For a lot of people it was one swan song too many. It was too many crossings of the bar in too short a time. Carl Bucky, Arlene Pott, Philip Shooky, Thad Boland, Rosemary Hill, Agatha Palmer, Percy Donlevy, and Bill Molyneux—how many was that? Eight! Eight funerals in six weeks!

Flo Terry, the reference librarian, was bleakly triumphant. When Homer crept into the library on the morning of Bill Molyneux's funeral, Flo looked at him with an expression of solemn elation, as if she were thundering like Jeremiah, *The Lord has opened his armory, and brought out the weapons of his wrath. Woe to them, for their day has come, the time of their punishment. Hark!*

But Homer, too, was oppressed by the large number of final departures. "It's like the Black Death," he said gloomily to Arthur Spinney as they came out of church together after the burial service for Bill. "You know, back in the fourteenth century, when three quarters of the living souls on the continent of Europe were cut down."

"It reminds me of those little graveyards in remote New England towns," said Arthur in melancholy recollection. "You wander around from stone to stone and suddenly realize that whole families were wiped out in one terrible winter." Arthur was plainly upset. "Listen, Homer, I'm not about to go to the police, but I've got a funny feeling somebody's playing God around here, and I don't like it at all."

"Playing God?" said Homer, raising his eyebrows. "You mean you think most of these deaths weren't natural, after all?"

"Well, of course there's no question about Rosemary Hill's suicide. She told me about those pills in her letter. But I'm pretty suspicious of some of the others. No apparent cause for death but simple heart failure? It's happened too often. And I'm curious about the needle marks on their arms. Of course most of them had hypodermic injections of one kind or another anyway—Agatha, Phil, Percy, Bill—because they all had nasty illnesses. They were having their blood tested all the time. But who knows what else might have been pumped into them with a syringe? Some of those needle marks looked pretty clumsy, as if an amateur had been at work."

"Were there any hypodermic needles lying around?"

"No, so it could have been a conspiracy. Somebody else was helping. Somebody gave the injection, then went away with the needle. It's a plot. They're helping each other out of their terminal diseases ahead of time. Phil Shooky, the veterinarian, I'll bet he showed them how. I swear, that's what I think."

"Is that so bad?" murmured Homer.

"Of course it's bad. There's always the chance for new cures. And some of them had a good deal of life ahead of them. They could have lasted for months, possibly years."

Homer looked at Arthur Spinney reproachfully. "Like Howie Sawyer and Claire Bold?"

Dr. Spinney turned holier-than-thou. "Playing God is a dangerous practice, Homer Kelly. You should know that. *Thou shalt not take the mantle of the Lord upon thy shoulders.* That's what it says in the Bible."

"Oh, go on," said Homer. "Where does it say that? I think you made that up."

The matter was admittedly complex. Homer said goodbye to Dr. Spinney and turned away to watch Joe Bold hurry down the hill, stooped over in a painful crouch. Homer wanted to run after

Joe and find out what he thought about the appropriation of the mantle of God. As an ordained Christian minister, trained in the niceties of ethical behavior, would Joe regard such a conspiracy as the merciful connivance of consenting souls and a work of virtue? Or would he think it was mass murder, kindly but misguided? Homer raised his long right arm and opened his mouth to shout at Joe, then thought better of it. This was no time to discuss mortality with Joseph Bold.

But Ed Bell was another honest Christian. What would Ed think about the mantle of God? Homer went back to the house on Fairhaven Bay and made himself a lonely lunch, because his wife was taking her turn with Claire Bold, and then he drove back to Nashoba to Ed Bell's house on Acton Road.

There was no room for Homer's car. Four other cars were taking up all the space in Ed's driveway. Homer recognized most of them. One belonged to the Bells, one was George Tarkington's old Chrysler station wagon, the one at the back was Bo Harris's old wreck. Only the fourth was a stranger.

Homer parked in the street, with two wheels up on the sparse grass of the Bells' front lawn, and walked up the driveway. When he saw Eleanor, he stopped short and gasped. She was part of the October spectacle. The sun was dappling her gold-red hair in the same lavish way that it scattered itself in splendor on the yellow leaves of the maples around her. Eleanor's lips were as pink as berries spilling out of a seedpod. She was crying. She looked up at Homer, tears running down her cheeks. Then Homer saw the reason for her tears. A pair of big feet in enormous sneakers was sticking out from under Bo Harris's Chevy. Bo must have said something cruel.

Homer squatted in the driveway and tried to see the talking end of Bo. "Hi, there," he said. "How's she coming?"

In the shadows under the car, Bo lifted his head, his eyes white in his greasy face. "Oh, it's just the hangers on the goddamned muffler," he snarled. "I can't make the goddamned things stay put."

"Anything I can do to help?" said Homer, conscious of the spotless cleanliness of his Sunday suit.

"Oh, no, thanks, Mr. Kelly." Bo heaved at something over his head and cursed savagely.

"Well, okay, then, if you say so." Homer struggled to his feet. "I'm a butterfingered jerk anyway." He turned to Eleanor and inquired politely, "Is your father around?"

Eleanor nodded at the house. "He's inside," she quavered. "There's a meeting."

"A meeting? Oh, that's what those other cars are here for. I see." Homer patted Eleanor's shoulder clumsily and walked around the house to the front porch. Then he dawdled on the steps, and stared into the living room.

There they were again, silhouetted sharply against the windows on the other side of the house. There were only three of them this time, three people standing in a small circle with their heads down, holding hands. Only three? Last time there had been more than that—eight or ten of them, Homer was sure of it.

Inside the Bells' living room, Ed and George and Eloise were sitting down. Ed told a joke, and then they got down to brass tacks. They were seasoned veterans by this time, at ease with each other, unruffled too by the other presence in the room, which now seemed like an invited guest.

Eloise Baxter was timid, that was the only trouble. She would need help when the time came.

Ed assured her the help would be there.

George Tarkington wasn't going to need anybody. He laughed. "Wait and see," he said. "No problem. I've got it all worked out."

When the doorbell rang, they didn't look up. Lorraine answered it, hurrying out of the kitchen with her coat on.

"Meeting going on again, like last time?" said Homer Kelly inquisitively, staring through the screen door at the closed sliding doors of the living room.

"Oh, yes, Homer. I'm sorry. Did you want to see Ed? How about tomorrow? Forgive me, Homer. I'm on my way to my volunteer job at the hospital."

"Oh, I see. Well, never mind. Tell Ed never mind."

On the way back to Fairhaven Bay, Homer drove blindly, lost in thought. When he slowed down at the end of his long driveway, he was surprised to see another car pulling up at the edge of the turnaround, its front wheels mashing the low pink blueberry bushes and yellowing ferns.

It was Parker Upshaw, in his gleaming new Subaru. Parker got out of his car and stood in the driveway. Homer was astonished to learn that Parker had come to him for the same reason Homer had gone to Ed Bell. He was troubled by the sudden excess of deaths in Old West Church.

"One from natural causes," said Parker, "then a murder, then six other deaths right on top of each other—one an accident, one a suicide, four completely unexplained."

"One from natural causes?" said Homer doubtfully, running the melancholy list over again in his mind.

"Carl Bucky's, of course," said Parker.

"Oh, Carl Bucky's." Homer wanted to tell Upshaw that Carl Bucky's death had been about as natural as Arlene Pott's, but he refrained.

"What does it mean?" said Parker, staring in philosophical despair at the choppy blue water of Fairhaven Bay.

"Damned if I know," said Homer, who was in no mood to engage in metaphysical speculation with Parker W. Upshaw. Courteously he waved at the high steps, followed Parker onto the porch, and opened the house door.

Heaving a deep sigh, Parker sat down on the edge of the sofa in the front room. He clasped his knees, then unclasped them. He put his hand inside his blazer, then withdrew it. He smoothed his hair. "What we want to avoid, you see," he said earnestly, "is the intervention of the police."

"I think you'll find," said Homer dryly, "they've already intervened. After all, they've locked up Wally Pott."

"Oh, of course, Wally Pott. Good grief, that was bad enough. It's the others I'm worried about. We mustn't allow Old West Church to acquire a macabre reputation." Parker Upshaw raised his voice and thumped the coffee table with his fist. "These deaths must stop!"

Homer was overjoyed. "Why, certainly!" he cried. "Stop them, by all means! Stay the hand of the grim reaper! Halt mighty death in his tracks! Let there be no more unseemly kickings of the bucket! No longer shall the tired warrior bend the bow in the happy hunting ground!" Homer's enthusiasm knew no bounds. As Parker stalked out of the house, Homer ran after him, babbling, "I mean, you're right. There's been altogether too much of that kind of thing down through the ages." Leaning over the porch railing, Homer bawled the first verse of an old hymn as Parker stamped down the stairs and got into his car:

Ten thousand times ten thousand, in sparkling raiment bright,
The armies of the ransomed saints throng up the steeps of light;
'Tis finished, all is finished, their fight with death and sin;
Fling open wide the golden gates, and let the victors in!

"I mean, ten thousand times ten thousand—it's too many, right, Upshaw?"

Parker started his car and swept it around the dirt circle. Then he leaned out, his face red with anger, and shouted, "Your driveway is a disgrace!"

Homer was still in a transport. "I mean," he bellowed, "who wants to throng up the steeps of light when he could be drinking a beer and eating a hamburger? Or gazing from a mountaintop at some stupendous view? I mean, I ask you, Parker," shouted Homer as Upshaw's Subaru tore up the steep hill, "why don't we all just go right on being alive?"

But it was no joke. When Mary Kelly came home from a long afternoon session with Claire Bold, worn out and discouraged, she listened with her head in her hands as Homer described Dr. Spinney's conspiracy theory.

"Spinney doesn't know it," said Homer, "but he's absolutely right. The conspirators meet every Sunday afternoon at Ed Bell's house. Did I tell you I saw them all before? I walked right in on them. It was a bigger bunch the first time. I was so ashamed of myself for interrupting I dodged right out again, but I swear I saw Phil Shooky and Rosemary Hill among the rest. Now Phil and

Rosemary are gone. I'll bet Agatha and Bill and Thad and Percy were there too. And now they're gone. So the group I saw today is just the tag ends that are left. I couldn't see who they were, but George Tarkington must have been one of them, because his car was there. I'll bet those people are going to be next. They'll turn up dead too. Do you know anybody else with a terminal disease who might want to be eased out of existence gently ahead of time? Somebody who might want to finesse the whole miserable final scene in the hospital, with hopeless surgery and bedpans and last-minute kidney problems and pneumonia and intravenous feeding and going into a coma and losing their wits entirely?"

"So that's it," said Mary slowly, looking up at Homer. "They're helping each other die."

" 'What a mercy,' everybody always says, have you noticed that? 'Isn't it a blessing!' Well, maybe the blessing is prearranged. It's a Merciful Society of the Blessed Dead, that's what I think, a prayerful organization for the cheating of death. It's like a church within the church. They're getting together to help each other take care of the matter themselves, before some hideous disease tortures them the way it's torturing Claire Bold, before senility turns them into living corpses like Howie Sawyer."

"If you're right, Homer, then surely it's a good thing? It's what I would want if some awful disease happened to me. Or if I had a stroke that threatened me with senile dementia. Listen, Homer"—Mary stood up and looked at her husband fiercely—"you've got to promise to kill me if that happens. Swear you'll do it. Oh, I know, it's vanity on my part, I admit. I'm too vain to want to be remembered as a helpless vegetable. Too proud, too conceited."

"Is that a formal request?" said Homer. "I've got carte blanche? Anytime Maud Starr crooks her little finger?"

Mary laughed, and led the way into the kitchen.

"That's the trouble, you see," said Homer. "Who's to say when the moment has come? If you and I had a pact like that, we'd begin to be scared of each other. I can see you coming at me with a pill in your fist before I'm ready. I can see myself in bed, helpless and paralyzed from the neck down, whining, 'Not yet, woman, not yet.' "

They went out on the porch with their crystal glasses and their bottle of wine. Venus was still the ornament of the evening. Downriver it hung low between barred channels of gray cloud. Homer watched as the glittering point of light fell behind a cloudy strip, then reappeared below it, as though a woman were moving through a house, looking out of each of the windows in turn. Her piercing glance alarmed him.

"It's a serious thing, mercy killing," he said uneasily. "In court it would be murder. And when you think about the ethics of it, what a baffling mystery! Is it the right thing to do, or not? God knows. God only knows."

"Maybe it's just coincidence, after all," said Mary. "Just because eight members of the congregation of Old West Church have died, it may not mean anything out of the ordinary. After all, this is an elderly congregation."

"It's just coincidence, you mean, that all eight of them died at the same time?"

"Why not? It's perfectly possible. Anyway, it's only seven. You can't count Arlene Pott. That was something else entirely. So was Carl Bucky."

Then Mary went inside to get supper, and Homer strolled down the front yard, pushed the canoe into the shallows, and paddled out to look at the sunset.

It was cool on the water. The canoe rocked in the waves. Homer wished he had brought a jacket. Shivering, he tried to warm himself at the glowing fires of the display in the west, a clotted confusion of flaming archipelagoes, burning ships, blazing coral reefs, and raging forest fires on the slopes of fiery mountains. It was the steeps of light—Homer recognized them —those selfsame steeps toward which the armies of the ransomed saints were thronging, turning up their rapt faces, bouncing out of their graves with pious good sportsmanship. Homer's face was bathed in the sunset glow, but he scowled as he dipped his paddle into a puddle of pink sky. Ten thousand times ten thousand poor doomed souls died every single day of the year. God had certainly arranged things badly. He was the destroyer of every living thing, blandly arranging the extinction of every creature. His universe worked on a principle of mass murder. But now, at least, thanks to the Merciful Society of the Blessed Dead, some of the clever ones had outwitted him. With the kindly assistance of Ed Bell, they were marching in the direction of those horrid steeps of light with a firmer step than the rest.

Then Homer had an uncomfortable thought, and he missed a stroke and nearly lost his paddle. What was Ed's interest in all this? Why was Ed standing there in his living room with the rest of the society? Why did they meet at his house? Was Ed Bell going to die too? Did he suffer from some illness that was threatening his life? Or was he merely the leader, the man behind the conspiracy, the one who was playing God? Was he the inventor of the plan for saving the rest from pain and suffering and indignity?

Homer put down his paddle in the bottom of the canoe and let the wind-driven waves slop against the metal sides. The air smelled of mud and turtles and decaying pickerel weed and the fresh water of the river, spongy and dark with organic matter. Homer thought of Betsy Bucky, who had killed her husband with deadly intent, and was getting away with it. Betsy was the very opposite of Ed Bell. Ed was a genuine angel of deliverance. But might he not be accused of murder in the first degree, multiple murder, if anyone else found out? Even though it was not malice aforethought in Ed's case, but pure benevolence?

30

Farewell . . . our dear sister in Christ Jesus, farewell, but we trust not forever.

Reverend Charles Stearns
Lincoln, 1812

*I*t was nearly Thanksgiving before Claire Bold died at last. The November air was thin and chill, purified of the heavy airs of summer. The glaring colors of October had given way to somber umbers and deep reds. There had been a thick fall of leaves, opening up astonishing forgotten vistas along roads that had been dark tunnels of shade all summer long. The sun rose late every morning and hurried to an early decline.

Thanksgiving at the County Hospital was a difficult time. The head nurse on Howie Sawyer's ward confessed to Joan that the patients were especially troublesome. "They sense something is going on, that they're being left out. It's almost as tough as Christmas." The head nurse shuddered. "How I dread Christmas."

Joan looked around at the small company of broken men and women who had been shipwrecked on this antiseptic shore—Mr. O'Doyle was sitting on the floor against the wall, drowsily clutching his ball, Mrs. Beddoes was rocking in her chair, Mr. Canopus was talking to himself, his eyes bright, Miss Stein was smiling in her sleep, Howie was pacing heavily back and forth. "I'll help at

Christmastime," she promised the head nurse. "I've got a few days off."

"I thought you weren't married to Howie anymore," said the head nurse, looking at her sharply. "I don't expect to see you around here much anymore."

"Oh, it takes a while to get a divorce," said Joan. "And anyway it won't matter. I'll keep coming just the same."

"I'll bet," said the head nurse, but only to herself.

On the day before Thanksgiving, Joe Bold tried to focus his attention on the sermon for the holiday service. But he had been up with Claire all night. His papers kept sliding to the floor as he nodded off in the chair beside her bed. When Lorraine Bell knocked on the door, he jumped up and let her in, and they stood together looking down at Claire's exhausted sleeping face. Her wasted body was almost invisible under the blanket.

"I think she's a little better now," murmured Joe, hoping against hope.

Without a word Lorraine settled herself beside the bed and took out her knitting.

Joe walked up the hill to the parish house. There he found Felicia, his secretary, in a vexed state of mind. "You've had a phone call from Maud Starr," she said, frowning at him. "She wants you to call her back."

"Oh, Joe," cried Maud on the phone. "I'm all agog. I've had this idea. I want to start a singles group. What do you think? Could you come over and talk about it? I'm just brimming with ideas. If I don't tell somebody, I'll pop."

"Now?" said Joe hollowly, staring at the paper turkey pasted to Felicia's window. "You mean I should come now?"

"Why not?"

Joe's brow furrowed as he tried to think of a reason why not, but nothing occurred to him. "Well, all right, I guess so."

"You're going over there?" said Felicia, shocked and disgusted as he put down the phone. "To *Maud Starr's house*?"

"Look," said Joe anxiously, "call me over there if—if you need me."

"I certainly will," said Felicia sharply, giving him an accusing look. Then she punched the on button of the tape recorder, turned the volume way up, and began battering at her typewriter, pounding out last Sunday's sermon for the next issue of the church bulletin. The quiet opening of the outer door and the soft sound of its shutting were drowned out by the stammering noise of Joe's recorded voice echoing from the tall ranks of Felicia's file drawers and the potted plants on the windowsill and the calendar of the Holy Places of Jerusalem and the oddly shaped pipe-fitting Joan Sawyer had left for the sexton and the stack of worn-out hymnals Felicia couldn't bear to throw away.

Half an hour later, still hard at work, she almost didn't hear the phone. But on the last ring she hopped up and grabbed it. Lorraine Bell was asking anxiously for Joe.

"I'm sorry," said Felicia, "he's not here. But I can give you the number where you'll find him." Felicia knew it by heart, and she recited it for Lorraine.

Lorraine knew it too. "But that's Maud Starr's number. Is that where he is?"

"I'm afraid so," said Felicia angrily.

"Well, thank you, Felicia," said Lorraine. But a moment later she rang again, panic-stricken. "There's no answer at Maud's. Where can Joe be? I've got to find him. I think Claire is sinking. I've called Dr. Spinney."

"I'll try Mary Kelly," said Felicia crisply. "Mary might know what he was planning to do today."

But Mary was not at home. When the phone rang in the small house on Fairhaven Bay, it was Homer who answered it. "She's not here," he said, sensing the desperation in Felicia's voice. "Is anything wrong?"

The story tumbled out of Felicia. "He's supposed to be at Maud Starr's, but she doesn't answer her phone." Then Felicia couldn't help interjecting, "With his wife on her deathbed!"

"Where does Maud live?" said Homer.

Felicia told him, and in a moment Homer's pickup was once again lurching along Fairhaven Road. Maud's house was easy to find. With its butterfly roof, it was a crumbling example of the modish architectural follies of the nineteen-fifties. Inside, Homer suspected, there would be a conversation pit lined with shaggy carpeting.

He had come to the right place. Joe's car was in the driveway. And there was Joe himself, behind the house, sitting stiffly upright in the swing that dangled from a rangy oak tree. Maud was pushing him gaily back and forth.

Clever girl, thought Homer cynically as he threw open the car door. The old swing trick. Disarm the subject playfully, reduce him to the status of a vulnerable child, get the tender bird in flight, then pounce.

"Joe!" bawled Homer.

Joe looked up, sprang off the swing, lost his footing, and fell to the ground. Picking himself up, he ran limping across the yard. There was no need to ask why Homer was there.

"Hey, wait for me!" cried Maud.

But they didn't.

Maud was disappointed. She went inside and lounged in her conversation pit and called up a friend she had once lived with for five tumultuous months.

The friend was wary. He was, he said, terribly sorry that they couldn't get together, but he was just leaving for Cincinnati.

"When are you coming back?" said Maud sweetly.

"Oh, not for ages. I've got an *awful* lot to do in Cincinnati."

31

*No message will ever reach me from the cold grave
where they have laid you!*

James Lorin Chapin
Private Journal, Lincoln, 1849

Mary Kelly had spent the morn-
ing in the Concord public library among the busts of Hawthorne
and Thoreau and Ebenezer Rockwood Hoar. For Mary, the library was a familiar haunt. She had once been employed there.
Every day she had inhaled the gummy fragrance of glued bind-
ings, the good smell of dictionaries, the cold aura of marble ears
and noses, the healthy aroma of middle-aged librarians, along
with a certain indefinable transcendental essence like the scent of
a pine grove on some bleak and windswept crag.

When she came home with her arms full of books, she was
startled to see Homer looking down at her from the porch.
"Claire's gone," he said.

"Oh, no," cried Mary, bursting into tears. One by one the
books fell from her arms as she sobbed up the steps, overcome
by pity and anguished sympathy and, above all, by relief. "It's
over. It's over at last."

Mary's sense of sad deliverance was felt throughout the parish as the word went around. It was as if they had all been holding
their breath.

"No more suffering," said Imogene Gibby, breaking the

news by phone to Hilary Tarkington. "She won't have to endure any more of those awful operations."

"Oh, no, bless her heart," echoed Hilary, her eyes filling with tears. In the next room, Hilary's husband, George, was going through a bad spell, struggling to fill his lungs with air. "Has anyone said anything about the service for her? I suppose they'll have to bring in another clergyman."

But who should the clergyman be? In the end it was Ed Bell who made the arrangements, with the help of his wife and Mary Kelly. Joe Bold, the bereaved husband, roused himself from his brokenhearted misery long enough to suggest an old classmate at the Divinity School, and the old classmate agreed to come.

When it was over, the congregation fled in all directions, oppressed by the apparently endless burden of continuous sorrow. Parker Upshaw, for one, felt strongly that they had all endured enough. Striding out to his car, he turned the key and looked significantly at Libby as she climbed in beside him. "Well, thank God. Now maybe Old West can get on with its work. If the man doesn't shape up from now on, I'm personally going to see to it that we get ourselves a replacement. I'm not kidding."

"Oh, Parker, honestly," said Libby, genuinely disturbed. "At a time like this—"

"I mean it." Parker edged the new Subaru out onto Farrar

Road, then waited impatiently for old Mrs. Pomeroy to struggle to the curb with her cane. "Somebody's got to face facts. Nobody else seems to be willing to make the tough decisions. The nasty jobs always land on me." Parker wrenched at the steering wheel and the car zoomed past the church, fluttering the skirts of Mrs. Pomeroy.

"Like foreclosing on Jerry Gibby?" said Libby, pinned against the back of the seat, looking sharply at her husband.

"Well, naturally I'm foreclosing on Jerry Gibby. The man should never have had a franchise in the first place. Those financial supervisors, they were far too lax and permissive before I came along. Too easygoing, too pusillaminous."

"Pusillaminous?" Libby giggled. "Oh, I love it, pusillaminous. You don't say pusillaminous, you dumb cluck. It's pusillanimous. You don't even know how to pronounce pusillanimous."

The signal at the railroad crossing on Hartwell Road was flashing and ringing. Parker Upshaw could have killed his wife. He snarled at her ferociously and raced the Subaru across the tracks, as the descending gate wobbled over the car roof, savaging the perfect paint.

On the way home husband and wife engaged in gentle debate. Whose fault was it, really and truly? Husband's? Or wife's?

3 2

We have had a very severe snowstorm. . . .
James Lorin Chapin
Private Journal, Lincoln, 1848

*E*arly in December there was a heavy fall of snow. It was a Sunday morning. Everyone on the north Atlantic seaboard woke to a shadowless gray light, reflected on walls and ceilings from the snow-covered ground and the branches of snow-laden trees.

Snow was still falling on Nashoba and Concord, on Boston and Worcester and Manchester, on Bar Harbor and Burlington and New Haven. It fell on the ugly strip roads of Routes 9 and 1, it fell on gas stations and discount drugstores, on liquor stores and three-deckers, on condominiums and shopping malls. Schoolchildren in Massachusetts and Connecticut and New Hampshire and Vermont and Maine hoped the snow would last until Monday morning. They longed to hear the hoarse *bah-bah* that meant no school, sounding across neighboring rooftops and snowy fields.

In the woods around Jerry Gibby's house every twig was layered in wads and blobs of white, as though the world had been remade by some clumsier person. Between the trees the wind picked up the powdery snow in fountains and tossed it into the gray air. Snowflakes ticked on the brown leaves of the oak trees, they mounded on the rocks in Jerry's front yard, as if the big granite boulders were part of the natural landscape, as if they had been paid for by Adam in the Garden of Eden, as if Jerry didn't owe the landscape contractor a lot of money for lowering them into place with a power shovel.

"Pa, wake up, it's snowing." The three tubby Gibby boys were bouncing on the king-size bed.

"Oh, boys," said Imogene, pulling the sheet over her head.

"Hey, stop it," said Jerry. "Come on, you guys, get down."

They were bouncing in unison now, rosy and laughing. The bed creaked. Something went *crack.*

Jerry rolled out of bed and looked out the window and began worrying about the store. What if the storm brought a power line down somewhere? What if the power went out in the store?

"Isn't it pretty?" said Imogene, putting her hand out the window to catch a few flakes on the sleeve of her nightgown. "Oh, look, boys." Quickly she pulled in her arm to show them the tiny crystal wheels before they vanished.

Homer Kelly, too, admired the small frozen patterns melting

The parsonage

on his coat as he shoveled a path from the porch steps to his car. Looking out past the white pines, he could see snow stretching in a flat sheet across the brittle ice of Fairhaven Bay to the blue haze of the farther shore. Driving the shovel ahead of him, scraping it along the path, Homer muttered to himself as much as he could remember of Thoreau's rhapsody about the sweeping of heaven's floor and the mysteries of the number six.

In church that morning, a small but determined congregation assembled after floundering through snowdrifts on foot or driving along roads just cleared by the town plows. It was Joe Bold's first Sunday back on the job after his wife's death. Getting out of bed each morning in his empty house, Joe found the rooms larger, more hollow, more cavernous. The shade cast by the spruce trees in the front yard had thickened since Claire's death, and multiplied in all the concavities and hallways and alcoves of the house in tissues of darkness, concentrated smudges of gloom. The snow this morning had temporarily brightened his bedroom, and Joe was grateful for that. In church he gathered his small flock around the organ in the balcony and talked impulsively about Emerson's pastor who had preached the dry bones of theological doctrine while the beautiful snow fell outside. Even Parker Upshaw had to admit that the little spontaneous discourse passed muster.

The snow continued to fall, harder than ever, all through the service. During the final hymn, the wind made the windows rattle, and the lights went out. There was a dying drone from the organ. Everybody sang on anyway, thinking regretfully about cold stoves and furnaces at home, and kerosene lanterns and candles, and soup warmed up over cans of Sterno.

Jerry Gibby couldn't bear it. Nodding apologetically to Joe Bold, he nudged Imogene and drew her out into the storm before the closing rituals of the service. Then he dropped his wife at home and drove to Bedford, burdened by a hopeless sense of doom. Why was he still struggling? The ax had fallen. He was to be out of the store on the first day of the new year. And in the store itself things were going from bad to worse. His customers had begun to stay away in droves, as though they sensed Jerry's failure. The place had a curious uninhabited feeling, and Jerry could tell that his remaining customers were uneasy and anxious to get away, as they scuttled up and down the empty aisles.

This morning the store looked dark as pitch. The power was out, all right. Jerry unlocked the door and stared down the blind aisles, then groped his way up to his office to summon help by phone. But the phone didn't work either. Gazing down from his high window at the huge compartmented dimness below him, Jerry wondered angrily if any of his employees would come to his aid without being summoned. The meat manager, damn him— didn't he care what happened to all those expensive cuts of beef he had got in for Christmas? Or the turkeys? The whole Christmas stock was threatened. What if the pipes froze? Well, the hell with the meat manager. There was no time to waste.

Jerry found a flashlight, then ran downstairs and began ripping empty cartons and laying them flat over the open freezers.

"Hey, is anybody here?" It was a shout from the front door. "Is that you, Jerry?" Johnny Fallon, the meat manager, loomed up in his snow-covered parka, mopping his glasses, grinning at Jerry. "Nice weather for penguins," he said.

"Oh, wow, Johnny," said Jerry, clapping him on the arm. "Am I glad to see you."

33

Faithful parishioner, dear friend, servant of
Christ, farewell! Earth is better that thou
hast lived. Heaven shall gain by thy presence!
Funeral sermon
by Reverend Barzillai Frost
Concord, 1856

*O*n Sunday evenings, George Tarkington usually paid a visit to his brother Bob, who was confined to a nursing home in Norwood, way down Route 128. On this stormy Sunday, George insisted on going to see Bob just as usual, snow or no snow.

"Oh, George, I wish you wouldn't," said Hilary. "What if your old car breaks down? Why don't you call Bob and tell him you're not coming? He'll understand."

"Oh, I'll be okay," said George, pulling on his heavy parka. He patted the dog. "Goodbye, Pixie." He embraced his wife. "Goodbye, Hil, honey." Then he climbed into his car and took off into the blizzard.

Hilary watched him vanish in the snow. She could hear the bleat and rattle of his engine for a little while after she lost sight of the car altogether.

George never made it to Norwood. At midnight his wife made an anxious call to the nursing home, and learned that George had not been seen there. Frantic with concern, she telephoned Peter Terry at the police station. Pete had received no message on the teletype about a fatal accident on Route 128. "There's a lot of abandoned cars out there," he told Hilary. "It's

like the blizzard of '78. Remember that? You wait. He'll call you from somebody's house where he's taken shelter. You'll see."

But George did not call. All night long, Hilary kept starting up out of bed, thinking she had heard the phone, but she hadn't. She didn't find out what had happened until next morning.

"It was the end of my run," said the snowplow driver, an employee of the Sudbury public works department, explaining the whole thing to Pete Terry. He was shouting into the phone, and Pete could picture him calling from some snowy telephone booth, his big yellow plow throbbing at the side of the road. "I was just cleaning up the last side street. You know, I left it till last because it didn't go anywhere in particular. It was a dead end deep in the woods. And then I saw this buried car. I would have gone right on by, only I noticed it was sort of like shaking, as though the motor was on. Old cars, sometimes they shake when the engine's running. So I pulled up and got out of the cab and wiped away the snow that was stuck to the car window in front, and there was this shape in there, leaning up against the window as though the guy was fast asleep. I yelled and knocked on the window, but he didn't wake up."

"Exhaust fumes," said Pete Terry sadly. "Leaking up inside the car through all those holes in the floor. I told George that old car would be the death of him. I should have taken away his sticker so he couldn't drive." Pete closed his eyes in chagrin. "I blame myself."

Now he was going to have to pass the bad news on to Mrs. Tarkington. Informing wives that they were widows was not Peter Terry's idea of a good time. He wouldn't call her, he would go right to the door. But first he would stop at the house of the Tarkingtons' minister, Joseph Bold, and persuade him to come along.

Joe was dismayed at the news. He stood on his front porch, galvanized with shock. Then he pulled himself together and got into the chief's car with Pete. Together they drove to the Tarkingtons' house and knocked on the door.

When Hilary saw them standing solemnly on her doorstep, she cried, "Oh, no," and burst into tears.

34

*One day we are in the busy scene of life and the next
we are spoken of only as the things that were.*

James Lorin Chapin
Private Journal, Lincoln, 1848

*T*he continual succession of funerals in Old West Church was spoiling the Christmas spirit, just as people were trying to whip up their lagging enthusiasm for another annual orgy of festive insanity. George Tarkington's funeral was followed almost immediately by Eloise Baxter's. Eloise was found dead of kidney poisoning by a neighbor who noticed that her house was still snowbound long after the snow had stopped. The news of her death sped around the parish house during the Christmas Fair and cast a pall over the bright booths and the counters piled with home-baked food and potted plants and hand-knitted baby blankets. It was not so much shock that people felt anymore as a kind of numbness. It had been obvious to everyone that Eloise had been in peril for some time. Lately her trips to the dialysis machine in Boston had been increased to three every week.

Geneva Jones was beside herself with remorse. Geneva had been Eloise's best friend. She stood behind the table of home-made Christmas decorations and berated herself to Barbara Fenster. "I didn't call her. Oh, why didn't I call her? My nieces and nephews were with me, and I was busy, but I certainly could have called her."

Barbara struggled impatiently with one of Betsy Bucky's crocheted candle ornaments. "Was it the storm? Oh, I wish we had known. Charlie could have driven her to the hospital."

But Mary Kelly shook her head. "No, it wasn't the storm. Ed Bell says she just didn't want to go on. She'd had enough. She gave up before the snow began to fall. Look, Barbara, I think you're supposed to tie them on. What a pest."

"Oh, aren't they darling!" cried Mabel Smock, pouncing on Betsy's handiwork. "I'll take six."

Flo Terry went from the Christmas Fair straight to her husband's office in the Town Hall and told him about Eloise. "You've got to do something," she said to Pete. "It's a plague. It's catching. It's never going to stop."

"What can I do?" said Pete helplessly. "I can't arrest a dead woman for failing to go to the hospital."

"But some of those people were murdered in cold blood. Remember what you told me about Carl Bucky?"

"I only said what Homer Kelly said." Pete looked gloomily at his wife. "He said Carl's wife fed him to death. You want me to arrest Betsy Bucky? You want me to go over there and knock on her door and say, 'Sorry, madam, I'm taking you in on suspicion of being a good cook?'"

"What about Arlene Pott?" said Flo relentlessly. "Arlene was murdered in her bed."

"Well, that's right," agreed Peter solemnly. "And her husband is now serving a life sentence in Walpole State Prison. If this were Florida, they'd execute him with a lethal injection. Would that satisfy you? Why don't you go live in Florida?"

"That's two," said Flo, determined to carry on, holding up a third finger. "And Rosemary Hill, she was a suicide."

"That's true. The poor woman was suffering from cancer of the bowel."

"Four, Phil Shooky. Five, Thad Boland. Six, Agatha Palmer. Seven, Percy Donlevy. Eight, Bill Molyneux. Nine, Claire Bold. Ten, George Tarkington. Eleven, Eloise Baxter. Eleven people in Old West Church since September! What if it never stops? Suppose it goes on and on until there aren't any parishioners left?"

"Well, then they could use the church for a bowling alley," said Peter heartlessly. "Or the Baptists could take over. Why not?"

But Flo's nagging wasn't the only pressure on Peter Terry. One day the editor of the local paper, the Nashoba *Bee,* called him up.

"It's just these obituaries, that's all. So damned many of them. I had a letter the other day, a letter to the editor, only I suppressed it. Some fundamentalist wanted to know why all the humanists were dying off. I think she was hinting it was a judgment of God. But, you know, I can't help but wonder myself if something's wrong. Do you think all those people passed away from natural causes?"

"You're just like my wife," said Peter, leaning lazily back in his chair. "She thinks somebody's trying to wipe out Old West Church systematically. You know, picking them off one by one, until everybody's gone."

"Well, maybe she's right. I have a suspicious nature myself. I just thought I'd ask."

"Well, don't you worry. I'm looking into it," and then Peter hung up the phone and opened his desk drawer and took out his lunch, and ate it thoughtfully.

The undertaker, too, was jogging his elbow. Ralph E. Benbow was a clever and observant man, and a certain similarity among the corpses assigned to his care had not escaped him. Five of them—Agatha Palmer, Bill Molyneux, Phil Shooky, Thad Boland, and Eloise Baxter—had been marked with pinpricks in the same places on their right arms, just above their wrists on the inside.

"Eloise Baxter, too?" said Peter, surprised. "But she died from her own poisons, didn't she? Because she couldn't get to the dialysis machine in that big snowstorm? Or else she was tired of the whole thing, that's the rumor. I was there in her house afterward, and I can tell you there wasn't any hypodermic needle anyplace in that house."

"Well, maybe somebody else administered a fatal dose of something," said Ralph Benbow.

"In the middle of the snowstorm? But there weren't any footprints going and coming, just ours and that neighbor woman's, the one who discovered the body."

"Maybe somebody came in during the first part of the storm, and finished her off and went away again, and then the storm went on and the footprints were covered with fresh snow. She had a Bible, too, isn't that right? Like Agatha Palmer and Phil Shooky?"

Peter was feeling more and more unsettled. There had even been discreet inquiries from a couple of insurance investigators, who had wanted to be reassured that their policyholders had perished of natural causes. The Paul Revere Insurance Company had gone so far as to hold back its first payment to Judy Molyneux because of "unresolved difficulties." Outraged, Judy had stamped into Pete's office demanding a signed statement, and then she had stamped out again, heading for the hospital and a signature from Dr. Spinney. Judy was really mad.

As a police chief, Peter Terry was no ball of fire. But now, after all this prodding, he sought out Homer Kelly in the basement of Flo's library and asked him what he thought about the eleven funerals in the Old West Church.

Homer professed himself ignorant as a newborn babe. *He* didn't know what was going on. A lot of coincidences, as far as he could make out.

"But they keep happening. Do you think they will ever stop? This parade to the graveyard? My wife is giving me a hard time. She thinks I should do something about it. But what can I do? Stand up in church in my uniform and wag my finger and say, 'Naughty, naughty'?"

"Oh, I suspect it's all over," said Homer uncomfortably, and Pete thanked him and apologized for interrupting him in the course of his researches, and went away.

But Homer wasn't altogether sure the continuous procession to the cemetery had come to an end. There was still one member left alive in the Merciful Society of the Blessed Dead—Ed Bell. What if Ed were sick too? Would Ed Bell be found asleep one of these mornings, so profoundly asleep that he couldn't be waked up?

Homer cornered him the next Sunday after church and asked him point-blank. "Listen here, how *are* you?"

"Me?" said Ed, looking at Homer with surprise. "Oh, fine, I'm just fine. How are you?"

"How am I?" Homer was nonplussed. "Well, as a matter of fact, I haven't been feeling too well lately." Homer put a pitiful hand on his shirtfront. "Tendency to, you know, digestive upsets. Belching, that kind of thing."

"Belching?" Ed tapped Homer sympathetically on the necktie and told him about his own prescription for excessive belching, a mixture of baking soda and whiskey. "Sure cure," he said wisely. "And your good wife? She's well, I hope?"

Then Ed turned away, and Homer watched him move among the after-church crowd, while faces lit up at his approach, and hands reached out. None of those good people had the least idea that Ed was a fellow conspirator in the deaths of all those long-time members of the congregation. Suddenly Homer felt his insides clench and tighten, his sphincters squeeze shut, his digestive apparatus convulse in constipated spasm. Everything was rigidifying, coalescing. Peristalsis had abruptly ceased.

Homer groaned. He knew what was happening. It was a physical response on the part of his body to the new strictures he was laying on his mind, in his determination that no one must find out about the existence of the Merciful Society of the Blessed Dead. From now on he must make a mighty effort to keep his suspicions bottled up, to become a monument of impassive stone. Eyes, mouth, all bodily orifices must be sealed. No one must guess Ed's part in the long succession of funerals.

"Oh, Lord," whimpered Homer, clutching his vitals, picturing Ed Bell sitting in the dock while some hardened prosecutor for the Commonwealth of Massachusetts accused him of multiple murder.

Poor Ed, the angel of mercy, the saint of Old West Church!

35

Can we be indolent? Shall we not exert ourselves?
Dr. Ezra Ripley
Concord, 1792

*I*f Homer Kelly was determined neither to see, nor speak, nor hear any evil, Flo Terry was just as determined in the opposite direction. Flo was opening her eyes and ears as wide as she could; she was talking a blue streak. If her husband, the chief of the Nashoba police department, wasn't going to do anything about all the funerals in Old West Church, and if Homer Kelly, the famous detective, wasn't even curious about what was happening, then she, Flo Terry, a reference librarian by trade, was going to put to use her expertise at tracking down stray bits of information. It was something she was good at. Why shouldn't the facts she was looking for be sought in the minds of living people as well as in dusty old books on a shelf?

Self-righteously, Flo set out one Saturday morning to talk to all the bereaved husbands and wives. She would go straight to the heart of the matter by trying to find some common thread in the lives of the deceased.

"Tell me about Bill," she said to Judy Molyneux. "I don't even know what he did for a living."

Judy was glad to talk to Flo about her husband. She opened up right away. "He was a technical writer at Digital, in Maynard," she said. "He graduated from Bates and then he took a special course at Wentworth Tech in word processing. What else can I tell you? Oh, of course, he loved ballroom dancing. Well, we both did. We used to win prizes before he began to get so sick. He played jazz piano. Let's see, what else?"

"He was a member of Old West Church," prompted Flo.

"That's right. He was on the Parish Committee for a while. Lately he'd been going to church meetings at Ed Bell's house on Sunday afternoons."

"What sort of meetings?"

"Oh, I don't know. Social concerns, I think. Picking out charities for the church to give money to." Then Judy's face lighted up. "Stamps! He collected stamps. You want to see his collection?"

At the Shookys' house, Flo drank a cup of Deborah's orange-blossom tea and learned that Phil had earned his veterinarian's degree at Cornell after spending the Second World War wading ashore under fire at various islands in the South Pacific. He had been crazy about animals, from a child. He was especially fond of German shepherds, which he had been breeding for forty years. And of course there were the meetings of the local kennel club. Phil had been vice-president. "Before that he was president for years and years," said Deborah Shooky. "Oh, and the church, of course. He really believed in going to church Sundays."

"Did he do anything in the church?" said Flo. "Wasn't he an usher, lots of times?"

"He was head usher. He was supposed to arrange a regular schedule for the ushers, but often it was easier for the two of us to do it ourselves. And lately there was that Sunday-afternoon group at Ed Bell's. Bible study, I think they were doing. You know. The Epistles of Paul. Things like that."

For information about Arlene Pott, Flo Terry had to call on Arlene's neighbor Ethel Harris. Ethel apologized for knowing so little about Arlene, even though they had been good friends. "She loved her garden," said Ethel. "But everybody knows that. You should have seen her out there working on it every day, all through June and July. There wasn't a weed anywhere. It was neat as a pin. And she grew the most beautiful vegetables. Oh, poor, dear Arlene."

"She was really regular about church attendance, wasn't she?" said Flo. "How about Sunday afternoons? Did she attend something else on Sundays besides church in the morning?"

"Not as far as I know," said Ethel, wrinkling her forehead, trying to remember. "No, of course she didn't, because Fred and I used to drop in on Wally and Arlene Sunday afternoons, and the boys would watch football or baseball on the TV and we girls would sit in the kitchen and talk." Ethel's eyes widened. "Oh, if I'd known we were socializing with a murderer! Poor darling Arlene!"

Hilary Tarkington, like Judy Molyneux, was glad to talk about her dead husband. She went on and on, grateful to spill it all out. Talking about George was like dedicating a small memorial to him, it was prolonging his memory a little farther in time, it was doing him honor of a kind. So it just gushed out of Hilary.

Flo listened and scribbled it all down in her notebook— engineering degree University of Michigan, forty-two years employment with Ma Bell, Mason Third Degree, organizer Nashoba Little League, drinking problem, Alcoholics Anonymous, heavy smoker until five years ago, church work, school committee, Mr. Fixit, carpentry, car repair, his brother in the nursing home, Sunday-afternoon committee meetings on purposes and goals for the church at Ed Bell's house every week.

Flo's pencil stopped. She looked up. "Purposes and goals? Are you sure that's what they talked about?"

"Well, no, but it was something like that," said Hilary Tarkington.

Maureen Donlevy had been so shocked by her husband's violent death on Route 2 that she was still in a traumatized condition. But by probing very tactfully, Flo was able to garner a few facts about Percy. She learned that he had been an investment counselor by day and an enthusiastic member of the Nashoba

Players by night, specializing in grandfathers, patriarchs, and old geezers. "He just loved to clap on an old hat and snap his suspenders and talk like an old cowpoke in some Western saloon," said Maureen tearfully. "He was always trying to get a drama group going in the church, but nobody was interested."

"They just didn't have his talent," said Flo sympathetically. "What else did he do in the church? Didn't he sing in the choir?"

"Oh, that's right." Then Maureen remembered something else. "And there was the Sunday-afternoon retreat. He always went to Ed Bell's house every Sunday afternoon."

"A retreat? He called it a retreat?"

"That's right. You know, they got together and had sort of spiritual discussions."

"Oh, I see," said Flo, writing it all down.

Agatha Palmer's spouse was less forthcoming. Bob Palmer's principal regret about his wife was obviously that she had lost her figure early in their married life and given birth rather carelessly to seven children. Flo suspected he was casting his eye around for a new girlfriend. Relentlessly she made him rummage in his memory for recollections of poor departed Agatha.

"Church work?" said Bob, in answer to her question. "Oh, gee, I dunno."

"Wasn't she director of the Sunday school at one time? What about more recently? Did she ever go to meetings at Ed Bell's house on Sunday afternoons?"

"Oh, sure, Sunday afternoons, you're right, that's right. She used to drive over to the Bells' house Sunday afternoons. I don't know what the hell for."

Bob Palmer was a dreadful man, decided Flo, leaving his house in disgust. But Betsy Bucky was even worse. Betsy was gleeful rather than mournful on the subject of her life-partner's recent demise. "What did he do with himself?" she said scornfully, repeating Flo's question. "Nothing, that's what he did with himself. He just sat around wasting his time, that's all he ever did."

"But he went to church, didn't he?" protested Flo, wanting to stick up for Carl. "What about Sunday afternoons? Did he go to any sort of meetings?"

"Sunday afternoons? Carl Bucky? You bet your boots he didn't. Sunday afternoon was floor-washing time. He had to move all the furniture and scrub all the floors in the house, every single Sunday. You don't think he was going to get out of this house on a Sunday afternoon? No, ma'am, not my Carl!"

Driving away from Betsy Bucky's house, Flo calculated the totals in her head. The Sunday-afternoon meetings at Ed Bell's house had grown in importance as the day went on, only to let her down in the end. Perhaps they weren't the common thread after all. Bill Molyneux had attended the meetings, and so had Phil Shooky and George Tarkington and Agatha Palmer and Percy Donlevy. But Carl Bucky and Arlene Pott had not. Of course Arlene Pott didn't count. What about the others? There was no way of knowing about Eloise Baxter and Rosemary Hill and Thad Boland, because they didn't have mates to pass on the news.

Yet it was terribly *interesting*, Flo decided, that the people who did attend the Sunday-afternoon meetings explained the purpose of the meetings in such different ways. They had been an occasion for spiritual retreat, Percy Donlevy had told his wife. A time to discuss the goals of the church, George Tarkington had explained to Hilary. Bible study, the Epistles of Paul, said Phil Shooky. An examination of church charities, said Bill Molyneux.

Clearly they had lied to their wives. They were getting together for some other purpose. What could it have been?

It was the kind of question Homer Kelly was most afraid of. But at the moment Homer was engaged in another kind of investigation. "What do you suggest, woman?" he asked his wife, his face distorted in anguish. "What should I do? I mean, modern science must have come up with some sort of remedy, after all these centuries of human physiological malfunction. You must know of some kind of internal explosive material? Something to loosen up the system?"

"Bran flakes," suggested Mary Kelly. "Water. Lots of water."

"Oh, ugh," said Homer, wincing and holding his stomach.

"Prunes!" said Mary, brightening. "Nature's remedy for constipation. Stewed prunes!"

"Stewed prunes, good God," said Homer, closing his eyes in tragic self-pity.

36

You, my dear brother, will mourn, for you must; we censure not your grief.

Reverend Charles Stearns
Lincoln, 1812

*T*he next day was misty. Evaporating snow stood in the air in milky clouds. But the thermometer was sinking. Hiking down Farrar Road past Quarry Pond, Joe Bold saw crystals of ice fingering out in all directions from the floating skim that lay on the surface of the water like a plate. On the way home he chastised himself for his increasing sense of guilt. It was absurd, and he knew it, but somehow he had begun to feel obscurely responsible for the mortal shrinkage of his parish. Perhaps if he had not brought his trouble into the congregation in the first place, all those people might still be alive. It was as though he had opened his hand and cast down from the pulpit the seeds of disease and death.

When he got back home, he found Ed Bell on his doorstep. Gratefully, Joe invited him in. It was curious how Ed seemed to know when cheerful companionship was useful and when it was not.

But the truth was, even Ed Bell was sometimes driven to his limit. Only Ed's wife, Lorraine, knew the effort behind his continual good humor. Looking at her husband's haggard face as he sank into a kitchen chair after walking back from Joe's house, Lorraine asked a sympathetic question, "How long do you think it will be before he recovers?"

Ed shook his head. "I don't know. Maybe never."

"Oh, Ed, we've got to give him time. It's only been three weeks since Claire died. Wait till Christmas is over. You know how shattering the Christmas season can be. Surely he'll be better in the new year."

"It's not just that he's mourning," said Ed. "He's not just grieving for Claire. He wonders how he can have the gall to get up in the pulpit on Sunday mornings, he feels so futile and feeble. He tried to give me back his salary check just now. When I wouldn't take it, he tore it up. Now Felicia has to send him another one. He's going through a fragile time. On the one hand, he's teetering on the brink of resigning, and on the other, Parker Upshaw is whipping up feeling against him. Parker was going around town yesterday afternoon, did you know that? Collecting signatures."

Then Lorraine began mumbling about redemption. She had been brought up to believe in it. "Christ died for our sins, that's what people thought. They were saved by his blood, and they could be born again into a new life." Lorraine gazed thoughtfully out the window at the clearing sky. "Why couldn't it happen to Joe?"

Ed got up and put his coat back on and said something that surprised his wife by its cynicism. "Well, at least redemption would be free of charge. You wouldn't have to pay a psychiatrist a hundred dollars an hour to tell you something equally bizarre."

Lorraine was dismayed to see her exhausted husband heading for the door. "Good heavens, Ed, dear, where are you going now?"

"County Hospital. I just came home to get the car. I'm going to pick Joe up and take him over to see Howie Sawyer. I promised Joan we'd be there today."

"Howie Sawyer?" Lorraine shook her head in disapproval. "Don't you think the County Hospital will plunge poor Joe still further into despair?"

"Oh, no," said Ed airily. "I don't think so."

Lorraine watched her husband trudge down the back steps to his car. She was feeling conscience-stricken because she hadn't told him about the phone call. Lorraine was terribly frightened about the phone call. Peter Terry, the chief of the Nashoba police department, had phoned while Ed was out, asking for him.

"I'll tell him you called," Lorraine had said. "May I ask what it's about?"

"Oh, nothing special." Pete had sounded embarrassed. "It's just that my wife gets all upset. You know Flo. She gets these bees in her bonnet."

"Well, I'll certainly have him call you," said Lorraine again, gripped with terror. Flo Terry was a woman of keen mind and unyielding perseverance. The chief of the Nashoba police department might be no threat at all, but his wife was a different kettle of fish altogether.

"Oh, there you are, Mr. Bell," said the head nurse on Howie Sawyer's ward, grinning at him, hurrying up to shake hands with the Reverend Bold. Mary Kelly was there too, and so was Joan Sawyer. Joan smiled at them and said hello, and all the patients lifted their drooping heads. Mrs. Beddoes clapped her hands gaily. Miss Stein opened her eyes. Mr. O'Doyle fired his ball at Joe, hitting him in the solar plexus. Joe gasped, clutching the ball to his stomach, then timidly threw it back. Mr. Keizer and Mr. Canopus and Howie Sawyer crowded around Ed, grabbing at his sleeves, his coattails, his pantlegs. Joe Bold stood aside and watched as Ed swept them all into the corner beside the battered piano.

The piano was new. It had been discovered by Ed in the basement and hauled up to Howie's floor, where its little wheels had gouged channels in the asphalt tile. Joan was the pianist. Under her clumsy fingers the piano tinkled and thumped, crazily out of tune. Some of the notes didn't play, but nobody cared. Nor did it matter that everyone sang on a different pitch, or that the words were mixed up, or that Miss Stein was singing the wrong song. Howie Sawyer made up for everybody else. He had the tune right, and all the words. He sang at the top of his lungs.

Joe opened his mouth to sing too, but nothing came out. He tried again and got a croaking tenor, "Dashing through the snow."

Afterward Joan and the head nurse and the social worker thanked them for coming, and Joan said something impulsive. "A Christmas pageant, we could have a pageant. Mrs. Beddoes could be Mary. Miss Stein could be a shepherd. Howie could be Joseph. Mr. Keizer and Mr. O'Doyle and Mr. Canopus could be the three kings."

"Mr. Keizer is Jewish," said the nurse, "but who cares? We'll celebrate Hanukkah too."

"I'll bring my menorah," said the social worker.

"I'll find some costumes," said Mary Kelly.

"I'll get Augusta Gill to help out," said Ed eagerly, "if she can spare the time."

Of course Augusta couldn't spare the time. *Christmas? Did Ed know what her schedule was like at Christmas?* But she came anyway and helped out. Augusta was a specialist in baroque music, she had conducted festivals of sacred song and written a thesis on Scarlatti, but now she was perfectly willing to play "Rudolf, the Red-Nosed Reindeer" on the beaten-up piano in Howie Sawyer's ward. Tirelessly, Howie's ex-wife, Joan, rehearsed the actors over and over. Mary Kelly collected costumes, lengths of blue flannel for Mrs. Beddoes, striped curtains for the kings, a doll for the baby Jesus. Ed manufactured a manger in his basement workshop, although it wasn't an easy task because most of his tools were scattered around Bo Harris's car in the garage.

The performance was a success. All the relatives came, and a bunch of people from Old West Church. At the piano Augusta provided musical continuity, running along from one tune to the next, while Miss Stein held her toy lamb and pointed excitedly at the cardboard star and knelt beside the doll in the manger. As one of the three kings, Mr. O'Doyle tossed his ball and caught it, and tossed it again and caught it. Mr. Keizer lit the menorah with extreme care. Mrs. Beddoes was a lovely Mary, rocking the doll in her arms. In the middle of the performance there was a crisis when the Virgin suddenly stood up in a panic and dropped the doll on its head and flapped her hands.

"It's all right, Mrs. Beddoes," cried the social worker, rushing her out of the room, and in a minute Mrs. Beddoes was back, kneeling in the straw, holding the doll, looking tender and holy.

The real star of the show was Howie Sawyer. Howie was amazing. He leaned over Mrs. Beddoes with husbandly pride and gazed at the baby and clasped his hands in rapture and condescended grandly to the three kings in the person of Mr. O'Doyle and, to the astonishment of all, burst out at the end in an appropriate song, "Away in a Manger." He was lost in his role, he carried the conviction of a professional performer.

The pageant was over. The visitors clapped and clapped. The relatives were pleased. Joan passed a plate of cakes. There was a distribution of presents.

"They'll feel let down tomorrow," said the head nurse. "I hope you won't forget us."

"I'll come back tomorrow," promised Ed.

"So will I," said Mary.

"Well, I will too," said Joe Bold, to his own surprise, not sure whether he had been cornered or whether, perhaps, he had actually volunteered.

"Listen, we could have another pageant," said Augusta enthusiastically, wondering if she had gone clean out of her mind. "You know, Santa Claus at the North Pole, with cotton batting and paper snowflakes. Howie could be Santa. I mean, I haven't got time for this, but it's okay. The other stuff can wait."

"Ho, ho, ho," shouted Howie, falling in with the idea right away.

37

Oh that I had a complete control over my feelings!
Then would my face always be clothed in smiles.
James Lorin Chapin
Private Journal, Lincoln, 1849

*T*he shrill sound of the doorbell frightened Police Chief Peter Terry on the porch of the Bells' house as much as it did Ed and Lorraine Bell upstairs in bed. It was the Sunday after New Year's Day, very early in the morning. "You've got to get over there before church," Flo Terry had said to her husband. "Otherwise they'll be out all day, doing one thing or another."

So here he was, in person, being ushered into the living room by Ed, who was tying the string of his bathrobe and waving him into a chair beside the Christmas tree.

Pete looked sheepishly at the tree, which was glowing with funny lights that bubbled up from the bottom to the top. "It's just that Flo thinks there was something queer about the way a bunch of those people from Old West Church who died this fall always came to a meeting at your house on Sunday afternoons."

"Coffee?" said Lorraine, suddenly appearing in front of Pete in a rumpled nightgown and bed jacket, her hair on end.

"Coffee?" Pete looked up in surprise. "Oh, no, thank you. Well, maybe. Well, yes, I guess so. But not if it's any trouble."

"Coffee, Ed?" said Lorraine, looking at her husband fiercely, her eyes brilliant with unspoken messages.

"Why, yes, dear," said Ed mildly.

"So, ha-ha, she thought maybe the meeting had something to do with the fact that they all died." Pete flapped his hand to dismiss the ridiculous notion. "Maybe she thinks Lorraine was, ha-ha, feeding them poisoned cookies or something."

"You hear that, dear?" said Ed, calling to his wife, who was grimly slamming pots around in the kitchen.

"Anyway, Flo just wanted me to ask you what the meetings were for. She says Judy Molyneux said they were charitable, and Maureen Donlevy thought they were some kind of retreat, and somebody else thought you were all getting together to study the Bible. I mean, everybody thought they were for something different."

"They were right," said Ed. "All of them were right. It was all of those things at once, you see."

"Oh, no kidding!" Pete slapped his knee. "Oh, I get it. That explains it. Well, so that's it. Well, well. Okay, I see. Oh, sure. Well, never mind. Say, never mind about the coffee. Hey, Lorraine! Never mind about the coffee! I won't stay for coffee. I'll just be on my way. Hey, I'm sorry to have bothered you, ha-ha, so early Sunday morning. Hey, you people, Happy New Year!"

Peter Terry was a willow reed, thought Lorraine, looking out of the kitchen as the front door slammed. He would bend with every wind. But his wife was still a menacing threat. Flo Terry was a rod of iron.

The Gibbys had sold their house. They were walking around it for the last time, their footsteps noisy in the empty rooms. The kids were already in Cambridge at Imogene's mother's house in Porter Square. Imogene was trying not to cry. She stroked the trash compacter and ran her fingers down the frame of the bay window in the family room.

"Oh, Imogene," said Jerry, "I'm sorry."

"It's all right," said Imogene. "Someday we'll have a place like this again. You'll see."

"Are you sure you want to go to church?"

"Oh, yes." Imogene dabbed at her eyes at the kitchen sink. "I'm okay now."

Parker Upshaw was in church that morning, just as usual. Parker never missed a Sunday, because he was keeping tabs on Joe Bold. Sitting with folded arms, he took mental notes, listening for hesitations and falterings, grading the sermons on a scale of one to ten, recording the evidence in a folder on his desk at home. He was preparing for another approach to the Parish Committee, making a case for the dismissal of the Reverend Joseph Bold. His wife, Libby, looked at him sideways when he whipped out his pencil during the final hymn to make a note on his order of service. "It's like the Spanish Inquisition," she whispered. "You'd think the man was a heretic."

"I suspect the Inquisition had a bad press," murmured Parker smugly, pleased with himself, reflecting that the Spanish inquisitors had probably been a bunch of good hard-nosed guys who made tough decisions in a time of crisis. They had probably saved the church in the long run. If it hadn't been for them, the whole Catholic Church might not have survived. The Pope would be digging potatoes in Poland. The Vatican would be a collection of high-priced condominiums.

Parker bowed his head for the final blessing, then walked to the door with Libby, suffused with self-righteousness, vowing to run uphill to the car to improve the shining hour. But outside he came face-to-face with Jerry Gibby. In Upshaw's state of exaltation, Jerry was little more than a blip on the screen of his own self-satisfaction. Looking right through him, Parker shouldered past Jerry and descended the steps, buttoning his coat.

But Jerry Gibby was not a stream of electrons in a cathode-ray tube. He was an overweight mass of suffering flesh, racked with rage and frustration, encased in a too small suit. Superimposed on Upshaw's arrogant face Jerry could see Imogene's plump hand stroking the frame of the window. Maddened by vexation and resentment, he struck at his tormentor, hitting him clumsily in the right shoulder. Then, screwing up his face and shutting his eyes, he pushed Upshaw down the steps and punched the top button of his coat.

Imogene screamed. Ed Bell and Homer Kelly pulled Jerry away from Upshaw, who was bending over, holding his middle, his face contorted. "Don't think I won't do something about this, Gibby," he gasped angrily. "Unprovoked assault and battery. You'll hear from me."

And, of course, Jerry did. Next day the doorbell rang loudly in Imogene's mother's house in Porter Square. The man at the door was wearing a blue uniform. He was an old friend of Jerry's from high school. A sob rose in Jerry's throat when he saw the big envelope in his friend's hand.

"Sorry, Jerry," said the officer, handing him the summons.

"Gee, thanks," said Jerry bitterly.

38

Oh lovely woman! Truly thou art a helper!
James Lorin Chapin
Private Journal, Lincoln, 1849

Flo Terry was, naturally, entirely dissatisfied with her husband's Sunday-morning attempt to solicit information from Ed Bell, and she told him so in no uncertain terms.

"Look, Flo," said Pete helplessly, "I admit I'm no detective. Why don't you talk to Homer Kelly? He used to do that kind of thing for a living."

"I've already tried Homer," said Flo. "But, all right, I'll try again."

So the next time Homer ventured into the Nashoba public library, Flo was waiting for him at her desk in a shadowy nook overhung with carved mottoes of an inspirational nature. Rearing up from the desk, Flo stalked over to confront him as he sat down and opened his notebook. "Move over, Homer," she commanded, and then she sat beside him and grilled him on the subject of the Sunday-afternoon meetings at Ed Bell's house.

But Homer seemed distracted and inattentive, as if he were in some kind of pain. "Meetings?" he said. His face twitched. He was holding himself around the middle. "At Ed Bell's? Sunday afternoons?"

"They were all there together, you see," said Flo. "Five of them anyway. Phil, George, Bill, Agatha, and Percy. And they all died within a few weeks of each other. Isn't that strange?"

"Well, I don't know," whined Homer. "They all went to church together too. I'll bet they all had toast for breakfast. Maybe they all had the same favorite hymn." Lifting his anguished face, Homer raised his voice in musical pleading, "Open now thy gates of beauty!" Then, suddenly excusing himself, he shot out of his chair and disappeared in the direction of the men's room.

Baffled, Flo made up her mind once again to pursue the matter on her own. She would go to the Bells herself. Poor old Pete, he had been overawed by the shining reputation of Ed Bell as a sort of *chevalier sans peur et sans reproche.* Well, Ed's wife was no saint. Lorraine Bell was an ordinary human woman. Flo homed in on Lorraine as if she were a book in the library or a standard resource like the microfilmed *New York Times,* or the

Harmony of the Gospels, or *Bartlett's Quotations,* or the *Dictionary of National Biography.*

"Lorraine," said Flo, waylaying her at Gibby's General Grocery among the boxes of dry cereal, putting her finger on the bosom of Lorraine's parka as if to mark her place on the page, "what was that Sunday-afternoon meeting all about, that group that used to meet at your house last fall? Who was in it?"

But Lorraine was a book without an index, an encyclopedia with a missing volume. "I don't know anything about Ed's meetings," she said firmly, looking past Flo at the Rice Chex and Sugar Smacks. "I had things of my own to do every Sunday afternoon."

"What things?" said Flo suspiciously, flipping Lorraine's pages, looking for the right paragraph.

"Volunteering at the hospital, for one thing," said Lorraine, giving her basket a strong shove so that it sailed down the aisle in the direction of the housewares department and knocked over a wastebasket full of mops and brooms.

So of course Flo pursued this clue to its primary source, the director of volunteers at Emerson Hospital, and the director corroborated Lorraine's story. Oh, yes, Lorraine Bell was one of their steadies. She had worked in the hospital lunchroom most Sunday afternoons last September, October, and November.

So that was a dead end. But Flo refused to give up. She had a small breakthrough when she remembered that Rosemary Hill's good friend Marigold Lynch was back in town, having spent the first two weeks of January in the Virgin Islands. Marigold didn't know what Rosemary did on Sunday afternoons, but she knew she did something. "We used to play golf every Sunday afternoon, and then she couldn't make it anymore, so we stopped. I assumed it was because of her illness. We got together Sunday nights instead, to have supper and watch television."

Flo was pleased. It was a small success, but it encouraged her to try to run down the friends and acquaintances of Thad Boland and Eloise Baxter. She had no luck finding anyone who knew what Thad had done on Sundays, because Thad had been pretty much of a loner, and even his daughter didn't know whether he was at home or not on Sunday afternoons. But Geneva Jones knew a lot about Eloise Baxter. "We used to get together on Sunday afternoons, but after a while she stopped being available, and I thought maybe she was mad at me. But whenever I asked her to go to the movies in the evening, she always said yes, so I felt better about our friendship. I mean, she was my oldest friend!"

"So that's seven out of the eleven," declared Flo to her husband, Pete, pounding on his desk during her lunch hour. "What do you make of that? They all met at Ed's house every Sunday afternoon and they all died mysteriously from things they weren't sick with, even though they were all terminally ill. It was a conspiracy, some kind of conspiracy. It was some kind of death pact. The whole parish may be in danger. Who will be next? You've got to look into it."

If Flo had been anyone but his wife, Pete might have taken her warnings seriously. But a prophet is sometimes without honor in her own country, and Pete had been withstanding Flo's energetic pestering so long, it was second nature to resist. "Do you want me to accuse Ed Bell of murder? Is that it? Do you want to see him behind bars? Just because he comforted a lot of dying people on Sunday afternoons?"

"*Comforted* them? How do you know he wasn't killing them? They had help, Arthur Spinney said. Somebody stuck a needle in them and then took the needle away. That's what he told you."

"No, he didn't. He didn't say that. He said they had needle marks on their arms, that's all. But desperately ill people are always having blood samples taken. The needle marks don't mean a thing."

"That's not the way I see it," said Flo darkly. "Well, never mind." Stalking grandly out of Pete's office, she turned dramatically at the door for a final statement. "I will pursue this investigation all by myself."

Pete stood up and made an ironical bow. "Go right ahead. Be my guest."

39

*A very fine, and excessively warm day, so that
I have taken off all my flannels.*
James Lorin Chapin
Private Journal, Lincoln, 1849

*W*inter in New England is not a
level plain of cold. First there is the freezing ascent of November
and early December, followed by a dangerous assault on the
tinseled plateau of the Christmas season. Then all cautious trav-
elers must negotiate the treacherous ice of the last week on the
calendar, only to stub their toes on the new year and plummet
into the glacial crevasse of January. The months of February and
March are a slow struggle upward with rope and pickax, until at
last everyone surfaces on the spring hillside of April and runs
gladly down into May.

Flo Terry spent the entire month of February and the first
two weeks of March exasperating Arthur Spinney, ruffling the
fragile composure of the bereaved friends, husbands, and wives
of the deceased, and exacerbating the tortured physical condition
of Homer Kelly, whose thirty feet of constipated bowel were
linked in some mysterious and abominable way with his clenched
jaw.

On the next to last Saturday in March, the sun struck warmly
through the trees as if summer had come at last like a perpetual
balmy bower of flowers, as if the rest of the spring would not be
a mixed bag of sun, sleet, hail, rain, drizzle, and snow. All over

Middlesex County pale-faced people who had been housebound all winter burst out-of-doors to ramble on the yellow grass or stroll along the sidewalk, their spirits rising with the temperature, their bare arms white as celery stalks. On the surface of Walden Pond, the last floating pieces of ice grew smaller and smaller, until nothing was left but sparkling ripples on the water. The little brooks that rose in Nashoba's swamps and rocky hilltops ran downstream to Bateman's Pond and Quarry Pond and Icehouse Pond in rushing torrents.

Flo Terry, too, experienced a fresh eruption of energy, a spurt of renewed zeal. She rushed out of her house, plumped herself into her car, and took off for Ed Bell's house. She would confront him directly, decided Flo; she would ask him the questions that were teeming in her breast. Saint or no saint, he would have to look her in the eye. She couldn't understand why she hadn't had the courage to face up to him before.

But when she drove up beside the Bells' house and looked at the purple crocuses under the laundry line and walked up the cement path and mounted the porch steps and knocked at the door, there was no answer. From behind the house she could hear tunking, clanging noises. Flo went around to the garage and found young Eleanor and the Harris boy working on a car.

Eleanor seemed vague and faraway. When Flo asked her when her parents would be back, she didn't seem to know.

"Is it okay if I wait inside?" said Flo impetuously, suddenly seizing a golden opportunity.

"Oh, sure," said Eleanor. "Just go right in."

Thus Flo Terry found herself alone in Ed Bell's house, the very house in which the conspiracy to bring to an end the lives of seven people had been hatched. For a while she sat by herself in the living room, looking around inquisitively. Then, after peering out the window to be sure Ed and Lorraine were not driving up, she nipped upstairs and explored the two bathrooms. Then she examined the bedrooms. Then she looked out the window again and ran down two flights to the basement.

The basement was large and cavernous. In the middle loomed the huge old-fashioned coal furnace, with large dusty pipes growing out of it like the branches of a tree. Beside it stood the small oil furnace that had taken over the job of heating the house. Beyond the two furnaces was a workbench. Flo looked everywhere among Ed's tools. She looked in the drawer where the hammers were stored. She pulled open the drawers labeled SCREWDRIVERS, PLIERS, C-CLAMPS. She examined the coffee cans in which Ed stored miscellaneous nuts and bolts.

She found nothing. Frustrated, she stood in the middle of the basement and looked around for the last time, ready to give up and go upstairs. Then, struck by a thought, she approached the coal furnace and opened the heavy cast-iron door into which coal had once been shoveled to keep the fire burning, tons and tons of it in the old days. Ed had probably shoveled a lot of it himself.

The interior was dark and cold, but something showed white within. Bending over, Flo saw a white plastic jar and a package wrapped in polyethylene. Excited, she reached in and extracted them. The package contained plastic syringes. The jar held some kind of liquid. It slopped invisibly inside the bottle when she shook it. Her heart began to beat quickly. She had found what she was looking for.

At Fairhaven Bay, Homer Kelly walked slowly along the shore, trying to keep his mind off his physical dilemma. In Pleasant Meadow he stood on the bank of the little stream and watched enviously as the water tumbled over the amber stones on its way into the river. Everything was flowing, running, splashing, squirting, gushing, surging, loosened at last from winter's icy grip. Only Homer himself was still blocked and cramped, grappled by sluggish intestinal stagnation.

He looked up as Mary hallooed at him. She was accompanied by Flo Terry. Flo was scrambling from one grassy hummock to another, waving something over her head. As she drew closer, Homer's heart sank. She was brandishing a bottle of some kind and—what were those other things? Not syringes? Please God, not hypodermic syringes!

"He had them in the furnace," cried Flo. "I told you, I told you! I found them in the furnace. Ed Bell, he's got this old furnace in the cellar."

"Oh, God," cried Homer. He clutched at his wife. All his juices had suddenly begun flowing at once, like the water in the brook. Mighty volcanic forces were suddenly releasing inside him the pent-up surge of his frozen intestinal tract. The dam had burst. "Oh, Lord in heaven," cried Homer, leaping across the brook and galloping for home. "Oh, Christ. Oh, Jesus. Oh, Jesus X Christ."

40

. . . by sin, we are fallen from God and our happiness; have incurred his holy displeasure, and deserve his wrath.

Reverend Daniel Bliss
Concord, 1755

*P*eter Terry had to admit himself defeated. He had never felt more wretched in his life.

"All right," he said, "all right. We'll have the stuff analyzed. Can you wait until then to destroy the finest guy in town? My God, Flo, I don't understand you. I just don't see what's got into you."

Flo threw up her hands, calling upon heaven to witness this folly on the part of her husband. "Even now? Even now you don't understand? You who are responsible for the health and safety of all the citizens of Nashoba, Massachusetts? You don't understand why we have to stop someone who is killing his fellow men and women? Who is ready to do it again? Why didn't he throw those things away? He's keeping them handy, that's why. He's ready to use those needles again."

"But the man is a saint," grumbled Pete. "You want to make him a martyr? That's what he'll be, a martyred saint."

"A saint?" cried Flo. "A saint? Some crazy kind of saint, to be taking God's power into his own hands. You call that being a saint?"

Then Pete accused the wife of his bosom of being no better

than Pontius Pilate, or those people who had burned Joan of Arc at the stake. Flo's feelings were terribly hurt.

Next day the promise of Saturday's basking warmth was repeated in the mild dawn of Sunday morning. Homer and Mary Kelly paid an early pre-church visit to Ed Bell. Homer sat down with Ed in his living room and told him gloomily what Flo Terry had discovered in his basement.

Ed seemed more amused than anything. "Oh, she found them, did she?"

"I'm afraid so."

"Clever girl. I must say, I thought her husband let me off far too easily."

"But, Ed, do you know what this means?"

"Oh, I can imagine." Ed smiled at Homer genially. "And maybe in the long run it will make a point. At least maybe some people will begin to think about it."

Homer looked at him solemnly. "Isn't the loss of your freedom a high price to pay for making a point?"

"I don't know, Homer." Ed looked at Homer candidly. "I'll find out, won't I?"

Out-of-doors Mary Kelly and Lorraine Bell stood in the bald sunlight of mid-March, watching Bo Harris work on his car. The Chevy had been rolled out of the garage, where it had spent the winter while Ed's car sat outside in the snow and cold. Bo had been unable to work on it through December, January, and February, but now he was coming down the homestretch. His repairs were almost done.

Lorraine stared at Bo's feet, which, as usual, were sticking out from under the Chevy, twitching and jerking as he struggled with something under the chassis. Then she looked suspiciously at Mary. "What are you people here for? What does Homer want with Ed?"

Mary hesitated, unable to tell a comforting lie. Looking up at the back porch, she said, "May we sit in the kitchen? I'll tell you what he told me."

As they walked up the steps, Paul Dobbs came out on the

porch. He was running a comb through his hair. He said good morning cheerfully to Mary and Lorraine, then bounded briskly down the steps and stooped to look under the car at Bo. "Hey," said Paul, "when you going to finish this pile of junk?"

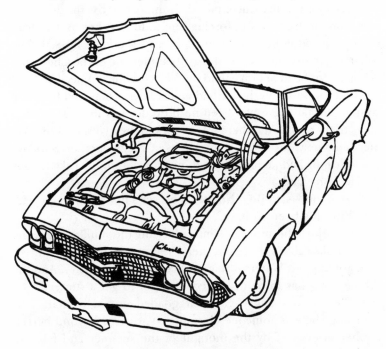

"Pretty soon," said Bo, crawling out from under. "I'm just bleeding the hydraulic system."

"Gimme a break," said Paul. "You been bleeding the whole goddamn car for a year. That heap's never going to get on the road. Who you kidding?"

"Next weekend," promised Bo, springing to his feet. "Just a couple more little bitty details, that's all."

Eleanor came out on the porch and leaned on the railing, dressed for church in an outfit of pink bandannas. She had run it up quickly on the sewing machine yesterday after finishing at the copy center. Then last night she had braided her hair in dozens of pigtails, and this morning she had undone all the pigtails, and brushed them out so that now her hair was a bright tangled thicket, pouring over her bare arms. Her lips looked wet because of the varnish in her lipstick.

Paul whistled, appreciating the result of all her hard work. Bo Harris didn't even look up.

Eleanor was in a queer mood. Stumping across the driveway, she stood in front of Bo, forcing him to look at her. But instead of a pink-and-gold vision staring him in the face, Bo saw only what was in his mind's eye, the gritty underside of the Chevy and a hoped-for bead of brake fluid on the hydraulic nipple. The bead of fluid would mean the air had at last been exhausted from the system. So far there had been no little drop of fluid. He would have to try again. And there was a crack in the hydraulic hose. He needed a new hose. Was the Icehouse Garage open on Sunday?

Eleanor had knocked herself out for nothing. "Take me for a ride," she said.

"Oh, no," said Bo. "Not yet. This car's not ready to go yet."

"But it's been so long."

"It's just the brakes. That's all. And the muffler. And the hand-brake cable's shot. And then I've got to get the car insured. I've got to go to Watertown, get a license at the registry. And the whole thing has to be inspected. I've got to get a sticker."

Eleanor was angry. She felt goaded out of herself. This morning she was someone else entirely, carried beyond herself by her grievance, by the thought of the summer and fall and winter she had spent making herself beautiful for Bo. All those cold Sunday afternoons in the freezing garage trying to help, all those Saturdays in the copy center earning money for makeup and clothes to dazzle Bo Harris, who cared for nothing but his stupid car, who never saw her at all, who treated her like a stick or a stone! To Bo, she was only a pair of hands to shine a flashlight on something, or extra arms for carrying the other end of the transmission, or an extra foot to hold down the accelerator while he checked a connection under the hood. He never saw the person to whom the hands and arms and feet belonged. He never saw the girl whose name was Eleanor Bell. He never saw what Eleanor saw in the mirror every day, a pretty girl, a pretty, *pretty* girl—everybody said so! She was really, really pretty! And Bo didn't see it. He didn't see her at all.

"Listen," said Eleanor, her voice tight in her throat. "You could drive around the school parking lot. Why not? Nobody would see you on the road. It's only a mile away. Why not? Why not? Take me for a ride."

But Bo was back under the car, taking a last loving look at the brake shoe on the left side. Hauling himself out again, he stood and picked up his bicycle. "I've got to find a hose. I'll be back sooner or later." Putting one foot on the pedal, he coasted gracefully down the driveway standing up, then put the other leg over and floated onto Acton Road, poised on the light frame of his bike. Once again Eleanor stared at his disappearing back, her face burning. She wanted to scream.

"Big jerk," said Paul, looking sympathetically at Eleanor. "Listen, you want a ride? I'll give you a ride."

Eleanor looked at Paul. "But he said—he said something isn't finished yet."

"Oh, sure, *he said*. He doesn't want to give you a ride. First time out in that car, he'll take some other girl. What do you want to bet? After you been helping him all this time, he's not going to give you no ride."

Eleanor stared at the fresh tufts of grass springing up in the driveway. *It wasn't fair. It wasn't fair.*

She looked up to see the big Ford pickup that belonged to Mr. and Mrs. Kelly turning out of the driveway onto Acton Road. Her father was running down the porch steps, calling to her, "Ready for church, Ellie? Where's your mother?"

Eleanor walked stiffly around the house to the front door, and found her mother scrabbling in her pocketbook in the hall. She looked anxious and absentminded, as if her mind were on something else entirely. "Here, dear," she said. "Here's something for the collection plate."

"Listen, Mom, I'm not going to church today. I feel sort of awful. I mean, I think I'll stay home."

"Why, Eleanor." Lorraine Bell suddenly focused her attention entirely on her daughter. She reached out a hand to feel her forehead. "Well, I don't know."

"Hey, you girls, are you coming?" shouted Ed. The car door slammed.

"Well, all right, dear," said Lorraine. "Just as you wish. You want to lie down on the sofa?"

"Maybe I will," said Eleanor. "I guess so. Maybe I'll just go lie down."

41

Truly it is a solemn thing to die.
James Lorin Chapin
Private Journal, Lincoln, 1848

*O*n this first day of spring they were all in church—the Kellys, the Bells, the Harrises, the Upshaws, the Fensters, the Sinclairs, the Otts, Joan Sawyer, Arthur Spinney, Donald Meadow, Geneva Jones, Maud Starr, Mollie Pine, Mabel Smock, Priscilla Worthy, Jill Marx, Marigold Lynch, the widows Deborah Shooky, Judy Molyneux, Betsy Bucky, Maureen Donlevy, and Hilary Tarkington, and widower Bob Palmer. The Gibbys were there too. They had driven all the way out from Cambridge.

In the pulpit Joe Bold conducted the service and surveyed his flock. He was still like a man cut off at the knees, but his vision had cleared. When the hospital bed had been taken out of his living room, along with the jars of morphine and the wheelchair and all the other desperate paraphernalia of the sickroom, it had been like coming out of a cocoon into chill, biting air of an amazing transparency. This morning, looking over the reading desk at his congregation, he was surprised by their resemblance to animals. With her little topknot, Betsy Bucky was a Celebes crested ape. Ed Bell was an American river otter, Dr. Spinney looked exactly like a kinkajou, Homer Kelly was a rough-coated dingo, and Parker Upshaw was *remarkably* like a Bactrian camel.

Joe gazed in startled appreciation at Upshaw, wondering why he hadn't seen the resemblance before in Parker's heavy eyelids, his immensely long nose, his supercilious expression. Then Joe caught sight of Augusta Gill in the balcony. She was glancing over her shoulder at him questioningly. Immediately, Joe leaped to his feet, late for the call to worship, seeing out of the corner of his eye the flash of Parker Upshaw's silver pencil in the sunlight. What was Upshaw scribbling in his pocket notebook?

Joe's sermon was a little delayed too, but this time it was the fault of the car that roared past the church up Farrar Road. Joe had to pause and wait until the noise died down. The congregation waited too, flinching at the rending clash as the driver shifted gears, waiting for the end of the grinding racket as the car picked up speed and thundered up the hill. Parker Upshaw grimaced at his wife. *Why didn't people have the courtesy to slow down, passing a house of public worship on a Sunday morning?*

It wasn't until the service was over and everyone had emerged into the glare of outdoors to stand basking in the unaccustomed warmth, shaking hands with the minister, exchanging the time of day, that the car came back. This time it was lunging down the hill out of control, swerving around the curve of Farrar Road, veering off the pavement. There were shrieks, and people flung themselves left and right as it bounded across the grass and thumped violently up the steps of the church. Lorraine Bell cried out as she saw her daughter's white face behind the windshield, but Ed turned only in time to throw himself at Joe Bold, who was in the way.

"Ed, Ed," screamed Lorraine.

As the car struck, the shaft of the steering wheel burst the spleen of Paul Dobbs and broke his back, and the door popped open, tossing Eleanor to the side like a morsel from a vending machine. As for Ed, he was pinned and crushed between the crumpled hood of Bo Harris's Chevy and the easternmost pillar of the church.

42

*The firmest pillar of the church has fallen . . . that full,
warm, generous heart, ever true to friendship, has ceased
to beat.*

Reverend Barzillai Frost, Concord
on the death of Dr. Ezra Ripley, 1841

*A*ll the children came for the funeral, gathering at the house on Acton Road, Stanton and his wife and kids from San Diego, Barbara from New York City, Margie and Cap from Milwaukee, Roberta and Lewis from Orono, Maine. They found their widowed mother still enraged. Over and over she kept saying the same thing, "What right has that boy Paul to be alive instead of your father?"

"Now, Mom," said Stanton, "it doesn't do any good to talk like that."

And Barbara said, "At least Ellie's all right." And they all embraced, while Eleanor sobbed remorseful tears and Lorraine, dry-eyed, tried to control her fury.

On the day of Ed's memorial service, they entered the church with Joe Bold in a parade of Bells, filling the first two pews across the middle of the chamber. The church was packed. The basement common room was jammed. People stood on the grass outside, mourning for Ed.

The service was short. Joe Bold held himself together and read the words he had written the day before in a convulsion of sorrow and affection. Afterward everyone collected on the lawn, anxious to speak to Lorraine and her family.

"Oh, Lorraine," said Flo Terry, embracing her in a paroxysm of sobbing. "I'm so sorry. I'm so sorry for everything."

Flo's husband, Peter, shuffled past Lorraine in his turn, taking her hand wordlessly. Peter had endured a difficult week. His wife had fallen completely apart, and it had been up to Pete to put her back together. On first hearing the news of Ed's death, Flo had been utterly dismayed. Then she had persuaded herself that this solution to Ed's troubles was really the best thing in the long run. Then doubt had begun to creep in, and finally Flo had succumbed to regret and self-recrimination.

Bo Harris was next in line. Working his way past Mrs. Bell to Eleanor, he looked at her red eyes and swollen tearstained cheeks.

"Hey, listen," he said. "Are you really okay?"

"Oh, I'm all right," said Eleanor. "Oh, Bo, I'm really sorry about your car."

"Oh, never mind the car." Bo looked dreamily at the plywood that had been nailed over the broken door of the church. "Mrs. Tarkington's giving me her husband's old Chrysler. It needs a lot of bodywork. You know, fiberglass repair. You want to go to a movie sometime? I can borrow my dad's car."

Eleanor blew her nose with her mother's handkerchief. "Well, all right, I guess so."

"How's Paul?" said Bo politely.

Eleanor shook her head. "Pretty bad. Paralyzed from the waist. I've seen him. He wishes he were dead."

Bo refrained from saying that he agreed with Paul, that Paul should have been killed instead of Mr. Bell.

But it was what everyone was thinking. Parker Upshaw said it out loud to his wife, Libby, but he blamed the whole thing on Ed, rather than Paul. "It's bound to happen every time, when you're too permissive with criminals. When that kid had his accident with the stolen motorcycle, they should have dumped him right back in prison. But Ed insisted they should give him another chance, right? Well, see what it led to. The whole thing was Ed's own fault. Now, don't look at me like that. It's true. Face facts. Ed Bell was a sentimental old fool."

43

This is the great end of the gospel, of the ministry,
of the church, that sinners may be saved.
Reverend William Jackson
Lincoln, 1848

*E*d Bell's death was the twelfth in six months in Old West Church. Devoutly everyone hoped it would be the last for a long time. But not until the Fourth of July was it apparent that circumstances in the three church communities of Nashoba had fundamentally changed.

At seven o'clock on the morning of the Fourth, Frances Mary Huxtible slipped on the braided rug in her kitchen while preparing a soft-boiled egg and broke her hip. An hour later, Roger Dolby fractured his skull when he fell off the roof of his house while attaching the lanyard of his American flag to the eaves trough. Mrs. Huxtible, a member of the Catholic parish of St. Barbara's, died twenty-three days later. Mr. Dolby, a lay reader in the Lutheran congregation of the Church of the Good Shepherd, was dead on arrival at Emerson Hospital.

The spell was broken. In Old West Church, death was no longer triumphant. During the month of September, Joe Bold baptized two infants, and in October he performed three marriages. One was the wedding of Bo Harris's sister. Louise Harris walked up the aisle of Old West during a thunderstorm in a seven-hundred-dollar wedding dress, preceded by eight bridesmaids.

And membership was on the rise. A few people said the influx was the result of the Reverend Bold's preaching, which was regaining its original fervor, others thought it was merely a reflection of the increase in the town's population because of the new real-estate development off Hartwell Road.

Jerry and Imogene Gibby were still diligent in their attendance at church on Sunday morning. Their rented house in Waltham was a lot closer to Nashoba than Imogene's mother's house in Porter Square. And before long Jerry was back at his desk in the office above the courtesy booth in the Bedford franchise of General Grocery.

Mary Kelly was surprised to see him at the store when she walked in from the parking lot one chilly morning in late October. There he was in person, standing on a tall ladder, attaching plastic bunting to the ceiling.

When he saw Mary, he climbed down off the ladder and shook her hand.

"Jerry," said Mary, "I can't believe it. I'm so glad to see you back."

"You bet I'm back. It's the pastry chef's doing. I got this idea for a new gimmick. You know, a pastry chef in a big chef's hat." Jerry patted an imaginary hat in the air high over his head. "And I sold it to top management. I mean, all I had to do was go to Boston with a bunch of samples, and top management bought the idea and gave me a new lease on life in the store. Here, come on, you've got to see this."

The aisles were festooned with bunting and bright Day-Glo arrows pointing toward the back of the store, to the pastry chef's domain, a small kitchen boutique with striped awnings, surrounded by a crush of customers. At first Mary could see only the tall white hat of the pastry chef, but when Jerry pulled her around the end of the counter, she was astounded to see Betsy Bucky's knobby little face beaming at her below the hat.

Betsy didn't have time to talk. She was too busy presiding over her simmering kettle of lard. The girl beside her was busy too, bagging Betsy's sausage fritters as fast as Betsy's tongs could whisk them out of the pot.

"Betsy," gasped Mary, "how wonderful. Congratulations. I understand you saved the day for Jerry."

Betsy glanced up from her boiling fat. "Well, like I always say, why are we put here on this earth in the first place? I mean, we come this way but once, isn't that right? Whoops!" One of Betsy's sausage fritters eluded her tongs and frisked to the side of the pot. Viciously she jabbed at it with her fork, and dropped it into an open bag. "Here, take some home to hubby."

"Go right ahead, take a dozen or two," said Jerry proudly. "It's on the house."

"Well, thank you," said Mary. She took the bag reluctantly, holding it at arm's length like a poisonous snake.

"Hey, Mary," said Jerry. "Listen, there's something else." He was tugging at her again, moving her away from the pastry boutique, guiding her into an isolated corner of specialty items, pickled onions, Scottish marmalade, smoked clams. "Listen," Jerry went on in a loud whisper, "You know Upshaw? Parker W. Upshaw? Guess what happened to him!"

"I don't know," said Mary, her eyes alight. "Tell me, what?"

"He's out in the cold. Fired from General Grocery. Will Daly told me, friend of mine. Will just got his job back too, just like me. Everybody Upshaw fired has been rehired."

"No kidding," said Mary, delighted. "Why did they fire Parker?"

"The chairman of the board finally caught on to what he was doing. Upshaw went over top management to the board just once too many times, trying to wangle himself into somebody else's slot, and this time the chairman persuaded the chief executive officer of General Grocery to get rid of him and reinstate everyone else."

"Well, what a good man, that board chairman," said Mary. "Who is he, anyway?"

"Who was he, I'm afraid," said Jerry solemnly. "You know who it was? I'll tell you who it was. It was Ed Bell."

"Good God," said Mary, awestruck at the wild oscillation of the tipping scales of justice, at the miraculous redemption of the murdering Betsy Bucky, at the resurrection of Jerry Gibby as a successful businessman, at the reincarnation of Howie Sawyer as a thespian performer, at the abasement of the mighty Flo Terry and the descent of Parker W. Upshaw into the abyss. "It feels like Judgment Day around here, the separation of the sheep from the goats at the last day."

"Well, Upshaw was a goat, all right," said Jerry in vengeful triumph.

"Some of us knew that from the beginning," said Mary Kelly. "Right, Jerry?"

But to Libby Upshaw, Parker's wife, the news that her husband was no longer among the upwardly mobile blessed ones of the earth was a horrifying discovery. At first she couldn't believe it.

"You mean," she said, staring at her husband, "I am married to a man who is unemployed? The top, you said! When I married you, you said you were going straight to the top."

"Shut up," said Parker Upshaw. He kicked the coffee table. He tipped over his Nautilus machine. He tossed a stack of books to the floor, his French grammar and every volume of the complete works of Plato, his new matched set, gold-tooled and bound in leather. Perfection as a life-style faded from his horizon. Parker W. Upshaw was once more as other men.

44

The heart . . . is not a superficial sensibility,—
the shallow pool that changes with every change
of temperature. The well is deep. . . .
                    Reverend Barzillai Frost
                    Concord, 1856

*J*oe Bold plucked his robe off its
hook and darted a glance out the window. The cloudburst that
had been going on all morning was over. The cold gray sky was
punctured by cavities of blue. Crossing the back entry, where
umbrellas lolled on the floor and coats hung dripping from the
rack, he opened the door of the sanctuary and mounted the steps
of the pulpit to face once more his gathered parish.

Homer and Mary Kelly were present, as usual, although
Homer didn't know how much longer he would be a loyal member of the congregation. He was finished at last with his history
of the spread of the faith from the town of Concord. If God
wanted to put the roof back on the church, it was all right with
Homer. Let Him reach out with his stupendous hand and turn off
the stopcocks of all those gushing faucets. But of course the final
result of Homer's researches was disappointing. His history
wasn't at all what he had intended. Oh, the Reverend William
Lawrence of Lincoln was in there with all his recorded possessions—his six chairs, his eight-day clock—and so was Ezra Ripley,
who had preached in the Concord church for sixty years, and so
were all those other august ministerial presences, looming out of
the histories of all these little towns.

But where were Rosemary Hill and Betsy Bucky? Where was Ed Bell? Where was Bo Harris? Where were the Farrars and Wheelers and Bloods and all the rest of the nameless congregations of yesterday? Well, of course a lot of sermons had survived, and Homer had taken dutiful note of them. How those old ministers had talked and ranted from their several pulpits! The congregations must have listened at least some of the time, and taken it all in, while out-of-doors the thick rushing life of their parishes went on just as it did right now, and the sow farrowed, and the horse died, and the barn burned down, and the price of apples rose and fell, and the baby cried, and the wife grew troubled in her mind, and the orchard blossomed, and the rugged trunks of the sugar maples were flooded with sap, and in Icehouse Pond the fish darted and the Canada geese came down to feed. It was this urgent life that had spoken in one voice from Parson Bulkeley in Concord in 1635, and in another from Reverend Stearns in Lincoln in 1795, in still another from Reverend Stacy in Carlisle in 1835, and in yet another from Reverend Joseph Bold in Nashoba right here and now. It would never stop talking, it would forever keep up its ceaseless murmur, its hoarse musical shout. Translated in the pulpit, the words would come out different, odd perhaps, peculiar often, sometimes dead wrong. And yet all of these reverend clergy would go right on cocking their ears and whispering, "Listen, did somebody say something? I could have sworn I heard something. Listen to that! Right now! Hear that?"

For Homer, then, the taps were turning off. But for Joseph Bold they were turning on. Looking over the pews this morning, he no longer beheld his parishioners as creatures of field and jungle. His vision had been increasing in severe acuity for months, and now he saw them magnified, as if he were gazing through an enormous hand lens. Clearly visible were individual pores and freckles, wens and pockmarks. It was painfully apparent that they were a spotted flock. Then, as they stood up to sing the first hymn, their troubles rose up too, and smote him, and Joe rocked back on his heels. Good God, there in the front row was Parker Upshaw, his dignity mortified by the loss of his job, and behind him sat Lorraine Bell, still embittered and unreconciled

to the accident that had killed her husband. And smack in the middle of the rows of pews was that extraordinary moral enigma, Betsy Bucky. And Arthur Spinney had been cracking up lately, and Deborah Shooky looked wretched, and Maud Starr with her hungry face was a perpetual nuisance, and how could a person be of use to Jerry Gibby as he clawed his way up the polished glass hill of middle-class prosperity? Then Joe blinked as a light flared up in one of the box pews. Good heavens, what was that? Oh, it was only Joan Sawyer, sitting directly in the path of the sun as it burst out from behind the clouds and hurled a burning ray through the window.

The words of the hymn were by John Bunyan:

> *He who would valiant be*
> *'Gainst all disaster,*

Let him in constancy
Follow the Master. . . .

Joan Sawyer was blinded. She couldn't see the words on the page because the sunlight had kindled her lashes like sparks. Looking past the glare from her hymnbook, she could dimly perceive the dark robe of the minister on the pulpit. His head was lowered. His lips were barely moving:

No foes shall stay his might,
Though he with giants fight;
He will make good his right
To be a pilgrim.

The plate was passed, the dollar bills dropped in, and behind the reading desk Joe fell back on the velvet chair, assailed by another frightful thought. What about Paul Dobbs, the boy who had been driving the car that killed Ed Bell? It occurred to Joe that he was going to have to do something about young Paul. And once he started, he would have to go right on doing it. And Paul was only the beginning. Joe's head reeled with the monstrous statistics of human poverty, inadequacy, wretchedness, and self-destruction. It was as though the glittering surface illusion by which he had so long been mesmerized had parted like a veil to reveal the tortured condition of his fellow men and women. The bright illusion was still there—the watery images of the windows creeping across the wall, Joan Sawyer glowing like a torch—but these elegancies were of no particular use to anybody, except perhaps as a voiceless congratulation of some kind. *Bully for you,* said the rainbow as you helped an old lady across the street. *Not bad, if I do say so myself,* twittered the singing bird. The impassive majesty of nature was what you got for dogged acts of kindness. Well, the truth was, you got the majesty anyway, kindness or no kindness. But looked at as a bargain, it made some kind of balance in the world, tit for tat.

Standing up again, Joe turned over his sermon notes, transfixed by this discovery, while outside the window the leaves clinging to the oak tree fluttered in felicitation, *Many happy returns of the day,* and the sun clapped its hands in sarcastic tribute, as if to say, *What a jerk! You finally figured it out. You certainly took your time.*

After supper on that chill November day, as the lid of clouds drew off over the ocean, leaving the bony landscape of southern New England without protection from the cold, Homer and Mary Kelly bundled up and drove back to Nashoba to visit the place where Ed Bell was buried.

They found it in the new part of the Old West cemetery at the top of the hill, not far from Arlene Pott's gravestone, and Carl Bucky's and Agatha Palmer's. As they stood silently looking at it, Homer was distracted by something over his shoulder. Glancing back, he saw the full moon coming up beyond the thicket of trees to the east, flattened into an oblate spheroid. The other way, above the crest of the hill, the sky glowed with the remaining shreds of the sunset. It was like that moment on the river when Joe Bold had plucked out of the advancing evening the instant

when sunlight and moonlight were equal. It was that time again.

Through the thick twilight, Homer walked out of the cemetery with Mary, remembering Ed's comic dance with straw hat and stick. As the moon rose and the sun declined, the memory struck the same celestial balance. It was a joke in sidereal time, and the laughter echoed from west to east, from sunset to moonrise.

The man's death was a calamity. But he had lived a good life. He had set an example. Surely there was no question about it, that Ed Bell had been a lasting monument of generosity and righteousness?

EPILOGUE

We are not surprised that the young pastor soon found among the fair daughters of the parish one who became a true helpmeet.
            Reverend Edward G. Porter, 1899
        on the marriage of Lincoln's first minister,
        William Lawrence, to Love Addams, 1750

*P*erhaps it is sad when a be-reaved husband puts aside his grief and observes that there are other women alive in the world. In Joe Bold's case the discovery was slow. The convergence of Joseph Bold and Joan Sawyer was like the approach of shy elephants, weaving and turning aside, slowly waving their trunks and shifting their huge feet.

The courtship, such as it was, went forward by widely separated leaps and plunges. There was the morning in church when a random streak of sunlight turned Joan into a Roman candle. And the day, months later, when Joe was fascinated at a Parish Committee meeting by the spiral whorls of her left ear. Half a year after that he was charmed at the County Hospital, where Joan was now working as an occupational therapist, by the nimble way she caught a ball tossed by Mr. O'Doyle. From then on, the small jolts of tender noticing happened more frequently, until at last Joe could think of nothing else.

Matters came to a head at another meeting of the Parish Committee. Joan was holding the floor that evening, explaining the problem of the overflowing septic tank and the need for another bathroom in the parish house.

"You mean we need another septic tank as well as another

bathroom?" said Lorraine Bell, who was running the meeting. "How much would it cost?"

Joan explained. Lorraine listened, and soon it occurred to her that something other than sewage was brimming under the surface of the discussion, a substance more ethereal than the

noisome contents of the septic tank. But Lorraine kept her eyes on her notes and jotted down lists of figures.

"What is the precise location of the present septic system?" said Joe ardently, his long hands rapidly shuffling his budget sheets.

Joan looked carefully at her diagrams and told him that the septic tank was buried at the curve of the driveway behind the parish house near the maple tree. Diligently, Joe scribbled the word *tree* on his budget sheet, then tumbled his papers wildly once again.

Lorraine decided sensibly that it was time to end the meeting. Sweeping her notes together, she called for a vote to adjourn.

"But we haven't decided what to do about the toilets," said Fred Harris, looking at her in astonishment.

"Sorry," said Lorraine. "Next time." Rapidly she led the way out, hauling on her parka, clearing the room of all the extraneous members of the committee.

Joe Bold and Joan Sawyer were left alone. Joan fumbled for her notebook, her rolled-up diagrams of the parish house, her handbag, scarf, coat, and mittens.

Joe bent over to pull on his rubbers. "May I walk you to your car?" he said in a muffled voice.

"Why, certainly," said Joan, fumbling the strap of her bag over her shoulder. "I'm parked way down by the church."

Blindly they made their way down the hill, trying to avoid drains and other large invisible obstructions that might have erupted out of the pavement during the meeting.

"May I?" whispered Joe, enfolding her large mitten in his glove.

"What an impertinent clergyman," murmured Joan.

"No, no, it's not impertinence," exclaimed Joe, wrapping a second glove around the first. "It has a teleological significance, you see. A purpose above and beyond itself, an ultimate design."

"Well, I'm glad to know," babbled Joan, "that it's a rational

act"—she flourished her notebook with her free hand—
"founded on fundamental axioms." All the pages fluttered out of
the notebook and flew away in the dark like pigeons. "Oh, dear,
look at them go."

"Oh, Joan," said Joe in a strangled voice, gathering into one
armful notebook, floor plans, coat, scarf, mittens, handbag, and
woman.

Next morning when Parker and Libby Upshaw drove up
Farrar Road, Parker was offended by the litter of paper blowing
across the lawn of the public library and flapping in the oak tree
beside the parish house and spilling out of the bushes in front of
the church. "Look at that," he said disdainfully. "People are so
thoughtless. They drive out from the slums of Boston and throw
trash out of their cars."

But it wasn't trash. It was Joan Sawyer's precise notes on the
required alterations to the plumbing system of the parish house,
with exact specifications for lengths of copper pipe and new
fixtures. Joan had to take her tape measure back to the basement
of the building and figure out the whole thing all over again from
scratch.

As it turned out, Joan's love affair was not the only romance
in the congregation of Old West Church that spring. Maud
Starr's was another. When the house next door to Maud's was put
on the market, who should buy it but Pulsifer Rexpole? Rexpole
was a famous Harvard professor, a poet, a recipient of the Nobel
Prize. Peeking out at him through her windows as he strode in
and out of his house after the moving men, carrying cartons of
his possessions—light fixtures, spare tires, broken chairs—Maud
could almost see the laurel wreath on his head, its ribbons
streaming behind him. She was thrilled.

Famous and talented Rexpole might be—he was also ugly,
crafty, unprincipled, and thrice divorced, a bird of prey of fiercer
visage and sharper beak than Maud herself. He was also a slob.
His front yard was soon a dump.

Maud didn't care. Into her life her new neighbor brought
instantaneous excitement, bliss, trouble, disaster, and final utter

catastrophe. What more could an adventurous woman ask of almighty God?

> *Lord, dismiss us with thy blessing;*
> *Fill our hearts with joy and peace;*
> *Let us each, thy love possessing,*
> *Triumph in redeeming grace:*
> *Oh, refresh us, oh, refresh us,*
> *Traveling through this wilderness.*
> —Pilgrim Hymnal

AFTERWORD

*N*ashoba is an invented town, its Old West Church an imaginary institution. A gusset was inserted in the map of Massachusetts on the northern border of Concord, stretching the towns of Bedford and Acton to east and west, and outraging the history of Carlisle to the north. The name Nashoba harks back to an actual community of Nipmuck Indians who lived somewhere between the Concord and Nashua rivers.

Most of the illustrations in this book are drawings of real buildings in the towns of Concord, Acton, Bedford, Harvard, Carlisle, Lincoln, Mattapoisett, and Cambridge, picked up by some sort of literary tornado and set down again around Nashoba's town common and along her streets and roads.

Many of the epigraphs at the beginnings of chapters are taken from sermons by ministers in Concord's First Parish and by pastors in the related churches of Lincoln and Carlisle. They were collected by Homer Kelly for his book *Hen and Chicks,* his history of the Concord church and its daughter parishes in other towns. Other epigraphs are chosen from Homer's notes on the journal of young James Lorin Chapin. Chapin was a farmer rather than a minister, but he attended Lincoln's Congregational church and commented in his journal on the sermons he heard there every Sunday in the years 1848, 1849, and 1850 (except for those Sundays when he stayed home in bed).

B·8

B2

LANGTON, J
GOOD AND DEAD

DEC 2 2 1986

RODMAN PUBLIC LIBRARY
215 East Broadway
Alliance, OH   44601